# HIS TO DEFEND

—

## Sharon C. Cooper

HARLEQUIN
ROMANTIC
SUSPENSE

# HARLEQUIN®
## ROMANTIC SUSPENSE™

Recycling programs for this product may not exist in your area.

ISBN-13: 978-1-335-75956-6

His to Defend

Copyright © 2021 by Sharon C. Cooper

This edition published by arrangement with Harlequin Books S.A.

For questions and comments about the quality of this book, please contact us at CustomerService@Harlequin.com.

Harlequin Enterprises ULC
22 Adelaide St. West, 40th Floor
Toronto, Ontario M5H 4E3, Canada
www.Harlequin.com

**Printed in U.S.A.**

Award-winning and *USA TODAY* bestselling author **Sharon C. Cooper** writes contemporary romance as well as romantic suspense. She's been nominated for numerous awards and is the recipient of Romance Slam Jam Emma Awards for Author of the Year 2019, Favorite Hero 2019 (*Indebted*) and Romantic Suspense of the Year 2015 (*Truth or Consequences*), to name a few. When Sharon isn't writing, she's hanging out with her amazing husband, doing volunteer work or reading a good book (a romance, of course). To read more about Sharon and her novels, visit www.sharoncooper.net.

### Books by Sharon C. Cooper

### Harlequin Romantic Suspense

*His to Protect*
*His to Defend*

### Harlequin Kimani Romance

*Legal Seduction*
*Sin City Temptation*
*A Dose of Passion*
*Model Attraction*

Visit the Author Profile page at Harlequin.com for more titles.

## Dedication

To my amazing husband, Al, thank you for your unwavering support and unconditional love. I love you more than words can ever express.

## Acknowledgments

Huge shout-out to Brenda, Carolyn, Yolanda, Claire and my Authors Who Brunch crew. I can't imagine this writing journey without you ladies! (HUGS)

To my amazing readers: thanks so much for your continued support of my work! Your sweet (and oftentimes funny) emails and DMs keep me going. You make me want to keep writing! Love you all!

# Chapter 1

Police Sergeant Maxwell Layton stared out the passenger-side window as the Las Vegas scenery went by in a blur. Riding shotgun with one of his officers was not what he'd had planned for the day. A mound of paperwork on his desk was begging for attention. Yet here he was babysitting a man he *used* to call friend. Now a man he could barely stand to share the same space with.

"Does the chief want me gone?" Jeremy Kelly asked from the driver's seat of the squad car. "Are you the only thing standing between me and the unemployment line?"

"No. If it was left up to me, your ass would've been off the police force a long time ago."

A wicked sneer spread across Jeremy's mouth. It brought attention to a small scar marring his reddish-brown skin. "Oh, so it's like that?"

"Yeah, it is."

Maxwell huffed out a breath. With the back of his hand, he blotted at the tiny beads of sweat popping out on his forehead. They had the air conditioner blasting on high, but it was no match for the hundred-and-ten-degree temperature outside.

"Jay, I don't know what's going on with you, but I suggest you straighten up or look for another job. You got off lucky with only the three days suspension for fighting."

The captain had ordered the suspension. Had it been up to Maxwell, he would've terminated both officers involved. Granted, that would've been harsh considering the indiscretion. But he had no tolerance for grown men, especially police officers, fighting each other while on duty.

"A.J. started it," Jeremy said of the other officer, Aaron McCallum. "His redbone ass shouldn't have come at me like that."

Maxwell jerked his head to look at him. "Are you serious right now? You sound like a damn five-year-old. We committed to serving and protecting this city, but instead, you idiots were trading blows as if you were in a boxing ring. During a briefing no less. The sad part is, it was probably over some stupid mess."

"It wasn't stupid," Jeremy snarled, and gripped the steering wheel tighter. "It was personal."

Maxwell didn't bother asking what the fight was about. Hell, he didn't care. All he cared about was the safety of his officers, and how that fight could've gotten way out of hand. As it was, it made his department look bad.

Both men were being tight-lipped regarding the reason behind the dispute, which was no surprise. Cops stuck together, even if they didn't agree with each other. However, Maxwell had no intention of letting either of them make a mockery out of his department, and if it happened again, they would definitely be terminated.

"Aaron might've thrown the first punch, but I didn't miss the way you were glaring at him from the moment you stepped into the room. And then to start taunting him…in front of everyone…" Maxwell shook his head. "It was stupid *and* childish."

His irritation with Jeremy went way beyond the senseless fight the other day. No, it had everything to do with the guy's apathetic attitude toward the job lately and his disrespect for authority.

The two of them had gone through the police academy together almost fifteen years ago. From there, they'd been tighter than blood brothers and had planned to move up the ranks side by side. Maxwell stuck with that plan and was currently in line to be promoted to lieutenant.

But Jeremy? At first, he'd walked the straight and narrow, worked hard and was conscientious about the job. Yet, the last year or so, he had changed. Not just at work, but personally too. Gone was the easygoing, funny and all-around nice guy. In his place was a competitive, trouble-making, mean-spirited man with a short temper. He had turned into someone Maxwell didn't recognize.

"Do the crappy assignments you've been giving me have anything to do with Mina?"

Maxwell glared at him as anger simmered just below the surface. "Leave her out of this!" he said of Jeremy's ex-wife and one of the sweetest women Maxwell had ever met. "This situation isn't personal."

The words felt like sandpaper on his tongue, but Maxwell wanted to believe that they were true. He tried to be professional and never let personal issues get in the way of decisions made with any of his officers. Yet, if he was honest with himself, it was possible that his and Jeremy's past troubles might be fueling some of the disgust he had toward the guy.

Maxwell shook his head, refusing to believe that. He was professional if nothing else. "Me riding with you is about your jacked-up attitude and poor performance out here on the streets," he said with conviction.

"Max, don't even try and front. You've had it in for me ever since you made sergeant, and even more after I married Mina. I can't help it if I'm a better man than you are, or that she chose me over you. So, if you think I'm going to apologize for getting the jump on you, then you—"

"Dispatch, unit 14," a female voice called over their radio. "What's your 20, over?"

Maxwell responded to the call, agreeing to check out a disturbance at an apartment complex that was seven minutes from their location.

When he was done, he turned his attention back to Jeremy. "The assignments you receive from me are always about police business. I have *never* and will never make it personal. Again, as for me riding with you this week, that has everything to do with you being a screwup. I don't know what's going on with you, but this is your last chance to get yourself together."

Jeremy tsked. He made a sharp U-turn, ignoring the way the tires screeched or the fact that he cut in front of another vehicle. Irritation gnawed on Maxwell's nerves as Jay drove faster than necessary, flying down the street toward the apartment complex.

Maxwell gritted his teeth to keep from saying anything, silently fuming as he held on to the door handle. And did the jerk have to bring up Amina? A woman who was never far from Maxwell's thoughts.

He and Jeremy had met her at the same time, on the same night, at a party that a mutual friend had thrown. Maxwell would never forget the moment he spotted her. He didn't believe in love at first sight, but that night he had reconsidered his stance on the subject. Amina was the most beautiful woman he had ever laid eyes on.

Smooth bronze skin with dark eyes that slanted when she smiled came to the forefront of Maxwell's mind. And, God, what a smile. Amina had been like a bright star lighting up the gloomiest sky. He still remembered what she'd worn that night—a strapless light blue dress that hugged her generous curves and stopped just above her knees. Legs that seemed to go on forever had been accentuated by high-heel shoes.

Maxwell also recalled her first words to him in that melodious tone that was like a caress over his skin. *Can I buy you a drink?* she'd asked, shocking the hell out of him. No woman had ever offered to buy him a drink. He and Amina had talked and laughed for much of the evening, giving him an opportunity to see that her personality was just as beautiful as she was.

But little had he known that Jeremy had been eyeing her too.

"I have a lot going on right now," Jeremy grumbled next to him, cutting into Maxwell's thoughts.

"Then take time off. Man, you've got too many years in to screw it up by being stupid."

Maxwell might not like the guy, but he'd hate to see anyone put in as many years as Jeremy had on a job, then lose everything because of doing something outrageous, like fighting a coworker.

Jeremy didn't respond. He made a right turn and crept down the tree-lined street that had an apartment building on one side and townhomes on the other. As they drove, Maxwell assessed the urban neighborhood that was just outside downtown and was currently undergoing gentrification. Late afternoon in the middle of a weekday, there weren't many people milling about. Probably because it was hot as hell. With this heat, no one in their right mind would be hanging outdoors if they had a choice.

They stopped on the side of the six-story beige-and-tan stucco building and parked. Before exiting the car, they both glanced around the exterior. The 911 caller complained of loud rock music that had been playing for the last hour. Maxwell was surprised that there hadn't been more than one call since he could hear it even with the car windows rolled up.

"Dang. If you're going to blast music, at least pick something that people know the lyrics to," Jeremy grumbled as they climbed out of the vehicle. "I don't know what's up with this place. The last few months I've gotten dispatched here at least once every couple of weeks. If it's not a break-in, it's some drunk camped out in the hallway harassing tenants. It always seems to be something."

"Maybe it's under new management and they're letting just anyone lease from them," Maxwell said.

He loved almost any type of music, but he never could get with hard rock. Other than the tunes blaring, the block was fairly quiet with barely any traffic on the street.

He continued to take in their surroundings as they moved down the sidewalk and around to the front of the building. Well-maintained shrubbery and flower beds made up the landscape as they strolled up the double-wide walkway. The music grew louder. Maxwell couldn't tell which apartment the ruckus was coming from.

"Just so you know, it was never my intention to hurt Amina," Jeremy said. "I just didn't wa—"

"Save it. What took place in your marriage is your business. Not mine."

Jeremy released a humorless laugh. "Yeah, but you wanted it to be your business. I knew how you felt about Mina before I stepped to her, but I needed to show you that you're not all that. She chose *me*, and you're still pissed."

"And then she saw you for the lowlife that you really are and divorced your ass," Maxwell said with a calmness that didn't match the annoyance swirling inside him.

He started to say more, but slowed as an ominous sensation settled around him. He wasn't sure if it was because of the direction the conversation was going or if there was really something wrong. Either way, he never ignored his gut and right now something felt off.

"Hold up," he said, stretching his arm out to stop Jeremy from moving forward. His other hand was on the handle of his holstered gun.

"What is it?"

"I'm not sure, but…"

Maxwell startled when breaking glass splintered the air and jagged shards rained down on them. He whipped out his gun and took a few side steps to his left as he aimed up at the broken window. He couldn't see whoever was in the unit. Besides that, the blaring of the music was more than irritating. It was also a distraction.

"You got anything?" Jeremy asked as they moved in unison.

Before Maxwell could respond, a shot rang out.

He flinched.

Jeremy gasped.

Maxwell jerked his head toward his friend, who dropped to his knees.

"D-damn," Jeremy murmured, and fell onto his side.

They were both wearing bulletproof vests, but even then, getting hit could knock the air out of you. But...

*Blood.*

Maxwell's heart slammed against his chest, and he moved as if on autopilot. With his gun in one hand, he frantically waved it back and forth as he grabbed the back of Jeremy's vest. He dragged him down the sidewalk and headed back the way they came. Instead of going to the car, he cut around the corner of the building. That would give them more coverage. The grass, flower bed and tall hedges would also help, but not much.

Maxwell knelt next to Jeremy who was squirming, his rapid, shallow breathing causing his chest to rise and fall as he struggled for air.

*Aw, hell.*

The bullet had missed the vest. Caught him in the side of the neck. Blood spilled from the wound and his mouth.

"Hang on, man," Maxwell said, his pulse racing in sync with the shrieking of the rock music still booming from the building.

His throat tightened and nausea swirled inside him as he set his gun on the ground close enough to easily grab if needed. He placed his hand on Jeremy's neck, applying pressure on the wound, hoping to slow the bleeding.

*So much blood.*

His hand, coated with the warm, sticky, scarlet substance pouring from the hole in Jeremy's neck, wasn't helping in stopping the bleeding. No amount of training could've prepared Maxwell for this…for seeing a friend shot and fighting for his life.

"Just hang on," he mumbled, his body trembling as he used his free hand to press the button on the walkie-talkie that was hooked on his shoulder. "Shots fired! Officer down! Need backup," he muttered into his radio mic. He gave his location and information about where the shots came from, and prayed backup and an ambulance could get there quick. He didn't know if whoever shot at them would try again.

Maxwell picked up his weapon and anxiously surveyed the area. Still, no one was in sight, but in between sounds of an electric guitar and drums, someone was yelling. Sirens could barely be heard in the distance.

"Sor-ry about Mi-Mina." Jeremy panted and coughed, blood sputtering from his mouth. "I—I was wro-wrong."

"Be quiet," Maxwell said between clenched teeth. His heartbeat was racing faster than a locomotive flying down the tracks. "Tell me later about how much of an asshole you are, but right now I need you to hang on. Your ass better not die on me."

Jeremy tried to laugh, but coughed up more blood. "I'm sor-sorry," he stammered, and his eyes drifted closed while he continued struggling to breathe.

"Come on, man. Hang on. Just hang on."

\* \* \*

Amina Kelly listened as Dr. McPherson, a pediatrician, explained to six-year-old Sophia and her parents the proper way to care for the child's cast.

"Try not to get it wet. You can buy a cast cover to protect it. Or you can use a couple of plastic bags and tape to wrap it before bath time."

Amina smiled when Sophia walked over to her while the doctor continued giving instructions to her parents. As a pediatric nurse, she had the pleasure of working with children, calming their fears and connecting with them on a level that others might not be able to. Most days she loved her job, like today.

Sophia was absolutely precious. All of their patients were, but every now and then Amina found herself drawn to certain children, like Sophia. She wasn't sure what that lure was this time, but there was something special about the little girl. Or maybe it was Amina's biological clock ticking louder than usual. One hazard of being around children all day was that she was reminded of what she wanted more than anything in the world. A family of her own.

At thirty-four, she thought by now that she'd be happily married with at least three children. She had foolishly tried the marriage thing once, only to make the biggest mistake of her life. As for having kids? That might not ever happen, now that she couldn't see herself getting married again.

Amina bent down to Sophia's level. "I have something for you." She dug through her pocket and pulled out a blue magic marker. "This is so your friends can write on your cast, but you can't use it on anything else. No walls. No floors. You can only use it on the cast. Okay?"

Sophia nodded. Her unruly blond curls covered much of her face, and Amina couldn't help but laugh each time the little girl brushed them away. They seemed to bother her, but when her mother tried pulling the hair back into a ponytail, Sophia protested.

Her gaze bounced from her cast to the marker, and her brows dipped into a frown. "I can write my name on it?"

"Yes. Do you know how to spell your name?"

Sophia nodded.

"How about this?" Amina removed the cap from the marker. "I'll sign my name on your cast first, then you can write yours. Would that be all right?"

"Okay."

Sophia watched in awe as Amina not only wrote her name, but drew a flower next to it. The fluorescent pink short-arm cast that stopped just below her elbow was so small. There wouldn't be much room for many other signatures.

"Now you try."

She held the little girl's arm steady and smiled as Sophia concentrated on writing. She wrote something, but Amina couldn't be sure if it was her name. It looked nothing like it.

"I did it! You like my flower?" Sophia pointed at what appeared to be a blue blob.

"It's beautiful, sweetie." Feeling her legs stiffen from the crouched position, Amina stood upright and stretched them out. "Be sure to save space for others who might want to sign your cast."

"Okay."

"Sophia, it's time to go. Tell Dr. McPherson and Nurse Mina thank you," her mother instructed.

"Bye," Sophia said softly to Amina, her sad hazel eyes staring up at her. Then she lunged forward, practically knocking Amina off-balance when she wrapped her good arm around one of Amina's legs. "Thank you for my marker."

Amina bent slightly and hugged her back. "You're very welcome. Remember, the marker is only for your cast, no walls or floors."

Sophia bobbed her head, and Amina hoped giving the little girl a marker didn't backfire. The last thing she wanted were angry parents calling and complaining about unwanted wall art in their living room.

She and Dr. McPherson walked out of the room behind the family. They all said their goodbyes and Amina watched as Sophia and her parents headed down the hall.

"You're wonderful with kids," Dr. McPherson said as he finished typing something into the computer tablet that he was holding. "They all love you."

"I love them too. That was one of the reasons why I decided to become a pediatric nurse."

"Dr. McPherson, your next patient is ready in room three," one of the nurses said from the station that was directly across the hall from where they were standing.

"Thanks, Katie. That'll be my next stop." He tucked the tablet under his arm and turned to Amina. "Do you mind walking with me?"

"Sure."

He didn't speak as they headed to the room, but a few minutes into their stroll, he slowed and glanced around. Amina almost groaned. She knew what was coming next. He had asked her out to dinner the week before.

When she turned him down, claiming to be tied up that evening, he'd said maybe another time. Since she hadn't seen much of him since then, Amina had forgotten about that invite and the one from a couple of months ago.

"I was wondering if you were busy Saturday night. I have two tickets to the Motown Review and would love to take you."

Caleb McPherson was not only one of the most respected doctors at the hospital, he was also super nice and *GQ* gorgeous. Most of the nurses referred to him as Dr. Mc*Fine*. Of course, they didn't address him like that to his face, but when they were huddled together it was always Dr. Mc*Fine* this or Dr. Mc*Fine* that.

Amina couldn't much blame them, though. At forty-something and around six-two, with a runner's build, and smooth dark skin with a dimple in the left cheek, he was definitely nice to look at.

Amina wanted to say yes. Not because of those qualities, or the fact that her mother would absolutely love the idea of her dating a doctor. No, she only wanted to say yes because she'd been wanting to see that show since it first arrived in Vegas. Outside of that, she wasn't interested in him. Besides, she had a rule about not dating people she worked with and had no intention of breaking it now.

She gave him a closed-mouth smile. "Thanks, but I can't."

He nodded, and his dark gaze held hers. "That's the third time you've turned me down. Are you seeing someone?"

She was almost positive he knew that she'd gotten divorced six months ago. Most of her friends and family had been surprised that her marriage hadn't even lasted a year. With so many wonderful examples of happily married couples in her life, the last thing she wanted was to get divorced. But months after marrying Jeremy, the funny, kind and generous man she'd vowed to spend the rest of her life with had turned into a world-class asshole.

The verbal abuse had been enough to let her know that their marriage wouldn't last long, but the moment he'd put his hands on her, she'd known it was over.

"Are you?" the doctor asked again, pulling her back into the conversation.

Instead of answering his question, Amina said, "Though I appreciate the invitation, I have a rule. I don't da…" Her words trailed off and her heart did a little giddyap when she saw a familiar face exit the elevator.

*It can't be*, she thought, needing for the man to lift his head so that she could get a better look at him. When he did, a wave of excitement crashed through Amina at the sight of him.

*Maxwell Layton.*

Amina's pulse amped as he ambled down the hall in her direction. She hadn't seen him in a while, but occasionally, she'd think about him. He was a hard man to forget, but at the moment, he was glancing everywhere but at her. She wondered what he was doing at a children's hospital. He didn't have kids, but he did have a niece and nephew. Had something happened to one of them?

"Amina?" Dr. McPherson said. "You were saying?"

"Oh… I'm sorry. Excuse me, doctor. I need to check on something," she said in a rush, and left him standing in the hallway.

She wandered toward Maxwell, giving him a quick

once-over along the way. He almost didn't look like himself. His laid-back, easygoing personality normally showed in his confident gait and the upbeat way he carried himself.

Right now, though, even with the distance between them, his anxiousness was almost palpable. His usual smile that could easily light up a room—nonexistent. Despite those observations, he still was one of the most handsome men she'd ever laid eyes on.

Maxwell kept his hair cut close to the scalp and often wore a baseball cap when he wasn't on duty. Not today. Today she had a clear view of his attractive face and the way his smooth mahogany skin glistened under the fluorescent lights. Amina took in the gray T-shirt that stretched across his wide chest, molded over his broad shoulders and hugged his thick biceps. Dark jeans covered his powerful thighs and made his legs appear ten feet long.

When her attention returned to his face, she realized he had spotted her, and her steps slowed. It was so good to see him again, but at the moment, his hooded gaze looked past her. She glanced over her shoulder where McPherson was still standing. The doctor gave her a slight nod before walking away. When Amina returned her attention to Maxwell, he was zoned in on her.

The intensity of his stare had her rooted in place. It was as if he was peering deep into her soul, searching for what, she didn't know. Then just as fast, his eyes softened. He regarded her in that way he usually did. As if she was the only person in the room. Amina often thought it was her imagination, but it was the same expression she'd seen the last few times they'd run into each other.

He moved forward, and her anxiety increased as his expression turned troubled and worry lines formed on his forehead. Suddenly a sense of foreboding settled in her chest. Before she realized it, her hands were in a praying stance under her chin.

"What's wrong? Did something happen to Trinity? Gunner? The kids?" The words flew from her mouth like rapid-fired gunshots. Maxwell's family meant everything to him. A family he would kill and die for. "Tell me."

"It's Jeremy."

Stunned, Amina dropped her hands and took a step back. She searched Maxwell's face again in confusion. He and Jeremy were no longer friends, but surely, he knew that she wasn't in contact with her ex-husband and rightfully so. The last months of their marriage, Jeremy had made her life a living hell.

Maxwell cleared his throat. "He was shot in the neck. He didn't…"

The blood flowing through Amina's veins turned into ice as his unspoken words altered the cadence of her heartbeat. He didn't have to say anything else. As she regarded him more, his red-rimmed eyes and the way his shoulders suddenly slumped while he rubbed a large hand over his chest said it all.

Jeremy was dead.

Amina didn't know how to respond as what felt like a two-ton boulder pressed down on the top of her head. Growing up with a police officer as a father, a strong, courageous man who was also her hero, she'd wanted to marry someone just like him. Not necessarily a cop, but someone who embodied bravery and strong morals.

Even though she knew how dangerous his job was

and that there was always a chance her dad wouldn't return home to them, that hadn't stopped Amina from marrying a cop. She'd become fearless and tough while growing up, feeling as if she could handle anything. Yet, nothing could've prepared her for this moment.

A range of emotions warred inside her. Shock. Fear. Sadness. Anger. Her mind and body couldn't seem to settle on just one. Her brain filled with questions that her mouth couldn't quite form.

Amina's gaze stayed on Maxwell, and her heart broke for his loss. She'd lost her ex-husband, but he'd lost so much more. A fellow officer. A man who was once like a brother to him. She might not have been in love with Jeremy anymore, but it was awful that his life was taken by a bullet.

"He's…he's dead. He died on the scene." Maxwell's voice was hoarse as if he'd been screaming or crying. "I was there," he continued. "I—I… I…"

Amina barely felt herself move. All she knew was that one minute she was a couple of feet from him and the next, her arms were around his waist. She rested her head against his chest, and the erratic tempo of his heart would've caused her concern, but was expected in this instance.

*Jeremy's gone.* Shocked didn't begin to describe what she was feeling. It just…it just didn't seem real.

At first, Maxwell stood rigid. Then he swung his arms around her, holding her tight enough to cut off all circulation.

"Everything happened so fast," he mumbled against her hair. His tear-filled words held so much anguish, and Amina ached for him.

"Shh," she crooned, still stunned by the news herself but wanting to offer some type of comfort. "I'm so sorry you had to go through that, but it's going to be okay. Everything will be okay." It had to be.

# Chapter 2

*What the hell is wrong with me?*

Maxwell scrubbed his face with his hand, shocked at how he almost broke down in front of Amina. He usually did a good job at controlling his emotions in front of others. Yet today had been tough.

As a police officer, he knew every day that they stepped out on the street could be their last. That mental preparation was no match for reality, though. There was no way he could've prepared for losing someone he had once been so close to. The situation was made even worse because he and Jeremy hadn't been able to settle their differences. Differences that should've been squashed. But no, he'd held on to the hurt that Jeremy had inflicted, and Maxwell regretted that more now than ever.

To Amina's credit, instead of letting him stand in the

hallway and further embarrass himself, she had ush-
ered him into a nearby stairwell to the top landing. She
excused herself to get someone to cover for her and returned within minutes. That was when it dawned on him
that he hadn't considered how his visit would pull her
attention from her work. When he apologized, telling
her that he'd leave, she ignored his protests.

A door from somewhere below slammed, and Maxwell stiffened.

"Relax," Amina said quietly, her hand on his back.
"Staff seldom come up here."

Maxwell nodded and released an exhausted breath.
He rubbed his forehead as if that would relieve the
pounding inside his skull.

"Can I go and get you anything? Soda? Coffee?
Water?" she asked. There was a slight tremble in her
voice, but other than that, she was handling the news
better than him.

"No, I'm good. Thanks."

They were sitting on the top step of the landing that
led out to the rooftop where a helipad was located. His
senses were hyperaware of her nearness. Each time he inhaled, his nose got a whiff of her fragrance—something
floral with a hint of vanilla. Their thighs were touching,
which wasn't helping his peace of mind. Even though he
wasn't at a good place mentally, heat bloomed inside him
and need spread to every cell in his body.

Damn, his attraction to her was stronger than ever.
And he hated himself for it. Lusting after Jeremy's ex-
wife felt wrong.

*The man just died.*

Maxwell rubbed his chest as if that would loosen
the guilt swirling inside him. This was not the time for

those intense feelings he once had for Amina to resurface. Yet, he couldn't stop them. Her presence did something to him, *still*. This was the woman he had once envisioned hooking up with. Granted, at the time, he hadn't known her well, but some things you just knew. The two of them clicked.

From the moment he and Amina met, there'd been a powerful connection between them that he couldn't explain. Conversation had flowed easily as if they'd known each other forever, and he'd sensed her interest in him. But Maxwell had missed his opportunity thanks to receiving a telephone call from work.

He'd been a detective at the time, and the call had been in regard to a huge break in one of his cases. He'd had to leave immediately to follow up on the lead.

Of course, that had been the same moment that Amina had gone to the ladies' room with her girlfriends. Rather than wait for her to return, he had jotted down a short note and his telephone number, and had asked Jeremy to pass it along to her.

Maxwell never did hear from Amina. He thought that maybe he'd read things wrong and had imagined their connection. He later found out that Jeremy never gave her the note. Instead, his so-called *friend* had taken advantage of the situation by pursuing Amina relentlessly. It was months later that Maxwell had seen them together and learned what Jeremy had done.

*But now he's gone, and he's never coming back.*

The words taunted Maxwell. *He's gone.* Amina was no longer his. Technically, she'd been free of Jeremy months ago and could be with whoever she wanted. Maxwell glanced at her, wanting…needing to say something, but he couldn't believe he was there, at a children's hospital…with her. They were both leaned forward with their elbows on their thighs. Dark, soulful eyes stared back at him as his gaze took in her beauty. She had cut her hair since the last time he'd seen her. The pixie style was short in the back and on the sides, and was long in the front. Her bangs were swept to the right side and hung almost over her eye. The style complemented her oval-shaped face and bronze-tone skin. She was such a stunning woman.

He probably shouldn't be there. Another officer could've delivered the news about Jeremy, but considering their history, Maxwell thought it best to come from him.

"It's good seeing you," he said quietly.

Amina bumped his shoulder with hers, and the corners of her alluring lips tilted up. "It's nice to see you too. It's been a while. I just wish we didn't have to come together under these circumstances."

He'd seen her off and on during her and Jeremy's short marriage because they all had mutual friends. It had been tough hanging out with them at parties and cookouts, but Maxwell always tried to act like it didn't bother him. He and Amina would talk at those occasions, and still, that intense vibe between them had been just as strong as the first time they met. He sensed that she'd felt it too, but she wasn't the type of woman who would step out on her husband. And Maxwell wasn't the type of guy who would ever disrespect anyone's marriage.

That was one of the reasons why he'd had to distance himself months ago. It had gotten too hard to see the two of them together.

"I can't believe he's gone," Maxwell mumbled, struggling to wrap his brain around the fact that only hours earlier he was arguing with the guy.

"Yeah, I can't believe it either. No matter how things turned out between him and me, I wouldn't have wished this on him. I think I'm still in shock. Tell me what happened. That's if you're okay talking about it," Amina said in a shaky voice.

That was the last thing Maxwell wanted to discuss. For hours he had recounted everything to his superiors, reliving the last moments of Jeremy's life over and over again. But Amina wanted to know.

"We were following up on a call about a disturbance at an apartment complex."

As he told her about what went down, Maxwell wondered if he had missed anything at the scene. With him and Jeremy talking as they walked toward the front door, had he failed to notice anything of importance? Sure, there was that minute when his hackles had gone up and he felt something was off. But what about before then?

He had wanted to return to the scene to take part in the investigation, but his captain had insisted that he let the detectives handle it. Maxwell knew he wouldn't be able to sit on the sidelines, but earlier, he'd been in no condition to argue.

"Did you see anyone?" Amina asked.

Maxwell shook his head. "No, but everything happened so fast. We were there because someone had their music up too loud. I never expected…"

He let the words hang out there. They were always supposed to be on guard, no matter what type of call they were responding to. On the ride to the hospital, he had replayed everything over and over in his head, but still came up with nothing. That only made him want to return to the crime scene. He needed to know what the hell happened. He needed to determine if he could've prevented Jeremy's murder.

With all that was going on between cops and the public lately, he couldn't help wondering if they'd been targeted. Their job was tough on any given day, but over the past year, they'd taken on more scrutiny than usual. Maybe the shooting had been a setup…something to lure police officers to the building and…

Maxwell shook the thought free. He wouldn't know anything until they finished investigating. All he knew at the moment was that he wouldn't rest until they found the killer.

"It could've been me lying in the morgue," he said, his voice cracking on the last word. He cleared his throat, refusing to get emotional again. "It could've easily been me. I keep replaying everything in my head and—"

"And knowing you, I'm sure you did everything you could for him. Max, please don't blame yourself. We both know that some things are out of our control."

He released a noisy sigh. "I know, but it doesn't make the situation any easier."

"Only time will help with that."

Amina slipped her arm through his bent one and a powerful current of need traveled through Maxwell. He dragged in a deep breath when she laid her head on his shoulder. She might've been trying to comfort him, but even feeling like crap inside, he was loving the sensation of her lush body hugged up against him. Probably a little too much.

"How's Trinity and her family?" Amina asked of his sister. Maxwell could've kissed her for changing the subject.

"They're great. My niece Brielle is three months old and has to be the cutest baby I've ever seen."

Amina laughed. "I'm sure you're biased, and I think you said that about your nephew too."

Maxwell smiled. This was helping. Discussing family was taking his mind off of his reason for being there. This was what he needed to regroup, if only for a little while.

"You're probably right. I can't believe how fast they both are growing. Jonah just turned four and is as smart as a whip. Trinity and Gunner are going to have their hands full as he gets older. Now what about your family? I saw your dad at a retirement party last month. He's looking good. How is everyone else?"

Her father, a former police captain, had retired a few years ago after thirty-five years of service. A highly respected man. Maxwell had served under him for a short period of time before transferring to his current precinct. Little had he known that he'd meet Amina, one of the captain's daughters, at a party years later. He could see some of her dad's influence in her. She was tough, but compassionate. Strong in her convictions, yet gentle in how she dealt with people. Nursing was definitely a good fit for her.

"Everyone is doing well. Sabrina and her family," she said of one of her sisters who had a twin, "are on a fourteen-day cruise with my parents. They left the day before yesterday. As for Katrina and her husband, they're great and recently relocated to DC."

Maxwell nodded, but stopped when he realized what she'd said. "Wait. That means you're in town by yourself."

Amina shrugged. "Yeah. Wouldn't be the first time,

and it's not a big deal. I've been working so much lately I haven't had time to miss any of them." She gave a small laugh. "And my dad mentioned that he saw you. Of course, he couldn't stop singing your praises. In case you didn't know, he's a big fan of yours. He said you might be up for lieutenant soon."

Maxwell chuckled and some of the melancholy slowly lifted. "That's the rumor going around, but I haven't decided if I'll go for the position."

When he first joined the police force, the plan was to work his way up to chief. Now he wasn't sure if that was what he really wanted. At the moment, he wasn't sure about much of anything.

"As for your dad being a fan, the feeling is mutual. His name still comes up in conversation, and he's definitely missed."

"I think he wishes he was there. If he could, he'd probably return, but my mom isn't having that." Amina shook her head smiling. "According to her, she still has *big* plans for him."

Maxwell grinned. "Is that right?"

"Yup, but they're probably not as sexy as you're thinking. They are more like him finishing the *unfinished* back deck that he started years ago, and cleaning out the garage. Let's just say his honey-do list is long and grows by the day."

They both laughed and their conversation bounced from one topic to another. It reminded him of the past. He always enjoyed talking with Amina, and their discussions flowed easily.

"Has Jeremy's family been notified?"

Maxwell nodded. "They'll be flying in from Seattle in a couple of days. Do you ever hear from them?"

"No. Elaine used to call sometimes, but I haven't talked to her in a while," she said of Jeremy's sister.

"Maybe you'll see them at the funeral," Maxwell said, then wanted to snatch the words back. She'd been through enough heartache with Jeremy, especially those last few months of marriage. Maxwell wouldn't blame her if she didn't attend.

"I don't know," she said quietly. "I'd want to give my condolences to his family, but... I don't know."

Maxwell nodded and wrapped his arm around her shoulders. "Let me know if you do."

"Okay."

"We've touched upon everyone else, but how have you been?" Maxwell asked.

"All things considered I'm doing well. Working a lot of hours and just trying to stay positive and move on with my life."

She was probably referring to how Jeremy had dragged the divorce out though he knew he and Amina would never reconcile. It was just another way he'd made her life a nightmare. It was always something when it came to him. Now this.

Maxwell glanced at his watch. They'd been in the stairwell fifteen or twenty minutes. "I'd better let you get back to your duties. Sorry about just dropping by." He started to stand, but she touched his arm.

"I'm glad you did, but do you think..." Amina's words trailed off and she released his arm. Nibbling on her bottom lip, she ran her hands up and down the light blue smock pants. When she returned her attention to him, she was no longer worrying her lip, but the wary expression caught him a little off guard. One thing she wasn't was shy.

"What is it?" he asked.

"Do you think it's a good idea for you to be alone tonight? I get off in an hour. Maybe we can meet up for a late dinner. Or you can come by my place and we can finish talking."

Dumbfounded, all Maxwell could do was stare at her. Any other time, from any other woman, he would've loved hearing those words, but this was Amina. A woman he had fallen for at first sight. A woman who was too much of a temptation—still—to be alone with right now. There was no way he could hook up with her later and not want more than conversation.

Besides all of that, Maxwell would never step foot in her home again. It wasn't that he didn't want to, but it was the house she'd once shared with Jeremy. Being there would bring back memories he'd tried hard to forget. Not that this impromptu meeting hadn't drummed up old hurts.

"Or I can meet you at your place," she continued.

Maxwell stood and pulled her up with him, then wrapped his arm around her. Placing a lingering kiss against her temple, he inhaled her fresh scent. "There is nothing I would like more than to spend time with you, but I don't think that's a good idea, especially tonight. I'll give you a call tomorrow to check on you."

Amina smiled up at him and looped her arm through his. "I think *you're* the one who needs checking on. What you went through today couldn't have been easy, and I'm worried about you."

"I appreciate that, but I'll be all right."

Arm in arm, they slowly descended the stairs, and Maxwell hated for their time to end. Yet, he knew it was for the best. It would be too easy to fall for her again.

Granted, she and Jeremy had been over for a long time, but it would be too weird hanging out with her, for more reasons than one.

"For the record," Amina said, "I don't think there'd be anything wrong with us spending time together." It was as if she'd been reading his mind. He started to speak, but she lifted a finger. "However, I respect your decision."

Maxwell nodded. He was sure later he'd regret not taking her up on her offer. She might no longer be married, but she'd made her decision years ago not to be with him. For the most part he had come to terms with that, but he wasn't ready to risk his heart, knowing that she was the only woman who could break it…again.

# Chapter 3

Hours later, Amina padded into her kitchen in need of something stronger than wine, her usual wind-down drink of choice. She had showered and changed into a Nursing Is My Superpower T-shirt and a pair of too-short-to-wear-in-public shorts. Now all she had to do was calm her nerves.

She reached into the cabinet above the sink and grabbed a glass, setting it on the granite counter. Next up, the bottle of scotch that Jeremy had left behind when she'd kicked him out a year ago.

*He's dead. Jeremy is dead.*

It didn't matter how many times the thought jockeyed inside her head; it still didn't seem real. There was nothing like finding out someone had died to remind you of how precious every day of life was. She needed to make some changes. Her whole world couldn't be just about work anymore.

"Alexa, call Katrina," Amina said to the small electronic device that she used for everything from making calls to turning on the lights when she wasn't home. Between that and other modern gadgets, her life was practically run by machines.

*Okay, calling Katrina*, Alexa's robotic voice announced.

It was a little late, but Amina needed to talk to someone. Her sister was a night owl, assuming she was even home, and she loved nothing more than talking. She was an attorney by trade, but currently worked as a wealth management adviser at a Fortune 500 company in Washington, DC. She could talk law and numbers all night long.

"What's wrong?" Katrina answered by way of greeting.

"Sorry to call so late," Amina said. With Katrina living on the east coast, the three-hour time difference often proved to be a challenge, especially when wanting to chat. "What makes you think something is wrong?"

"Because this will make two times that we've talked this week when normally we can barely get in one call, and it's only Thursday. Besides that, you never call this late. So, what happened? Oh no, did you lose a patient?"

Whenever one of her patients died, she would normally stop at one of her sisters' houses instead of going home. They always provided a normalcy, a reminder that death was a part of life and she had to cherish her loved ones. She would even go to them when that happened during the short time she was married.

Reflecting on her failed marriage, Amina couldn't

help but think of Jeremy. "Jay was killed while on duty today," she said.

Her sister's gasp filled the quietness of the kitchen. "Oh, my goodness. That's awful! I'm so sorry. I know you guys weren't on speaking terms, but…man, that's awful."

"Yeah, I know. It still doesn't seem real, even though I hadn't talked to him since the divorce." She had seen him days after, for a few minutes, when he stopped by to pick up the last of his things. Even then, they didn't talk. She hadn't seen or heard from him since. "I think I'm still in shock. I feel horrible about what happened to him, but it's like I'm not sure what I'm supposed to be feeling. I haven't even cried."

As a human being, the news of his death broke Amina's heart and she'd feel that way about anyone's death. As Jeremy's ex-wife, who had felt nothing but anger toward him for so long, she was numb.

"It probably hasn't hit you yet. How'd you find out?"

"Max. He came to see me at the hospital, and he said it happened when he and Jeremy were responding to a disturbance."

Silence filled the phone line, and she had no idea what Katrina was thinking. Only her sisters knew how she felt about Maxwell. They'd been the ones she'd complained to after first meeting him at the party and how he'd left without saying goodbye. They were also the ones she had confided in months later after Max mentioned the note that Jeremy never gave her.

Amina sighed at the memory. How different would her life have been had she and Maxwell gotten together? By the time she had learned about the note, it had been too late. She'd already fallen for Jeremy, but couldn't believe the man she loved would treat his friend like that. When she confronted Jeremy, he'd said all the right things to justify his behavior.

Amina rubbed her temple, disgusted that she had believed him. Jeremy had told her that the moment he'd laid eyes on her, he knew they were meant to be together. He had treated her as such, catering to her needs and desires, showering her with gifts. She wanted for nothing while they were dating. She had gotten caught up in the fantasy that Jeremy had painted over the four months that they'd dated.

But then there was Maxwell. Every time Amina was in his presence, a passionate stirring swirled inside her. She ignored it for the sake of her marriage, telling herself that like others in their small circle, she and Max were just friends. But deep down, Amina knew it was something more. Even with the few times that they ended up in the same proximity, they developed a bond that she couldn't explain. Katrina had once referred to the relationships as a jacked-up love triangle where Amina had married a man she'd fallen in love with, when she'd been seriously attracted to his friend.

"How's Max holding up?" her sister asked.

"About as well as you would expect. I'm so used to seeing him strong and in charge, but today he seemed... he seemed... I don't know. He's taking it pretty hard and kept saying that it could've been him."

Staring down into the glass at the dark liquid, Amina brought it to her lips and gulped half of it. She winced when it burned her throat on the way down to her stomach. She hadn't realized the scotch would be so strong, but it was exactly what she needed. Something to knock the edge off, calm her nerves and maybe even make her forget what a long day it had been.

The effects of the alcohol were already working as warmth spread through her body. She recounted the details of the shooting to Katrina, only able to answer some of her questions. As they talked, Amina realized just how awful it must have been for Maxwell to have witnessed the incident. He'd been right. It could've been him. He could've died today.

That thought had Amina slamming back the remaining booze, wincing at the taste and the heat the way she'd done moments ago.

"Goodness, that's strong." She gagged.

"I guess that means you're drinking something other than wine," Katrina cracked.

"Scotch, and it tastes like it might be a hundred percent alcohol. It's *that* potent," Amina quipped.

She poured herself another two-finger glass of the amber liquid, since she didn't have to work in the morning. Her mind then went back to Maxwell. After spending a few minutes in his company, all the old feelings had come crashing back. Amina hadn't seen him in over six months and missed him. She hadn't realized just how much until they were talking in the stairwell.

She didn't dare tell her sister about how she had suggested to Maxwell that they get together tonight. When she proposed the idea, it had been strictly innocent. Yet, something in his gaze told her that he hadn't taken it that way. Actually, now that she thought about it, Amina wasn't sure if it was as innocuous as she'd wanted it to sound.

Did she want to spend time with Maxwell getting reacquainted? Heck, yeah. Would he ever allow that to happen? Probably not. Amina had missed her chance with him. That didn't mean she didn't want to at least rebuild what they once had. They'd been friends…at least that's how she saw him.

Amina sighed as she stared into her drink. If only she could have a do-over of the last year and a half. She'd take it in a heartbeat. There were so many things she would change, but too bad life didn't work that way. Sometimes you had to just accept your poor choices and hope for the best, especially when it came to matters of the heart.

"Are you still interested in Maxwell?" Katrina asked. "And before you answer, I'm not talking about as a friend. I mean are you still attracted to him?"

*Yes.* The word dangled on the edge of Amina's tongue, but she held back from speaking it aloud. What would be the point? Maxwell had made it clear that the two of them could never have more than a friendship. He'd felt betrayed not only by Jeremy, but also by her, despite the fact that Jeremy had screwed them both.

"It wasn't that hard of a question." Katrina's voice penetrated Amina's thoughts. "You're either attracted to him or you're not."

Amina sighed and traced her finger around the rim of her glass. "What difference does it make? Nothing can happen between us. I blew that opportunity when I chose Jeremy over Maxwell."

"Wait. You didn't choose him over Max. Jay took the choice out of your hands when his backstabbing ass—"

"Stop. We're not doing this, especially not now. That was the past. What's been done is done. Besides, you know that old saying. Never date your ex's best friend or your best friend's ex."

"None of that applies to this situation, and you deserve some happiness. If it means starting something up with Max to see if those old feelings are back, then I say go for it. Take a chance and open your heart again."

Amina wasn't sure if those old feelings ever really left, and she was too ashamed to admit that out loud. Maxwell was special, a perfect gentleman and the kindest man she'd ever met. What she wouldn't give for a chance to see if they could ever be more than friends.

"I can't." She hadn't meant to say what she was thinking. The words slipped from her mouth before she could pull them back. "Maxwell and Jeremy were once besties. It would be too weird. Besides, now is not the time for a conversation like this."

"Not to speak ill of the dead, but Max and Jay hadn't been close in a long time," Katrina continued, ignoring the part about not having that conversation. "Not since Max punched him for getting in your face at your birthday party last year. After that, they barely tolerated each other. Even I know that."

Amina closed her eyes and pinched the bridge of her nose. A heavy weight settled in the center of her chest, then nose-dived to her stomach. She never imagined that she'd be the cause of anyone's friendship imploding, especially theirs.

"Actually, Jay was lucky in so many ways that night."

Amina opened her eyes and her brows dipped into a frown. "Seriously? Are you kidding me? He lost me *and* his best friend that night all because of drinking too much and acting out. There was nothing lucky about it."

"Oh, but there was," her sister said in that nasally tone and cocky way that grated on Amina's nerves. Katrina should've been a trial lawyer with the way she enjoyed arguing. Always quick to bring out numerous points of view to practically every conversation. To Amina, she did it all for the sake of arguing.

"First of all," Katrina went on, "Jay was a jerk even when he wasn't drunk. I hated how you always made excuses for his sorry ass. As for him being lucky, if Daddy had seen the way he had grabbed your arm that night, he would've killed him on the spot. Then we would've had to visit our father in jail all because of Jeremy's stupid ass."

"Would you stop it! I can't believe how callous you're being right now. The man died today, Katrina! Killed while trying to serve and protect. We should be mourning his death, not discussing his mistakes," Amina snapped. A tear slid down her cheek, and she quickly swiped it away.

She had known within a few months of her marriage that it was doomed. That she had married wrong. Still, Jeremy was gone. She would never wish death on anyone. Not even him. They shouldn't even be discussing what happened in the past. It was done. Over. Yet, the time her family had thrown her a surprise birthday party would go down as one of the worst moments of her life.

The party had started out fun. It was great seeing family and friends, even some from high school. Her sisters had taken her to a spa that afternoon, and when they returned to her house, everyone except Jeremy was there. Tables overflowed with food dishes, there was dancing and celebrating, and guests were having a good time. Amina knew Jeremy's tardiness had been a source of contention with her family, but it hadn't bothered her. It gave her a chance to reconnect with people she hadn't seen in a while, including Maxwell. She'd been glad to see him that day.

Amina sipped more of the liquor and glanced around. Her home had an open floor plan, giving her a good view of the family room. Her gaze settled on the spot near the front door where Maxwell had knocked Jeremy unconscious. But in reality, in his drunken state, it hadn't taken much to knock out her ex-husband.

"I need to use the bathroom. Hold on a second," Katrina said. Amina was glad for the verbal break, but now memories of her last birthday party filled her mind.

The celebration had turned bad, really quick after Maxwell punched her ex-husband. It had taken a minute for Jeremy to come to, and when he did, his surly attitude only got worse. He would've probably tried to retaliate, but Maxwell left soon after the incident. And once Jeremy got his bearings, he had demanded everyone out.

Amina never thought she could hate someone as much as she had in that moment. Refusing to be alone with him in his condition, she had spent the night at her parents' house. That night, she had finally admitted to herself that her marriage was over. The day after the party, she had kicked Jeremy out of the house, and had filed for divorce a few days later.

It had been one of the most stressful times in Amina's life. For months, he had dragged out the process, insisting he would never let her go, but it had only been out of spite. That only made her hate him that much more. He hadn't been holding out on signing the divorce papers because he was still in love with her. No, it had everything to do with Maxwell. Jeremy was so sure that the moment he was out of the picture that she'd run into Maxwell's arms.

Amina rubbed her tired eyes, and her heart ached

realizing that those were the most prominent memories of her late ex-husband. How had their relationship gotten so far off track? She wanted to blame Jeremy for everything. She couldn't. She was the one who fell for his charming ways and his sweet words. He had the type of swagger that drew women to him, and she had fallen for it within months. All the while, ignoring the little voice in her head that warned her to tread lightly with him while they were dating. Or maybe it had been Katrina's voice. Her sister and their father never thought much of him.

Suddenly, her eyes filled with tears. She wasn't a crier, but when a couple of rogue tears slipped through, more soon followed.

"Alexa, hang up," Amina said on a sob, and the call disconnected.

Her sister would call back. In the meantime, Amina stood and snatched off a couple of sheets of paper towel from the holder on the counter. An acute sense of despair lodged inside her, and she was powerless against the uncontrollable sobs that shook her body. Maybe it was exhaustion combined with the alcohol that had her falling apart so abruptly.

But she knew it was more than that. Jeremy was gone. Dead. Killed in the line of duty. She cried for his untimely death. She cried for his family, and she cried for all that she'd never get to say to him. No matter how horrible their marriage had been, there were still a few happy times that had gotten overshadowed by the bad.

Amina's cell phone rang in the bedroom, but she didn't make a move to get it. She allowed herself a few more minutes to pull herself together. As the tears slowly dried, she released a shaky breath then went in search of the phone, assuming it was her sister.

When she entered the bedroom, she turned on the lamp that was on the nightstand and picked up her cell. Glancing at the screen, she had missed two calls from Katrina.

Amina huffed out another breath before hitting Redial.

"Why'd you hang up? I told you I'd be right back," her sister said. "Now, where were we?"

Amina sniffed. "I'm done talking about Jeremy. From now on, or at least for the rest of this conversation, can you please keep your opinions to yourself?"

After a short hesitation, Katrina said, "I didn't mean to upset you, sis. You're right. I was insensitive. It's just kind of hard to think kind thoughts about a guy who mistreated my little sister. He might've never hit you, but knowing that he had grabbed you during your party pissed me the hell off. And I can recall once when he belittled you in front of me…it was hard to watch."

Shame swelled inside Amina and she dropped down on her queen-size bed. Had she not married Jeremy, her family wouldn't have been dragged into the drama that had been her life. They wouldn't have been privy to the times that he had talked to her like she was a nobody. She also wouldn't have wasted even a few months of marriage with a man who didn't respect her.

"All I'm saying is Jay was…something," Katrina continued. "Daddy said it more than once that there was something shady about him, and you know he's rarely wrong. I'm glad you divorced Jeremy as soon as you did. Who knows what type of mess he could've eventually pulled you into? I only wished you hadn't gotten involved with his slimy ass in the first place. Heck, I wouldn't be surprised if his death rattles a few cages. That brother probably had all types of secrets."

"Katrina," Amina managed in a warning tone. "Can you please just stop?"

"Hey, don't get mad at me because I speak the truth. I know you don't want to admit it, but I'm just sayin' dude had issues. Something was up with him."

Amina released a noisy sigh. Yeah, Jeremy had problems, seen and unseen, but from what she knew of him, he wasn't all bad. Maybe if she focused on that for a while, the less-than-favorable memories would drift away.

"I wonder what Dad is going to say when you tell him what happened to Jeremy."

"Probably not much," Amina admitted reluctantly.

She didn't want to break the news to her parents while they were on vacation. Besides that, they'd be unreachable out in the middle of the ocean. They usually locked their phones in the cabin's safe the moment they started sailing and rarely checked in while cruising. This time probably wouldn't be any different.

"On another note, do you think you're still Jeremy's beneficiary?" Katrina asked.

"Seriously? Are you really asking me that right now?"

"Don't tell me you haven't thought about it."

No, she hadn't, and leave it to her sister to make an uncomfortable conversation even more unpleasant. Amina was pretty sure Jeremy would've removed her as the beneficiary on any of his work benefits, but they had purchased an insurance policy that was outside his job. It was paid annually, and she probably wouldn't have thought about the policy for another few months if it wasn't for Jeremy's untimely death.

Instead of answering her sister's question, Amina said, "As usual, it's been interesting talking to you."

Katrina gave an unladylike snort. "And by interesting you probably mean, *Why did I call you?* But that's all right. I'm sure I haven't said anything that you weren't thinking or will be thinking once the news of Jeremy's death sets in. Just promise you'll call me or Mark if you need us," she said of her husband. "Don't be down there suffering in silence. I might not have liked the guy, but I know at one point he was important to you. We're here for you."

"Thanks, sis. I appreciate that."

"Oh, wait. Are you planning to go to the funeral?" Katrina yawned, which made Amina yawn. It was after eleven her time and two in the morning on the East Coast. She didn't know how her sister functioned with limited sleep. Rarely did she go to bed before one in the morning, and she was usually up by five.

"Maxwell asked me that too, and I don't know. I feel like I should at least go and give my condolences."

"Why? Why put yourself through that since his parents didn't like you."

"They liked me enough," Amina defended. "They just didn't like hearing that Jay and I were having trouble. Then when we separated——"

"Which was when they started treating you like crap. I'm glad they don't live in Vegas anymore. Now you won't have to risk running into them."

That was true. Amina got the house in the divorce settlement, and Jeremy's parents used to live a few blocks away. After they moved to Seattle, she didn't have to worry about seeing them at the store or walking in the neighborhood.

"At least Elaine was kinda cool," Katrina said of Jeremy's sister, who was two years older than him. "I feel sorry for her. It's not going to be easy losing her only sibling."

No, it wouldn't be, and Amina's heart broke for her. Elaine was always kind, and unlike her parents, she didn't always take Jeremy's side of things. She knew her brother wasn't the man he should've been, and often called him out on his BS, but she loved him despite his shortcomings.

"I think I will attend the funeral. Maybe I'll arrive late and leave early."

"Then what's the point? You won't get to pay your respects to his family."

"True," Amina said on a groan. She hated funerals. Maybe not attending would be for the best. Then again, Maxwell might need her. "Once I get the details, I'll probably attend. Hopefully, I won't regret that decision."

## Chapter 4

The thick haze hovering over the city mocked Maxwell's gloomy mood as he sat outside the apartment complex where Jeremy had been shot. Despite his boss insisting he take a few days off, he had returned to the crime scene, parked in almost the exact spot where they'd been the day before.

Apprehension mounted inside him as he finally climbed out of his car. It probably wasn't a good idea to be there, especially since his boss had instructed that he take time off. Maxwell couldn't stay away. The sooner they found the person responsible, the better, and he wanted to help any way he could.

As he drew closer to the spot where Jeremy had been gunned down, his pulse pounded louder in his ears. *It could've been me.* The words taunted him with each reluctant step he took. Though he'd known plenty of people who had dealt with survivor's guilt at one time or another, he never had. At least maybe not until now. He couldn't be sure, but for most of the night and into the morning, he hadn't been able to stop thinking that he should've been dead too. He and Jeremy had been standing right next to each other. Why hadn't the gunman taken him out?

Operating on less than three hours of sleep probably wasn't helping his mood or the depressing thoughts flowing through is mind. The shooting played on loop inside his head. He needed answers. He had to determine whether he'd missed something the day before, which was why he was there.

Crime-scene tape stretched across the walkway to keep residents and visitors from using the front entrance. Maxwell's steps grew heavier as if his feet were encased in cement, but he didn't stop. He kept moving forward, determined to overcome the unease swirling inside him as he trudged up the walkway.

With each step he took, more questions than he had answers to plagued his mind. There was one that nagged him more than the others, though. Had there been more than one shot fired the day before? He couldn't remember. Had he blocked that detail out? And if there had only been one shot—why? Why hadn't the shooter shot him too? Everything had happened so fast, but wouldn't he remember something like that?

Frustration gnawed on his nerves, and without warning, the staccato rhythm of his pulse inched up. His heart was practically pounding out of his chest.

*Relax. Just calm down and keep moving*, he told himself, but the self-talk wasn't helping. His heart raced faster, and he balled his fists at his sides, pushing down

the sudden urge to reach for his gun. He was off duty
and in plain clothes instead of his uniform. His gun
was in his ankle holster and not easy to get to, which
was probably good, especially since there was no threat.

Maxwell slowed. He needed to pull himself together
before he came face-to-face with his team. He was about
ten feet from the main entrance when the door swung
open.

"Hey, Sarge," Peter O'Brien, one of Maxwell's officers, said from the doorway. "I'm surprised to see you."

Maxwell nodded at him and another police officer,
Kent Jackson, who was standing just inside the foyer. He
assumed the men were assigned to guard the entrances
while the team continued their investigation.

The two men couldn't be more different. Peter, a
clean-shaven blond with blue eyes and movie star good
looks, was around five-ten with a runner's build. His
easygoing personality stood out amongst some of their
more somber officers, like Kent. The six-four giant with
the maximum amount of facial hair the department allowed and a few tattoos on his arms rarely smiled. He
mostly only spoke when spoken to, and his and Peter's
personalities balanced each other and made them good
partners.

"You doing all right, Sarge?" Peter asked.

Maxwell willed his breathing to settle back to normal. "Yeah, I'm fine. How are things here?"

His gaze bounced to Kent. The officer studied him
as if he sensed Maxwell was trying to get himself together, but he didn't comment. They were all on edge.
Losing a fellow officer was hard. It reminded them of
just how dangerous their jobs were, and what happened
to Jeremy could easily happen to any of them.

"All things considered it's been fairly quiet here. I'll walk up with you." Peter fell in step with Maxwell. "Danny and Zeke have been here since daybreak, talking to some of the tenants," he said of a couple of their best detectives.

Maxwell wasn't sure why Peter thought he needed an escort, but he didn't comment. The limited amount of sleep the night before had him anxious and irritable. Not a good combination. It was possible his guys sensed that he wasn't himself at the moment.

He had received calls from a number of them after the incident expressing their condolences of him losing not only an officer, but a friend. With each call, more guilt settled inside him at how things ended between him and Jeremy. If only they could've made peace before…

Maxwell didn't bother finishing the thought. They headed to the stairs, bypassing the elevator that looked as if it had seen better days. They hiked the four flights of creaky stairs and strolled down the long hallway that looked and smelled as if it had been freshly painted. Though some parts of the building appeared to be going through renovations, other parts, like the scuffed tiled floor, still needed work.

"Most of the tenants on this floor have already been questioned."

"Anyone see anything?"

Peter shook his head. "A lot of them weren't home during the time of the shooting. Others barely let us get the questions out before saying they didn't see, hear or know anything."

That wasn't a surprise. Most of them didn't want anything to do with cops, even if it meant catching a killer. Some of them probably had warrants out. Others might've had previous bad experiences with police officers. Either way, Maxwell hoped that if anyone knew anything, they'd come forward.

They reached the end of the hallway and another officer was posted at the door of the apartment where the killer had been. Maxwell nodded and entered. Like in the hallway, the smell of fresh paint greeted him. He glanced to his left into the small kitchen and continued forward until he stood in the living/dining room combo. He wasn't sure what he'd expected, but he at least thought there would be furniture in the two-bedroom, one-bathroom unit.

"Hey, Sarge. I didn't know you were here," Danny, a short, middle-aged detective with a receding hairline and age spots covering his fair complexion, said as he exited what Maxwell assumed was a bedroom. "I thought you were taking a couple of days off."

"Where's the furniture?" he asked instead of responding to Danny's comment. His gaze bounced around, taking in everything from the carpeted floor to the picture window that was across the room.

"Yeah, so here's the thing," Danny said, adjusting his badge that was hanging from a silver chain around his neck. Then he tugged on the collar of his polo shirt as if it was choking him.

Due to the heat, the department usually allowed them to dress down in the summer. Instead of a suit or sports coat, detectives wore polo shirts and slacks.

"No tenants live here," Danny continued. "The apartment has been vacant for a couple of weeks and the assistant manager has no idea who might've been in here yesterday. She tried getting in contact with the manager, who's been out of the office the last few days. We did talk to the maintenance team, and they said that vacant apartments are always locked. The supervisor said they had no reason to enter this one since it's been ready to rent for weeks."

Glancing back at the door and the lock that appeared perfectly intact, Maxwell wondered how the shooter got in.

"We're guessing he picked the lock," Danny said as if reading his mind. "When we arrived yesterday, the door was pulled closed like nothing was wrong. Come on back—you can see the room where the window was busted out."

Maxwell followed him to the rear of the apartment. The windowpane hadn't been replaced and a large piece of plywood sat on the side. "Forensics brushed the window seal and a few other surfaces, but so far, we don't have much."

Careful not to touch anything, Maxwell glanced through the window and on to the front walkway. As he peered out, he ran his hand up and down his chest to help tap down the bile that was rising inside him. The gunman had a perfect shot of them. Maxwell swallowed hard, realizing now more than ever that he could've been lying in the morgue beside Jeremy.

*Why didn't the shooter shoot me too?* he asked himself again. *He'd had the perfect opportunity.*

Had the shooter prepped to take potshots at cops? Had it been someone with a grudge? Someone who'd had a run-in with him or Jeremy in the past? He didn't ask any of the questions out loud knowing the answers would come while they investigated. He stood there for a few minutes taking it all in, then moved to the window on the other side of the room.

Maxwell stared out and the view was of the street where his car was currently parked. "The shooter saw us coming," he mumbled, not expecting the detective to comment. "What about a radio or speakers, or whatever was used to blast the music? What was found?"

Danny shook his head. "Nothing was here. We've determined that the music came from another apartment on the other side of the building and two floors down. Zeke," he said of the other detective on the case, "has been trying to locate the tenant. Yesterday, when we didn't get an answer, we ended up kicking the door in. That's when we found an old boom box sitting near one of the windows with the music blasting."

Moments after backup arrived the day before, paramedics were on the scene. Maxwell had stayed with Jeremy, who'd been barely hanging on at the time, until he passed away.

"We got him," Zeke said as he strolled into the bedroom with a small notepad in his hands. He looked surprised when he saw Maxwell.

"You got who?" Maxwell asked, hope blooming inside him.

"Not the shooter," Zeke said quickly. "The tenant who lived in the apartment where we found the radio just showed up. Get this—he's saying that a guy paid him two hundred and fifty dollars to blast his music."

"Did he say why?"

"According to him, he didn't ask any questions when the guy flashed the money. He was instructed to turn the volume as high as it would go, then leave. He was also told not to return to his apartment until today. We're taking him in for further questioning."

"What about other witnesses? Surely someone must've

seen or heard something. There's no way someone could've shot at us and gotten out of here without someone seeing him."

"What are you doing here?" Lieutenant Grayson roared from the doorway. "I thought I told you to take some days off." He was huge and intimidating, looking like he should've been a defensive lineman on some professional football team instead of running a police department. Dressed in his uniform while glaring at Maxwell made him appear even more threatening, but everyone knew he was more bark than bite.

"I am taking time off," Maxwell said, unconvincingly as he continued glancing around the empty room. "I'm here in an unofficial capacity. I needed to see the space for myself."

He'd hoped by seeing where the shooter had been it would help ease the knot that had been lodged in his chest since the moment Jeremy dropped to his knees. It didn't. All it did was make him more anxious. Maybe he and Jeremy had been too relaxed and not vigilant enough when walking up to the building. Maxwell didn't think so, but that nagging feeling that he had missed something kept gnawing at him.

"Did you remember anything else?" his boss asked.

Maxwell rubbed his forehead, exhaustion starting to catch up with him. "Nothing I haven't already told you." He turned his attention back to Zeke. "You didn't answer me. Besides the guy you're planning to question, were there any more witnesses?"

"Go home. Get some rest, and that's an order," Lieutenant Grayson barked. "When we know more, you'll know more. Until then, I don't want to see or hear from you. Got it?"

Maxwell stared at him and tried to rein in his frustration before nodding. He wasn't good at letting others do what he felt he should be doing, and that was finding Jeremy's killer. Yet, he was no good to his guys if he didn't have his head on straight, and right now, he was so tired he could barely string two thoughts together. They had their best people on the case, and he had no doubt they'd find the person who murdered Jeremy. But what the heck was he supposed to do in the meantime?

After saying his goodbyes, he left the apartment. He might've been exhausted, but if he went home, he'd still be bombarded with questions running through his brain. He wouldn't be able to relax even if he wanted to. No, he needed a distraction. Maybe he'd stop by his sister's house and hang out with his niece and nephew. But as he trotted down the stairs, Amina came to mind. He could take her up on her offer from the day before and hook up with her.

As soon as the thought materialized, he knew it was a bad idea.

"A very bad idea," he mumbled.

# Chapter 5

Amina couldn't wait to leave work. She'd done an eight-hour shift that felt more like twelve, and the only highlight was knowing she had the next three days off.

"Hey, you. I didn't know you were still here. You look as if you're about to fall on your face," Samantha, a friend and fellow nurse, said. She was walking toward Amina and they both turned down the hallway that led to the locker room.

"It's been a long day and night." Amina pushed open the door to the room, and the moment she stepped in, she eyed the overstuffed sofa that was to the left of the door. Someone had recently donated it to the hospital, and Amina didn't know what it was made of, but it was the most comfortable piece of furniture she'd ever sat on. Tempted to stretch out on it, she thought better of the idea and went to her locker instead. Why settle for a temporary reprieve when she could be home and in bed within the next thirty minutes?

"I've only been here an hour, but it hasn't seemed that busy. Why do you look like you've been dragged behind a car down the interstate?"

Amina glanced over her shoulder. Samantha was sitting on the bench in front of her locker changing into a pair of white shoes that had a thicker sole than the black ones she'd walked in with.

"You haven't heard?" she asked.

Her friend glanced up at her with her brows furrowed. "Heard what?"

"Jeremy was killed yesterday."

Samantha gasped and her hands went to her mouth. "Oh, my God. Honey, I'm so sorry. I hadn't heard. What happened? How did you find out? Why didn't you call me?" She rattled off one question after another.

Even though Amina considered Samantha a friend and someone she trusted, she hadn't shared everything about her marriage. Partly because it was too embarrassing to admit how poorly she had chosen a mate.

As she filled Samantha in on the little she knew about the case, Amina's chest tightened. It still didn't seem real. The scotch might've helped her fall asleep, but the moment she'd opened her eyes that morning, she'd had to face reality again. Jeremy was gone…for good.

Samantha stood and pulled Amina into a bone-crushing hug that practically knocked the breath out of her. "I am so sorry," she said when she finally released Amina. "How are you holding up?"

"I'm doing all right. It helped that it's been so busy around here. So I haven't had much time to dwell on the what-ifs, the woulda, shoulda, couldas and just how things ended with us."

Who was she kidding? She might not have been thinking about those things throughout the whole day, but every few minutes, memories of Jeremy infiltrated her mind. There were so many regrets, but deep down, Amina knew that the two of them together were never meant to be.

"How'd it go dropping Tammy off at camp this morning?" she asked of Samantha's youngest child.

"You're not slick trying to change the subject, but I get it."

Amina listened while Samantha discussed her two daughters who'd been doing gymnastics since they were three. Now one was eight and the other ten, and according to her, they were future Olympians. A pang of longing always hit her whenever her coworkers discussed their families, especially their kids. She'd always wanted to be a wife and mother, and at the rate she was going, she'd never realize that dream.

"Listen to me going on and on. Girl, I'm sorry. I know you're trying to get out of here, but..." Samantha sighed and her eyes searched Amina's. "If you need me, call. I know your family is out of town, but they're not the only family you have. If you want to stay with us for a while, I'll get the guest room ready."

Amina wrapped her arms around her friend's neck. "Thank you. That's sweet, but I'm fine. Really."

"All right, but the offer doesn't expire. At least call or text me during your days off to let me know you're okay."

"Will do." She draped her large bag onto her shoulder and double-checked that she'd grabbed what she needed out of her locker. "I'm out of here," she said on her way to the door.

"Okay, see you later, and don't forget what I said. I want to hear from you."

"Yes, Mother," Amina cracked, and gave her friend a wave.

As she took the elevator down to the ground floor, she couldn't help but smile at the mention of Samantha getting the guest room together. That was code for *she'll declutter and sanitize the family room, then pull out the sofa sleeper.*

A few minutes later, Amina stepped outside and breathed in the warm air. Some of the tiredness of the day slowly drifted away as a breeze ruffled her short hair. *Three days off.* She needed a break and that would be just enough time to regroup and clear her mind. Now all she needed to decide was how to spend her free time. Instead of going straight home as planned, maybe she'd stop and pick up some kung pao shrimp and crab rangoon. Then she'd head to her sanctuary and camp out in front of the television until she fell asleep.

"Oh, that's exciting," she mumbled under her breath. She needed to make some changes.

Working so many ridiculous hours helped pad her bank account, but it was ruining her social life. Actually, that wasn't true. She was the one ruining her social life by not going anywhere or letting her coworkers fix her up on blind dates. She hadn't dated since before getting married, and until recently, hadn't felt like she was missing anything. But heading home to an empty house was getting old.

*Definitely time for some changes.*

Amina went down another aisle and wove between

cars. When her vehicle came into view, she pointed the key fob at her Toyota Camry and unlocked the doors.

"Excuse me."

Amina's heart slammed against her rib cage, and she spun around. "Oh, my God. You scared me," she said, her hand on her heaving chest.

There was just enough illumination from a nearby light pole to let her see that the man was a little taller than her five-foot-eight height. His dark clothes and the baseball cap pulled low over his eyes blended into the night. With her heart racing, she glanced around the lot. If anything went down, she was too far from the building for anyone to see or hear her.

"I didn't mean to scare you," the man said, flashing straight white teeth against his dark skin. "I was just wondering if you could spare a couple of dollars."

"Stop right there!" she yelled when he moved toward her. She positioned her car key between her fingers to use as a weapon if needed. Her other hand had a death grip on the handle of her oversize bag. "I'm not sure what you're doing out here, but—"

He lunged at her, and Amina screamed and swung her handbag at him. Anticipating the move, he shoved her against her car, then slapped a gloved hand over her mouth. In his other hand was a blade that he pressed against her throat.

Amina's bag dropped to the ground with a thud and so did her keys. She immediately grabbed on to his forearm, pulling down on it and trying to keep the knife from making contact with her skin as panic plowed through her body.

"I don't want to hurt you, but fight me and you're dead," the man said close to her ear, reeking of cigarette smoke. The deep rumble of his voice sent a chill scurrying down Amina's spine. An icy fear twisted inside her gut when he pinned her against the vehicle.

"Please don't," she cried out, her voice muffled against his gloved hand.

*Do something!* her brain screamed, but what? Her mind darted back to the hospital-sponsored self-defense class she had taken a few months ago.

*Just calm down. Just calm down*, she told herself. Scared to death and breathing hard, she slowly uncurled her fingers from around his thick arm and gradually lifted her hands in surrender.

"That's what I'm talking about. Cooperation," her attacker said, and his hand over her mouth loosened and his knife moved slightly away from her neck.

*Fight. If you don't fight, you're as good as dead.* She heard her father's voice as if he was standing right next to her. He had ingrained those words into her and her sisters from the time they learned to talk good.

*Fight.* The word played on repeat through her mind.

Without another thought, she jabbed her left elbow back as hard as she could, catching the man in his side. He cursed and his hand dropped from her mouth just as she jammed the heel of her foot on top of his instep.

He yelped. "Son of a…"

Amina started to run, but the guy recovered quicker than she expected. She screamed when his arm went around her like a steel band, pinning her arms to her sides. The knife was back at her throat, but that didn't stop her from twisting, turning and wiggling against the man's hard body. But he was too strong.

"Let me go!" she screamed over and over. She jerked

against him, moving left and right, trying to pull away as she forced him to back up from the vehicle.

"Stop it!" he snarled, and lifted her off the ground. She kept squirming, keeping him off-balance. She had to get away.

Tears blurred her vision. Her hammering pulse was deafening in her ears as he shuffled them forward again. When they got closer to the car, Amina kicked her leg out and connected with the back door. She pushed off the vehicle. The move caught her attacker off guard again causing him to stumble back.

"Dammit," he growled, trying to stay upright while still holding on to her, but his other arm jerked, causing the knife to slide across her neck. Amina shrieked at the initial sting and the shock of being cut, but used the downward momentum to her advantage.

Her deafening scream pierced the air.

"Hey!" someone yelled in the distance, and her assailant startled, loosening his grip.

Heart racing, Amina wrestled out of his grasp. "Help!" she screamed, and took off in a sprint; adrenaline propelled her forward and she darted in between cars and headed to the building. She didn't dare look back, just pushed herself to keep going. "Help me!"

When she got closer to the building, she spotted Dr. McPherson running toward her. More tears spilled down her cheeks as he got closer. She slammed into him, holding on as if he was a lifeline.

"What happened?" he asked in a rush, his arm around her shoulder.

"A ma-man attack—attacked me," she said, her words strangled on a sob. The faster she wiped at her tears, the faster they fell.

Two security guards came running and Dr. McPherson directed them to the middle of the lot.

"Come on. Let's get you inside." He hurried her to the building. "A little help over here," he called out once they were inside.

*I could've been killed.*

That overwhelming realization sent her mind spinning out of control. Amina covered her face with her hands when sobs engulfed her, and she dropped to her knees. Her body shook violently while chills raked over her skin and she struggled to get air into her lungs.

*I could've been killed.*

She wept uncontrollably as a flurry of activity went on around her. "Help me," she choked out, feeling as if she was being swallowed into a deep, dark hole.

"She's bleeding."

"Is that Amina?"

"What happened?"

"Get her into room thirteen."

Amina's head spun, and she couldn't stop the tears as everyone talked at once. It was as if her brain couldn't completely process what was happening.

Someone squeezed her hand. "Oh, honey. You're okay. We've got you."

# Chapter 6

"How do you feel?" Samantha asked when she finished taking Amina's blood pressure again.

Propped up against pillows on the hospital bed, Amina kept her eyes closed. "I'm embarrassed, and I'm exhausted. I also feel like I sprinted the New York City Marathon in ten minutes flat."

Samantha laughed. "Well, you have nothing to be embarrassed about."

Amina cracked one eye open and glanced at her friend. "Seriously? I made a fool of myself downstairs. I have never cried like that in my life, and of course it had to be in front of everyone. How am I ever going to be able to face them again?"

Samantha huffed out a breath and sat on the side of the bed. "Girl, you just went through hell. All of us would've fallen apart had we been in your shoes. As

far as embarrassment goes? Please, you had a panic attack. My butt would've passed out the moment that jerk
showed up out of nowhere at my car. Trust me—you're
doing amazing. You're way stronger than most of us
would've been in that situation."

Amina sat up straighter and linked her fingers in her
lap, trying to stop her hands from shaking. Physically,
she was fine, but mentally, she was still a nervous wreck.
*First Jeremy. Now this.* If she didn't know better, she'd
wonder if the mugging was connected to Jeremy's death.

Amina shook the thought free, mentally chastising
herself for going there. Clearly, she'd been watching too
many crime shows. Her imagination was getting the best
of her. Jeremy was killed in the line of duty. Of course,
the attack on her had nothing to do with his murder.

"I have never been so scared in all of my life," she
said.

"Thank God you got away. I only wished Security
could've caught the guy. But while you were being
checked out, they found your bag and keys next to your
car and brought them inside. Oh, and while they were
questioning you, you mentioned that he had on a baseball cap. Did you see any part of his face? Anything that
the rest of us should be looking out for?"

Amina shook her head but stopped when the cut on
her neck started stinging. It was a superficial wound,
similar to a scrape, but the prickling sensation was just
enough to be irritating. It was about five inches long, and
there was about a half an inch of it that was a little
deeper than the rest. It would probably leave a scar, but
nothing as bad as it could've been.

"It happened so fast, and even though the lot was
pretty well lit, I didn't see his face. All I know was that

he was a little taller than me. He had on all black and smelled as if he bathed with cigarette-scented shower gel." She pinched the bridge of her nose as she recalled the guy. "He came out of nowhere, but I fault myself for not paying attention. I'm so used to just going out there and hopping into my car. I never thought I'd get mu…" The rest of the word caught in her throat. She was beyond lucky that she'd gotten away.

There was a quick knock on the door before Dr. McPherson strolled in. "I just wanted to check on you. Are you all right?"

"Yes, I'm fine. I didn't mean to freak you and everyone else out."

"I'm just glad you're okay." He studied her in that way that he always did with his patients and their parents. Sometimes he appeared as if he was waiting for them to say more. While other times, it seemed he was debating on what other questions to ask.

"I'm ready to get out of here," Amina said.

The emergency room doctor wanted her to stick around a little while for observation. She rarely had headaches, especially those that were as strong as a migraine. She also didn't suffer from high blood pressure, but during her panic attack, she'd dealt with both. Her blood pressure had skyrocketed and it had taken a while for it to go back to normal.

"When was your last tetanus shot?"

That had been one of many questions the ER doctor had asked even though all of them were strongly encouraged to stay on top of their vaccinations.

"Two years ago," she told Dr. McPherson.

He nodded slowly. "You're shivering. Are you cold or is that nerves?"

Amina glanced down at her hands, noting that they were still shaking a little. How had he noticed that? He was on the left side of the bed, but still, there was a little distance between them.

"It's probably just nerves. I'm sure I'll be fine. Once I get home, shower and relax a bit, I should be back to normal."

"I don't think it's a good idea for you to drive," he said.

Amina had been thinking the same thing. She'd been there an hour. Though she felt better, he was right. Her nerves were frayed. The thought of driving home to an empty house had her wringing her hands even more. It wasn't that she was afraid exactly, but she was definitely on edge.

God, she hoped she wouldn't be looking over her shoulder all the time. That guy wouldn't have caught her off guard had she been paying better attention. Besides that, she should've waited for Security to walk her to her car at that time of night. The chief nurse had recommended that none of them go to their cars at night by themselves. Not that they'd had many problems in the lot, but there had been enough break-ins over the years to warrant caution. Amina had never had a problem before and hadn't thought anything of leaving the building alone.

Dr. McPherson shifted next to her, and she returned her attention to him. "I'm getting off in a few minutes. I'll be glad to give you a ride."

Amina could almost feel Samantha rolling her eyes. Her friend liked the doctor enough, but she had once mentioned that she didn't like the way he eyed Amina. Like he wanted to gobble her up and go back for seconds. Back then, Amina had laughed off the comment, but she had to admit that since Samantha mentioned it, she'd noticed the looks he gave her.

"I couldn't ask you to do that," Amina said. "I wouldn't want to put you out, but thank you."

"No, I insist. You've been through something traumatic. Driving you home wouldn't be a problem at all."

"Actually, her ride should be here in a few minutes," Samantha said, and Amina jerked her head to look at her. Her friend had been by her side the whole time and was standing to the right of the bed.

"Oh? Who's picking you up?" Dr. McPherson asked, his gaze steady on Amina.

She was going to kill Samantha.

"Umm," she said, trying to think of something without having to lie, but before she could respond, the door flew open. Amina's heart slammed against her chest.

Maxwell.

He stood just inside the room looking larger than life in an untucked button-up short-sleeve white shirt. The garment emphasized his huge biceps and put the corded muscles of his arms on full display. Well-worn blue jeans covered his long legs, and the Timberland boots on his feet added to the badass aura that surrounded him.

"*Dayum*, girl. You've been holding out on me," Samantha mumbled under her breath.

"Max?" Amina said, shocked to see him there. And like usual her body came alive the way it always did at the sight of him. Forgotten were the headache and the shivers that had consumed her for the past hour. Instead heat soared through her body at the way his gaze took her in.

"It appears your ride is here," Samantha said, humor lacing her words.

Maxwell gave her a cursory glance, but his attention held on Dr. McPherson a little longer than necessary. Almost like he'd done the night before when he came to the hospital to tell her about Jeremy. Amina couldn't decipher the expression, and at the moment, she didn't care. She was just glad to see him. Not only because he'd be her excuse for not needing a ride from the doctor. But it had everything to do with how happy and safe she felt with him around.

"All right, Amina. Take care of yourself," Dr. McPherson said on his way out the door.

"I guess I'll be going too," Samantha said, grinning as she backed her way toward the door and giving Amina a little wave.

"Not so fast," Amina said, stopping her friend in her tracks. "How'd you know Max was coming?"

"I'd heard there was an incident here and I called your cell," Maxwell said as he moved closer and took the spot next to the bed where Dr. McPherson had been standing.

"Actually, he called you three times," Samantha added, and pointed at an upholstered chair near the window that held Amina's oversize bag.

Amina hadn't even thought about her cell phone or whether anything had been stolen from her bag. Not even when she was trying to figure out how she was getting home.

"Please tell me you didn't call my family," she said to Samantha.

She probably wouldn't have reached her parents, but Katrina would've been on the next flight out. And Amina didn't want to bother either of them.

"I didn't, but I thought about it. Anyway, when your phone kept ringing and then stopping, I noticed the same name kept showing up on the screen. *Max*."

"She answered, asked a lot of questions then told me where I could find you," Max added. The worry lines that had creased his forehead moments ago were gone, but Amina didn't miss the concern in his eyes as he looked at her.

"Once I found out he was a cop and a friend, I figured it would be all right."

Amina could've kissed her. "Thank you." With her family out of town, she couldn't think of anyone else she'd want by her side.

"My pleasure," Samantha said sweetly, and grabbed the door handle but turned back. "Oh, and you will be hearing from me tomorrow." With that, she was gone.

Maxwell's gaze traveled the length of Amina, before his attention settled on her neck. "How bad is it?" he asked gruffly. He sat next to her and gently touched the bandage.

"It's a superficial cut. I might have a little scar, but it's nothing to worry about."

His hand moved up to her face and he cupped her cheek. "When Samantha told me you were attacked," he said hoarsely, then cleared his throat, "I couldn't get here fast enough. Are you sure you're okay?"

Unable to speak with the way the pad of his thumb was brushing over her suddenly heated skin, all Amina could do was nod. She couldn't believe he was there.

"Thank you for coming," she said quietly. Though she would've wanted him there, she wouldn't have called.

"Of course, I came. Just because I put some distance between us doesn't mean I stopped caring."

His admission stirred a longing inside her that she hadn't felt in a long time. She'd never wish Jeremy dead, but if his death caused her and Maxwell to start rebuilding their friendship, she wouldn't complain.

"I talked to Security and they filled me in, but why don't you tell me what happened."

For the next few minutes Amina recounted the incident. This time, though, her pulse might've beaten a little faster when she told him about the knife, but at least her heart didn't feel as if it would leap out of her chest.

"So he took off without stealing anything?" Maxwell asked, a frown marring his handsome face.

Amina's brows dipped as she let the question marinate in her mind. "I—I guess so. When someone in the parking lot shouted, it startled both of us and made the mugger loosen his hold. It was just enough for me to get away. I didn't look back." Her voice caught, but she pushed down the emotion swirling inside her. Repeating the story kept reminding her that she could've been killed.

Maxwell looked a bit pensive, but said, "I'm glad you're all right. I think I was holding my breath during the whole ride here. Knowing that you were hurt took at least ten years off my life."

Amina smiled and reached for his hand that was now resting on the mattress. "Sorry I worried you, but…" Now she was the one clearing her throat. She wasn't sure why, but having him there was making her get choked up. "Are you off of work, or do you need to get back?"

He shook his head. "My boss made me take a few days off after Jer…" He stopped abruptly. "Anyway, I was picking up something at the precinct, and when I was leaving, I heard that there had been a mugging here.

I wasn't sure if you were on duty. But when I called and couldn't reach you, all types of thoughts went through my head."

Amina was touched. If someone would've told her months ago that she and Maxwell would reconnect, she wouldn't have believed them. He'd made it clear that day at her birthday party that he wasn't coming around anymore. He told her that it gutted him each time he saw her with Jeremy. But even after her marriage ended, he still kept his distance, which had been understandable. He hadn't gotten over her choosing Jeremy over him.

He stood and offered her his hand. "You ready to get out of here?"

"More than ready."

Maxwell was still coming to terms with Jeremy's death. There was no way in hell he was taking Amina to her house. Not only because he had vowed never to step foot in the place again but also because he couldn't leave her. He had practically lost it when he learned that she'd been the one attacked. Not knowing what to expect when he arrived at the hospital, once he saw her sitting on the bed looking alert, he'd finally been able to breathe.

But his gut was still unsettled, especially after what had happened with Jeremy. Hopefully, the two incidents weren't connected, but the cop in him couldn't stop his mind from going there even for a moment. Until he learned more about both cases, he wouldn't jump to conclusions.

Besides looking a little tired in the hospital, Amina had seemed fine, except when his gaze had gone lower. The butterfly bandages on her neck that were keeping her wound closed stood out like a beacon in the night. Who could do that to a woman? Hell, to anyone? No matter how long he stayed on the police force, there were days he couldn't wrap his brain around the foolishness of the streets. Too many people didn't value human life, and it angered him more and more each day.

What if the knife had cut deeper into Amina's neck? Thinking about how she could've died tonight had him gripping the steering wheel tighter. What he wouldn't give to get his hands on the asshole who had attacked her and scarred her beautiful skin.

Now as he drove out of the parking lot, Maxwell thought about how they were only fifteen minutes from her house. He needed to figure out how to broach the subject of her going to his place instead.

He glanced to his right where she was sitting in the passenger seat looking straight ahead. Her hands were clasped tightly in her lap as if she was trying to hold herself together.

"Are you hungry?" he asked when he stopped at a traffic light. Moonlight spilled into the interior of the car, casting shadows across her face and letting him see how exhausted she was. Just then, she released a noisy yawn then quickly covered her mouth.

"Ah, man, excuse me," she said sheepishly, her beautiful brown eyes staring up at him. "It's been a long day."

It was after midnight, and she'd been through hell fighting off an attacker. Yeah, he would say it had been a long day.

"I'm starving, but I might be more tired than hungry." She gave a little laugh and turned more in her seat to face him. "I just want to crawl into bed and sleep for a week." Her stomach chose that moment to growl and they both laughed.

"What would you like to eat?" Maxwell asked.

"I had a taste for Chinese food earlier, but I'm not sure if any place is open. Besides, I don't want you going out of your way. If you drop me off at home, I'm sure I have something in my refrigerator that I can eat."

"About that, I'm not comfortable leaving you alone tonight. I was thinking we could go back to my place instead. I promise to be a perfect gentleman."

She hesitated for a moment, and the traffic light changed before she could respond. Maxwell split his attention between her and the road.

"What?" he asked when all she did was stare at him. "If you're not comfortable with that idea—"

"No, it's not that, never that. You've always been a gentleman."

"Then what? Clothes? We can stop and you can pack a bag."

"No, I have an extra change of clothes in the bag that I have. I guess I'm just surprised that you're okay with me going home with you."

Yeah, he was a little surprised too. Except for the night before when he had stopped by the hospital, it had been well over six months since they'd seen each other. After the incident between him and Jeremy during her birthday party, Maxwell knew he couldn't be around them. He had cut all ties even though it gutted him to know that Jeremy had been mistreating her. But he'd been glad to learn that she'd filed for divorce shortly after that incident.

"I don't think it's a good idea for you to be alone tonight," Maxwell said. "And I have plenty of space."

"Is that the only reason?" she asked quietly, no longer looking at him. Instead, she stared down at her hands that were still folded in her lap.

"Amina," he started, but didn't know what to say. He felt like a world-class asshole for still wanting his friend's ex-wife. Granted, Jeremy had made it clear on more than one occasion that he had only married Amina so that Maxwell couldn't have her. Yet, it felt wrong for him to be longing for her.

"Never mind, don't answer that," she said. "I appreciate the offer, and I'm going to take you up on it for a couple of reasons. One—I don't want to go home to an empty house. Two—more than anything, I don't want to be alone."

She was normally a strong, independent woman. Maxwell knew it probably took a lot for her to admit that. He reached over the console and grabbed her hand. "And I don't want you to be alone. You can stay as long as you need to."

She nodded and glanced out the passenger window. "Thank you."

"Now, let's go find you something to eat."

As Maxwell drove toward downtown, where he knew of a Chinese restaurant that stayed open late, he thought about the night he had fallen for Amina. If only Jeremy hadn't stabbed him in the back. Then again, Maxwell only had himself to blame. Like so many times, he had let his job get in the way of his personal life.

That night, at the party where he and Jeremy had first met Amina, right away, there had been something about her that intrigued Maxwell. To this day, he wasn't sure what it was. It could've been the fact that she worked twelve-hour days, yet still made time to volunteer at a nursing home where her grandmother stayed. It could have been her knowledge about professional sports and her hearty appetite. Or maybe it was how she shared hilarious stories about her twin sisters and parents. When she mentioned that she wanted a large family of her own someday, he became even more enamored. That was what he wanted, a wife and at least four kids. It also didn't hurt that Amina was absolutely gorgeous.

*If only I hadn't left without letting her know I was interested.*

He let the memory of that time drift from his mind and headed for the restaurant. Forty-five minutes later, he pulled his Dodge Charger into his two-car garage. Amina was sound asleep. She had started dozing on his way to the restaurant, and by the time he picked up their carryout meal, she was knocked out.

He parked next to his pickup truck and closed the overhead garage door.

"Amina," he said, gently shaking her shoulder. She moaned then turned and snuggled deeper into the soft leather seat. "Amina, wake up."

She startled awake and scurried away from him, her knees bent to her chest. Frightened eyes stared back at him, and Maxwell wanted to kill the man who had attacked her.

"It's me, sweetheart. You're all right." He slowly reached out and touched her hand, giving her time to wake up completely. "You fell asleep, and we just arrived at my place."

"Max," she croaked out, and visibly swallowed. "I—I…"

He still had a hold on her hand and didn't miss the way she was trembling. "Hey, it's okay. Come on. Let's go inside so you can eat and get some rest."

Instead of responding she nodded and slid her hand from his hold. Maxwell wasn't accustomed to seeing her this way—scared and unsure—but she was a fighter. He had no doubt she'd get through this. At least he hoped.

After helping her out of the car, he grabbed the food from the back seat and her oversize bag from the trunk. Guiding her into his home felt surreal. Amina had only been to his house once and only for a few minutes. It was how he had learned that she and Jeremy were dating. Maxwell had been shocked and livid.

Jeremy had stopped by his house to return tools he had borrowed. He claimed he was in the neighborhood, but Maxwell knew what he'd been doing. It was Jeremy's way of showing him that he'd gotten the girl. At the time that they'd all met, Maxwell hadn't even known the guy had been interested in her. If only...

Maxwell shook his head, wanting to stop that train of thought before it blossomed into anger. That was the past. He had to let that time in their lives go.

*If only it was that easy.*

# Chapter 7

Amina was glad she made a habit of carrying an extra change of clothes to work. Granted they were for working out, but the T-shirt and leggings were perfect for lounging around. Which was what she was currently doing. After taking a long hot shower in the guest bathroom, she'd felt somewhat human again. Flashbacks of the attempted mugging popped into her head but didn't freak her out as much. Probably because Maxwell had done a good job distracting her.

She glanced at him. Taking in his handsome profile while his attention was fixed on the sixty-inch flat screen hanging on the wall across from them. They were camped out in his spacious family room, sitting on the huge overstuffed sectional sofa eating kung pao shrimp and watching a movie. The large room was simply decorated with a brown, beige and splashes of orange color scheme. The decor was a bit masculine for her taste, but his home was comfortable and inviting.

Amina couldn't think of a better way to end a horrific night. Relaxing with good food and great company should be a requirement to conclude a stressful day. Especially if that company was Maxwell. It didn't matter how tired she was, she planned to relish her time with him despite the circumstances that brought them back together.

"You call yourself a fan of *The Fast and the Furious* franchise, but how is it that you've never watched *Tokyo Drift*?" Maxwell asked, dividing his attention between her and the big screen. He had searched through a streaming service, looking for an action flick since they both enjoyed them, and landed on this one.

"Good question. I've seen the other movies in the series. I'm not sure why I never got around to seeing this one. Now shush before you make me miss something."

They ate and chatted a little throughout the movie as if hanging out together was something they did all the time. It could've been…it should've been.

Amina's fork stopped midway to her mouth. The sounds of the television faded to the background as memories she didn't want to revisit bombarded her mind all at once. The party where they'd first met. The easy way conversation flowed between them. Their immediate connection. The hope that she and Maxwell could get to know each other better. The disappointment in knowing he'd left the event without saying goodbye. All of it sat at the forefront of her brain.

She sighed and went back to eating. Popping a shrimp into her mouth, Amina hoped she wouldn't choke on the food as she bitterly recalled how Jeremy had pursued her after that party. He'd caught her at a time in her life when she hadn't been in a serious relationship in years. Not because she hadn't wanted to date. No, it had everything to do with her waiting for the right man to come along. One who would love and cherish her like no other. She'd always hoped to one day have the type of relationship her parents shared, and the kind her sisters had with their spouses.

Instead, Amina found a man who had done everything right. Seducing her into believing she was someone special. It wasn't just the intriguing dinner dates, shows, weekend getaways or the romantic walks in the park that made her swoon. He played on her desires. Made her believe they shared the same dreams—a big house full of love and kids. Someone to grow old with. They had a plan, a future. No detail spared. A two-story Spanish-style home in Summerlin North. Three kids, Loretta, Rhamel and Gabriel. All the while, Amina never suspected it was a con, a ploy. The sole reason Jeremy stole her heart was to one-up Maxwell.

*If I knew then what I know now.*

"I'm going to get another beer," Maxwell said, interrupting Amina's thoughts. He paused the movie, then stood. "You want anything from the kitchen?"

"Uh, maybe some water."

His brows knit together. "What's wrong? You all right? You look a little…tense. If you're getting tired, we don't have to finish the movie. I know it's been a long day."

"Oh no. I'm fine." She wasn't ready for their time together to end.

"Okay. Let me grab our drinks. Be right back."

Amina tried to keep her thoughts from drifting back

to the past as she resumed eating, but it was hard not to. She felt so stupid…still. How had she not been able to see through Jeremy's crap before saying *I do*? She'd asked herself that question so many times during their short marriage and even after they were divorced. No answer she managed to come up with was good enough to endure the heartache that Jeremy had inflicted. The signs had been there, but she had ignored them all.

"All right, here you go," Maxwell said when he returned. He had his beer in the crook of his arm, and in his hands were a bottle of water and a mug with steam billowing above it. "I made you some chamomile tea thinking that maybe it'll help you relax."

"Aww, Max. Thank you," she said, accepting the mug that was warm in her hands. Even the small things he did made him stand out from any man she'd ever met. Which was probably why Jeremy had been jealous of Maxwell. He used to talk about how everything came easy for him, and how everyone at work loved him. That he was the golden boy who could do no wrong, and Jeremy couldn't stand that.

Maxwell set the bottle of water on the end table next to her, then reclaimed his seat. Considering how huge the sofa was, he chose to sit close enough, and she inhaled his freshly showered scent. It wasn't just how amazing he smelled. It was everything about the man that turned her on. The way he carried himself. His kindness. His sense of honor. And damn if the man wasn't *fine*.

An overwhelming current of heat charged through her and aroused a sensual need Amina hadn't felt for any man in a long time. If he was trying to torture her with his irresistible…everything, it was working. Add that to the fact that his leg was rubbed up against hers, and she was about ready to leap out of her skin.

*Goodness.* It had been a while since she'd been with a man, and right now Maxwell's presence had all of her girly parts tingling.

He pushed Play on the remote and the movie continued, but watching it was the last thing Amina wanted to do. What she really wanted was to have her whole body pressed against his, feeling every single hard muscle and…

"What are you thinking about?" he asked, his left eyebrow arched in a way that had Amina wondering if he could read her mind. Or did something in her expression give away that she was having sexy thoughts about how she wanted to touch him…*feel* him?

"Oh, um, nothing," she croaked. "Just enjoying your company and the movie."

Maxwell gave a slow nod, but the intensity of his powerful gaze and the awareness of his leg so close to hers sent a shiver through her body. If the desire in his eyes was any indication, she wasn't the only one affected by their physical closeness. Good. That meant the connection between them was still as powerful as ever. Now, if only he'd kiss her and…

*God, I've gotta stop this. We're friends. That has to be enough right now.*

Amina cleared her throat and forced her attention to the television, but she could still feel his heated gaze on her.

"Shouldn't you be watching the movie instead of me?" she asked without looking at him.

Maxwell chuckled and without another word they focused on the movie. Well, at least she tried to. Amina struggled to tap down the desire swirling within her. Right now, they were friends. And if she was patient, they could build from that and possibly she could have everything she wanted, and that included him. But she had questions. Questions she'd wanted to ask for a long time. Like why he hadn't sought her out after the party if he'd been interested. He was a cop. He could've found her easily enough. Jeremy had. He'd hunted her down then poured on the charm.

But did any of that matter now? She considered Maxwell a friend, and he seemed to feel the same about her. Shouldn't that be enough?

The questions faded away as she finished her meal, which had been delicious. Instead of dwelling on what she and Maxwell missed out on, Amina decided to concentrate on the here and now. Neither of them spoke until after the movie ended.

"What did you think?" Maxwell asked.

"I thought it was really good. Not as action-packed like the others, but definitely entertaining." As the credits rolled, she realized another *Fast and the Furious* movie was coming on next.

"Are you ready to call it a night?" Maxwell asked.

"No," she said without hesitation. "The tea was relaxing, but I'm not ready to go to sleep. If you're tired, though, you don't have to stay up with me."

Amina would be forever grateful that he showed up at the hospital when he really didn't have to. If she was being honest, not only was she enjoying his company, but she wasn't looking forward to going to bed. The last thing she wanted was to close her eyes and possibly dream about the attempted mugging.

Nope, she was staying up until she just couldn't keep her eyes open any longer.

"Do you like cheesecake?" Maxwell asked out of the blue.

"I like any type of cake. Heck, I like anything that has sugar. Why?"

"Because I picked up some while you were drooling in my car."

Amina's mouth dropped open, then she burst out laughing. "I do not drool," she lied, praying that he hadn't actually seen saliva sliding down the side of her mouth when she'd fallen asleep in the car. It was possible, though. She was sleeping hard, to the point of not knowing where she was when he woke her up. Those few minutes of shut-eye were just what she'd needed.

When the next movie started, he paused it. "I hate to be the one to break it to you, but yes you do."

She didn't miss the grin that spread across his tempting mouth as he headed out of the family room. Instead of letting him continue waiting on her hand and foot, Amina carried the remaining food and dishes into the kitchen. He pulled the cake from the refrigerator then grabbed small plates and utensils. While he did that, Amina began rinsing their dinner plates and putting them in the dishwasher.

"Can I ask you something?" she said.

He cut the cheesecake, giving them both healthy slices. "Of course. Ask me anything."

"Do you know Dr. McPherson?"

Maxwell's brows dipped, and he thought about it for a moment. "The name doesn't ring a bell. Why, should I know him?"

"Because yesterday and today, when you saw him at

the hospital, you looked at him as if you wanted to rip his head off." When he didn't appear to know who or what she was talking about, Amina continued. "He was the doctor in the hospital room with me and Samantha."

"Oh, him. No, I don't know him," was all he said. "Do you want to eat this in here or the family room?"

"In here is good. I want to finish loading the dishes first, but getting back to Dr. McPherson… If you didn't know him, why'd you look at him the way you did?"

Maxwell carried their plates to the glass kitchen table and took a seat before taking a bite of his cake. As he chewed, his forehead crinkled as if thinking about a response. "I don't know. There's something about him. Just a weird vibe I get from him."

"So it's a cop thing, huh? My dad gets like that with certain people, but usually they're actually criminals or thugs or people who warrant a glare. But Dr. McPherson is a nice guy. A little pushy maybe, but nice."

Amina dried her hands and sat at the table with him. She tried not to moan when she put a forkful of cheesecake into her mouth, but it was no use. The taste of lemon and raspberry burst onto her tongue. "Wow, this is amazing. Where'd you get it?"

"Let's just say, I know people."

She laughed. "Well, I hope these people will be willing to hook you up with another cheesecake in the near future. I'm definitely going to want one. Preferably with strawberries and/or white chocolate."

"Duly noted." They ate in a comfortable silence until Maxwell spoke again.

"You said this Dr. McPherson is pushy. How so? Has he asked you out and you said no, so he keeps asking?"

Amina's fork stopped halfway to her mouth and she

gaped at Maxwell. How the heck had he come to that conclusion? Instead of asking right away, she finished the final bite of her dessert. She knew he was observant and had been a detective before making sergeant, but still.

"I thought so," he said with a smirk.

"There's nothing going on between me and Dr. McPherson." Amina wanted him to know. Because if there was a chance that they could be more than friends, she didn't want anything or anyone to stand in their way this time.

"I didn't think you guys were involved, but I can't blame him for asking you out. You're a beautiful, compassionate and intelligent woman. No doubt he'd be interested."

Heat spread to Amina's cheeks and if her skin was fairer, he'd notice her blushing. That was one of the nicest things he had ever said to her. He occasionally complimented her even while she was married to Jeremy, but it was never anything inappropriate. Sometimes it would be regarding her perfume, an outfit, or even when he learned she had received a nursing award a year ago, he congratulated her. But hearing him describe her that way meant more than he'd ever know.

"Thank you."

"As for how I knew McPherson was interested in you, I didn't. I was mostly guessing, but the signs were there. It was in the way he looked at you both times I saw him."

Amina didn't say anything. She knew the look. Initially, it didn't bother her. Heck, she probably looked at Maxwell the same way. But now that others were noticing the doctor's attention on her, she'd have to talk to him. The last thing she wanted was for rumors to start spreading around the hospital. Especially since she wasn't interested in him and never would be. There was only one man she wanted to spend her time with, and he was sitting an arms-length from her.

"You think you can handle another movie?" Maxwell asked as he stood and gathered their dessert plates.

"If you can, so can I," she said, trying to hold back the yawn that was threatening to burst free. She wasn't fooling anyone, especially if Maxwell's crooked grin was any indication.

"All right. We'll see."

Twenty minutes later, Maxwell glanced down at Amina, whose head rested on his shoulder. So much for her staying awake for another movie. She had fallen asleep before the show started good. It was a wonder that either of them lasted as long as they had.

Maxwell knew his reason for staying up, and it wasn't just about having Amina there. No, it also had to do with his lack of sleep from the day before. Each time he closed his eyes, the shooting played over and over in his mind. Not wanting the same results, he was reluctant to head to bed. Amina being there was just the distraction he needed. Tonight, they were helping each other, because he was pretty sure that she hadn't wanted to fall asleep for similar reasons.

Maxwell eased forward, prepared to move and let her stretch out, but stopped when Amina groaned. It sounded more like a whine, and the death grip she had on the front of his T-shirt had him wondering if she was dreaming about the mugging. He would love to get his hands on the bastard and terrorize him the way he had done her.

*What good would that do?* Sure, it would make him

feel better and it would be one less thug out on the street. Yet, every day they put creeps away, more popped up.

Amina stirred, and Maxwell wrapped his arm around her shoulders. Now her head was resting against his chest, and she still had a tight grip on the front of his shirt. His goal, after bringing her home with him, was to make her feel comfortable and take her mind off what happened at the hospital. Unfortunately, there was nothing he could do about her dreaming, except to be there if she awakened.

*Might as well get comfortable.*

A long yawn escaped him as he propped his feet up on the coffee table. He'd watch a little more TV then get them both up the stairs. That was his last thought before falling into a deep sleep.

# Chapter 8

*Maxwell cupped Amina's face between his hands and stared into her gorgeous, toffee-colored eyes as the pads of his thumbs brushed the softness of her cheeks. He wanted to kiss her. God, he wanted to kiss her more than he wanted to do anything else at the moment. But tasting those tempting lips would only make him yearn for more.*

*No, he couldn't. It wouldn't be right. They couldn't succumb to the desire that had always been pulsing between them. What would people think? She used to be married to his best friend. Besides that, what if it changed the trajectory of his relationship with her? They were friends. Could he risk it? Should he?*

*Amina's gaze moved back and forth, searching his eyes just as he was doing to her. Was she thinking the same thing? Did they really want to take this chance?*

*He already knew one kiss wouldn't be enough, but if he couldn't have her forever, at least he'd have this moment.*

*To hell with it. Consequences be damned.*

*Maxwell's mouth greedily covered Amina's before he could change his mind. His arms encircled her, crushing her to him as he deepened their connection. Heat blasted through him, sending jolts of electricity to every cell in his body as she ground against his hard length.*

*Chest to chest, thigh to thigh, there wasn't any part of them that wasn't touching the other. And her mouth. Her sweet, soft lips were more than he could've imagined they'd be as she gave herself freely to the mind-numbing kiss. That was all the encouragement Maxwell needed to deepen their lip-lock.*

*His pulse pounded harder with each lap of her tongue, and it was as if he could hear angels singing in the distance. How many times had he imagined them together? Kissing. Hugging. Loving on each other.*

*He slid his hands down her sides, over her magnificent curves and didn't stop until he reached her butt. Never had a woman turned him on as much as Amina. He couldn't get enough. He wanted more. So much more.*

An erotic moan pierced the air. "Oh, Max, don't, please don't stop."

The lyrical voice sent waves of lust crashing through his body and…

Maxwell froze. His eyes popped open, and his breath hitched when he stared into the most beautiful eyes. Eyes that held so much passion and desire, and eyes that belonged to… Amina. His hands were palming her perfectly round ass while her curvy, lush body was stretched out on top of him.

They didn't move. They didn't speak. They held their positions and stared at each other. Maxwell couldn't seem to get his brain to catch up with what was happening.

*What. The. Hell?* Did he? Had they?

As if suddenly realizing their position, Amina's eyes grew large and the stunned expression on her face resembled the shock coursing through his veins.

Maxwell's heart raced as he continued trying to make sense of what had just happened. It hadn't been a dream. The desire in her eyes and her kiss-swollen lips confirmed that.

They had kissed. He and Amina had actually kissed.

One of them needed to say something. What could he say? *We kissed and I liked it? A lot.* No, at the moment he could barely think straight. He wasn't sure how she ended up on top of him, but it was safe to say that she felt his erection that was straining behind the zipper of his jeans. It was a little hard to hide when her body, an incredible body with large breasts, a tiny waist and a butt that fit perfectly in his palms, was flat against him. If it wasn't for their clothes, the only barrier between them, he'd be able to slide right into her sweet heat and…

*Aww, hell. Don't go there.*

Maxwell stopped that train of thought before his mind sent him right off a cliff. "Umm, this is awkward," he said. "I'm sorry. I thought I was dreaming and I'm not sure how—"

"I'm not sorry," Amina said just above a whisper, her heated gaze steady on him. "That was even more amazing than I imagined it would be. I'm just not sure how I…uhh…how we…"

"Yeah, me either, but maybe we should sit up."

Maxwell absolutely loved having her right where she was, but her tempting body was a little too much for his limited willpower. He was trying to clear his mind and imagine her not on top of him in hopes that his boner would go down.

"Oh, I'm so sorry." She wiggled, struggling to get up, which only made her rub against him more.

He groaned and grabbed her hips, forcing her to be still. Her core was lined up with his penis, which was about to punch a hole through his pants.

He breathed in and out grappling to get his body under control. "I, um…give me a minute," he croaked out.

"Oh… Ooh, I'm sorry," she said, her lips twitching as if trying to keep from laughing.

They lay there in silence for a few minutes with Maxwell maintaining a firm hold on her hips. Once his body had settled down, he let his hands fall away from her. "Now you can move…slowly," he said between gritted teeth.

This time Amina burst out laughing and eased off him. Maxwell forgot how much he loved her infectious laugh that was warm and throaty. Hell, he loved everything about the woman…still. And now that he had tasted her sweet lips, he wanted to find out how the rest of her tasted.

Once she was standing, he sat up and adjusted himself. Maybe he should've been embarrassed, but he wasn't. He was okay with her knowing the type of effect she had on him.

*She's Jeremy's ex-wife*, his brain taunted, and guilt stabbed Maxwell in the chest. *Ex* was the operative word, but deep down he had to admit, being with Amina felt wrong on some levels. On the other hand, he didn't care. He wanted her in his life. Always had. But…

"About what just happened," he started.

"Don't say you're sorry," Amina said as she dropped down on the sofa next to him.

"I hadn't planned to apologize," he said honestly. "I might be considered the lowest form of human life for what I'm about to say, but I've wanted to kiss you from the first night we met. Even when you were with Jeremy."

"Why didn't you?" she asked quietly, surprising the heck out of him. "I mean, why didn't you kiss me that first night? You had to know that I was feeling you."

"Yet, you ended up with my best friend," he said with a bite behind his words.

"Max, it wasn't exactly like that and you know it," she snapped, then huffed out a breath. "Listen, we've never had a chance to really talk at length about what happened. But I didn't pursue Jeremy. Even when he asked for my telephone number that night at the party, *after* you left without saying goodbye, I said no."

Maxwell knew the rest. Jeremy had gone behind his back and tried to get with her that night. When that didn't work, he sought her out and pursued her until she finally gave in.

"If I knew that he had no intention of passing on my information to you, I would've done it myself."

"You *should've* done it yourself anyway. Asking your *friend* to give me your number was a little high school-ish if you ask me."

Maxwell nodded. That was probably what pissed him off the most. She was right. He shouldn't have left that party without her digits.

"I always wondered," she said, wincing a little when she moved her neck. Not once had she complained about discomfort or pain, but he had noticed her periodically touching the small bandages.

She leaned forward with her elbows on her thighs, and her attention was on the dark hardwood flooring. "You were a cop—if you were that interested in me, why didn't you do whatever you guys do when you want to find someone?"

"Because the day after the party, Jeremy told me you weren't interested. Besides, I don't use the police department's resources to look up information on random women I meet."

Amina stood. "Well, I guess that was your loss then, huh?"

Maxwell grimaced. Maybe he could've said that better. Of course, she was right again. It had been his loss.

"I'm heading up to bed," she said. "Enjoy the rest of your night."

"Amina, wait." She stopped but didn't turn to face him. "For the record, not fighting for you back then is my biggest regret. If I had a chance to do that night and the months that followed over again, I would've fought to have you in my life. For that... I'm sorry."

She nodded, but still didn't turn. "Yeah, I'm sorry too."

Maxwell watched as she headed up the stairs. Now that that was settled, where did they go from there?

Hours later, Maxwell slowly opened his eyes and lifted slightly to glance at the digital clock on his bedside table. *Five thirty.* He'd hoped to sleep until at least eight, but his internal clock was consistent if nothing else. Normally, he was awake and up before daybreak every morning. Clearly, today was no different.

He released a tired sigh, turned onto his back and closed his eyes. The events of the last couple of days flitted through his mind, but none stronger than the one of him kissing Amina. One minute he thought he was dreaming, and the next, it was as if his fantasy had come to life. He didn't even remember stretching out on the sofa, let alone having her on top of him. Either way, it was one hell of a way to wake up.

His body temperature rose and his dick stirred remembering how his hands had roamed over her luscious curves. Damn if she didn't feel perfect in his arms… and in his hands.

He reopened his eyes, and a slow smile tugged at the corners of his lips. He wouldn't soon forget how glorious it was to wake up with his hands cupping her butt.

He had finally experienced what it was like to do more than just hug her, which back then was considered playing with fire. Once she and Jeremy were married, Maxwell had stopped embracing her, and barely wanted to look at her.

*Look but don't touch* had taken on a whole new meaning as it related to his feelings for Amina. No one could ever accuse him of coming between her and Jeremy. Yet, if their family and friends knew how much he had fantasized about her, they'd think he was some type of pervert. Maxwell had eased out of their lives, showing up for fewer and fewer events held by mutual friends. But when Amina's father had invited him to her surprise birthday party, he had to attend. One, because you didn't say no to Captain Hudson. And two, he longed to see her again. She'd been glad to see him too, and they'd picked up where they'd left off. Conversation flowed effortlessly, and they still vibed even after months of no interaction.

Of course, Jeremy had to ruin a perfectly nice occasion by showing up late and drunk to his wife's birthday party. Maxwell had never wanted to hurt someone as much as he'd wanted to destroy Jeremy that day. Not because he was late, but Maxwell hadn't been able to ignore the way he had disrespected Amina. Thankfully, it had only been the three of them in the room at the time. Everyone else had been in Amina's backyard.

Maxwell shook his head at the memory. After what went down, he'd had to extricate himself from their lives. He couldn't stand by and watch Jeremy's behavior toward her. Sure, he had to work with him, but he kept his distance as much as possible.

After their divorce, it wasn't that Maxwell didn't want to check in with Amina. It never seemed to be the right time. Not until the other day when he found her at the hospital to deliver the news about Jeremy's death.

Maxwell rubbed his forehead then pinched the bridge of his nose. *He's gone.* Jeremy was gone. Some moments it still didn't feel real, but he was gone, and Maxwell had every intention of hunting down his killer.

As for Amina, though, he was done feeling guilty about wanting her in every way a man could want a woman. Lusting after his friend's ex-wife probably made him a world-class asshole, but he was tired of smothering his feelings. Would he intentionally act on his attraction to Amina? Probably not, at least no time soon, but Maxwell was done with the remorse that always came with thoughts of wanting her.

His cell phone vibrated on the nightstand, and he

reached over, patted around until his hand landed on the device. Glancing at the screen, he sat up when he saw it was Danny.

"Hey, tell me you have something," Maxwell said by way of greeting. His lieutenant might've wanted him to take some time off, but those who reported to Maxwell knew he wanted to be kept in the loop on the case.

"We have something," Danny said, and the sound of papers rustled in the background. "Heard back from the medical examiner. She said you wanted a rush on the report."

"Yeah, I talked to Hayley last night. What did she have to say?"

"A couple of things. From her preliminary findings, Jeremy had drugs in his system. A low dose of fentanyl and traces of alcohol were found. She said the drugs could've been from a prescription and not recreational. Right now, that's unknown, but I'll request a subpoena to get access to his medical records to determine if he was on medication. But there's something else you'll find interesting. Hayley thinks that whoever the shooter was, might've been a professional or got seriously lucky."

Maxwell bolted upright in bed. "Wait. What?"

"It's too early in our investigation, but there's a possibility that Jeremy was targeted. Hayley said the gunman's bullet punctured one of the carotid arteries and a jugular vein. The reason she says that it might've been someone who knew what they were doing was because of the trajectory of the bullet."

Maxwell tossed the covers off and placed his feet on the cold hardwood floor. He barely listened as Danny talked about angles, distance and the precision of the shot. Several thoughts blasted him at once. Was the ambush done by a professional? If Jeremy had been targeted, that would explain why the shooter hadn't taken aim at Maxwell too. When he definitely had opportunity.

And drugs? Jeremy did a lot of stupid crap, but would he honestly put himself and those serving with him at risk like that? *Recreational drugs?* Maxwell didn't want to believe that. Besides, no way would Jay put his job and livelihood on the line. But considering Jeremy's erratic behavior the last few months, drug use was a possibility.

"I know you're supposed to be taking some time off, but can you come down to the station for a minute this morning?" Danny asked, breaking into Maxwell's thoughts.

"Sure, but why?"

"There's a situation surrounding Jeremy that popped up a little while ago that you're going to want to handle face-to-face."

Maxwell wasn't sure why the detective was being vague, but there was only one way to find out. "I'll be there in thirty minutes," he said, and disconnected the call.

Tossing the phone on the bed, he made his way to the en suite bathroom. As he showered and dressed, Maxwell replayed the conversation with Danny in his head. One of the most pressing questions he had was, *if* Jeremy was targeted, how had the shooter known that he'd be the responding officer? Granted, the neighborhood was part of the territory he was usually assigned to, but so were other officers. Also, if it was a setup, was someone in the police department a part of it? How else could the person ensure that Jeremy showed up?

And if this was the case, why would Jeremy be targeted? Even more important, by who? Those were questions Maxwell needed answers to, and he needed them yesterday.

He grabbed his badge and service weapon from the top drawer of his nightstand. Then rummaged for a pen and paper that he usually kept in there. He had learned the hard way about leaving Amina without saying goodbye. The last time he'd done that she had ended up married to Jeremy. He wouldn't make that mistake again, but assuming she was still asleep, a note would have to do.

With the sticky pad of paper in hand, he strolled out of the bedroom and down the short hallway to the guest room. The door was slightly open and Maxwell gave it a little push. Darkness greeted him except for a sliver of early morning sunlight peeking through the slats of the closed blinds.

He moved quietly across the room, and his pulse picked up speed as he got closer to Amina's sleeping form. It was mind-boggling the pull she had on him, like he was a chunk of metal and she was an industrial-strength magnet drawing him to her. It happened every time they shared the same space. A penetrating connection...a powerful bond that he hadn't experienced with any other woman.

*Clearly, some things are just unexplainable,* he thought as he took in the rumpled sheet and the lightweight blanket that hung off the bed but mostly on the floor.

Maxwell smiled. *So she's a wild sleeper.*

But as he stared down at Amina, his heart squeezed at the sight of her curled up on her side with her hands beneath her cheek. He gently brushed her long bangs away from her eyes, admiring the way her lashes fanned over high cheekbones. She was wearing the T-shirt and yoga pants from earlier and seemed so at peace. The sight of her, the vulnerability reflected on her beautiful face, unlocked something deep inside Maxwell's soul. A possessiveness he hadn't felt for anyone in a long time washed over him like a tsunami crashing onto the shore and taking everything out in its wake.

*God, he had it bad for this woman.* There was no doubt in his mind that he wanted Amina in his life going forward; he just needed to figure out what that would look like. Friend? Or something more? But if he was honest with himself, she was already something more.

As he covered her with the sheet and blanket, his gaze spied the butterfly bandages on her neck that were a constant reminder of the attempted mugging. The adhesive strips wouldn't be on for an extended amount of time, but even for a day was too long for him. He wanted to hunt down the bastard who did that to her, the man who dared put his hands on her.

Anger simmered inside him. There was something about the whole incident that wasn't adding up. Maxwell just couldn't quite put his finger on it, but it would come to him, hopefully soon.

He forced himself away from the bed and turned on the light in the guest bathroom. After scribbling a quick message on the sticky note, he stuck it on the mirror. No way could she miss it there.

He turned the light back off and, after one last glance

at her, left the bedroom. Hopefully, she'd be there when he returned. If not, he'd find her.

Amina might not know it yet, but he was never walking out of her life again.

# Chapter 9

A short while later, Maxwell entered the back door of the police station and jogged up the stairs that would take him to his department. He hoped to slip in and out without getting bombarded with questions or requests. That was going to be impossible since he had to walk past a few offices. His only advantage was that it was still pretty early in the day.

He turned the corner and almost ran into Aaron. The officer looked as if he had been up all night and had slept in his clothes. Maxwell had wanted to talk to him but just hadn't had a chance.

"Hey, you off today?" Maxwell asked.

"Yeah, I left something in my locker the other day and came in to get it." His tired eyes looked everywhere but at Maxwell. "Listen," he started, finally making eye contact. "I'm sorry to hear about what happened to Jay. I know you guys were good friends."

"Yeah, it's still unbelievable, but how are you holding up? You two were friends also."

Aaron released a humorless laugh. "Yeah, we used to be, but things changed, *he* changed."

"Actually, I wanted to talk to you about that." Maxwell stopped speaking when a couple of support staff members stepped out of one of the offices. Once they passed, he continued. "One minute you and Jay seemed pretty tight, the next you're fighting during a briefing. What was that all about?"

They had both been suspended, but Jeremy received one extra day since he had thrown the first punch.

"I'd rather not say. It was personal."

"What was the fight about?" Maxwell repeated, his no-nonsense tone warranting a response. Either he'd get answers now or he'd haul Aaron's ass into an interrogation room and make him talk that way.

"We didn't always see eye to eye, but I would never wish him dead."

"What was the fight about?" Maxwell asked again.

Aaron sighed and leaned against a nearby wall as if he could no longer hold himself up. "My sister. Jeremy was a dog, but you probably already know that. He would chase anything in a skirt. Anyway, I found out he'd been hooking up with Val, and I told him to stop. He said *make me*. More words were exchanged and before I knew it, we were throwing punches."

"And that's it?" Maxwell asked, sensing Aaron was holding something back.

"Yeah, that's it. The asshole was trying to prove he

could get any woman he wanted. I just didn't appreciate Val being one of them."

"How old is she?"

"Twenty-eight. I know she's old enough to do whatever and with whoever, but she's my little sister. I tried warning her away from him, but that was useless. If anything, it had the opposite effect."

Maxwell nodded and clapped Aaron on the shoulder. He knew better than anyone the influence Jeremy had on women. "Thanks for telling me. Now get out of here and go get some rest. You look like hell."

Aaron sputtered a laugh. "Gee, thanks, Sarge. Way to boost my morale," he cracked.

Maxwell grinned. "That's what I'm here for. Now go. Take care of yourself."

"Will do."

Maxwell sauntered into the bullpen, and the buzz of energy greeted him at the door and flowed through the space. Even with only ten of the twenty desks occupied by his detectives, the volume in the room was as amplified as usual. It was a wonder anyone could hear anything since it seemed everyone was talking over the other. Some had civilians sitting at their desks giving statements. Others were on the telephone or tapping away on their computer keyboards. He was glad to see everyone hard at work.

He addressed a few individuals as he wove around the nest of desks and office chairs.

"You slummin' today?" Officer Smith asked, nodding at Maxwell's attire.

He chuckled. "Yep, that's exactly what I'm doing," he said, and kept moving toward his office, which was at the back of the large room. Since he'd only planned to be there a few minutes, he had dressed casually in a T-shirt and jeans.

Maxwell didn't see Danny at his desk, but he did make eye contact with Zeke, who was on the telephone. The detective acknowledged him, lifting a finger signaling it would be a minute.

When Maxwell reached his office, he flipped on the lights and noted the pile of files on his desk. Files that needed his attention. That was the downside about taking time off. Even if you needed a mental or emotional break, work would still be there when you returned.

He picked up the top folder, but before he could open it, a knock sounded on the opened office door.

"Hey, come on in," he said to Zeke, then moved the mound of files to the corner of the desk. "How's it going?"

Zeke closed the door and strolled in rubbing the back of his neck. "It's going."

Maxwell wasn't sure what time the detective arrived, but he appeared to have pulled an all-nighter. Whenever they lost one of their own, especially in the line of duty, solving those cases took precedence and putting in long hours wasn't unusual.

"Sorry to have you come in this morning." Zeke dropped down into one of the guest chairs in front of the desk. "I figured you'd want to handle this particular situation in person."

The seriousness of his tone had Maxwell taking a seat in his desk chair. "What situation is that?"

"Jay's fiancée."

Maxwell's mouth gaped open. "Fiancée? *Jeremy?*"

The detective nodded. "Yep. There's a woman here

who's making that claim and says that Jay told her that if ever she couldn't reach him, to contact you."

Maxwell sat stunned. Nothing should shock him when it came to his former best friend. Yet, the surprises kept coming. The idea of Jeremy being engaged and not rubbing it in his face made him wonder if the woman's claim had any merit. Jay was always in competition with him or trying to one-up him, even when Maxwell didn't know they were competing. No way would the guy keep something like this to himself. Besides that, the ink on his divorce papers hadn't even dried yet. Then again, he knew from experience that it didn't take long to fall for someone.

"Do you believe the woman?" Maxwell asked.

Zeke ran his hands down his face, looking wearier by the minute. "Honestly, I don't know. She was pretty upset when she arrived. So, we only asked a few questions. I guess she's been out of town and only found out about Jeremy's death this morning."

"Where is she?"

"Danny took her to the break room for something to drink. He wanted me to fill you in a little before meeting with her. They should be back up here shortly. I also wanted to catch you up a bit on the case."

"Okay, good. What do we have?"

"You know we questioned the tenant who was blasting music, but when we got him here, he didn't have much more information. He insists the gunman gave him two hundred and fifty dollars to play music and disappear for a day. He was able to give us a general description of the guy. He said the man was African American, a little over six feet, and had on all black and was wearing dark aviator sunglasses. He doesn't know if he lived in the building or not, and the only other thing he said was—*money talks*."

Maxwell pinched the bridge of his nose. Some people were so desperate for extra cash, they'd accept it from anyone for any reason without asking questions. Two hundred and fifty dollars wasn't chump change and could probably cover a large portion of the guy's rent.

There was another knock on the door.

"That's probably Danny," Zeke said and stood.

"Come on in," Maxwell called out.

Danny strolled in, followed by an attractive tall woman with fair skin and long micro braids pulled into an elaborate twist on top of her head. Conservatively dressed, she wore a simple white blouse and tan pants. Her clothes were slightly disheveled and the dark circles under her eyes reflected that of a person who hadn't slept. But what totally floored Maxwell was the sleeping baby in the stroller that she was pushing.

He shot a glance at Zeke who only shrugged, knowing he hadn't given him the full picture of the situation.

"Sarge, this is Rochelle Tillman. Rochelle, this is Sergeant Maxwell Layton."

"Max is fine," Maxwell said, and shook her hand. "Nice to meet you, Ms. Tillman."

"You can call me Rochelle, and it's nice to meet you too." Her voice was quiet and her timid tone didn't match the confidence that she walked in with.

Now that he had moved a little closer, upon further inspection, Maxwell noted her red eyes and how worn-out she appeared.

"Come on in and have a seat," he said, and touched the back of a guest chair. He moved the one next to it out of the way to make room for the stroller. "Can I get you anything?" he asked.

She lifted the bottle of water in her hand. "No, thanks, I'm fine." Maxwell detected a slight accent, maybe from the Virgin Islands. "I'm sorry to just stop by here, but I wasn't sure what else to do. I just heard what happened to Jeremy."

"How did you find out?" Maxwell asked. If she was really his fiancée, why hadn't she been notified the other day? But maybe Jeremy hadn't updated his emergency contact information.

"On the news about an hour ago. I've been out of town and just got back this morning," she said, her eyes tearing up, but she blinked them away and pulled her shoulders back.

The move seemed to be some type of defense mechanism because a moment ago she appeared the bereaved lover. Now she looked like a determined woman who wanted answers.

"I called him several times the other day, and when I didn't hear back, I knew something was wrong. He usually always calls back within a couple of hours. I want to know what happened, and why wasn't I notified?"

Maxwell exchanged glances with the detectives who were standing to his left against the wall. They couldn't give the woman any information until they verified who she was to Jeremy. She wasn't family.

"Ms. Tillman, I'm sorry, but Jeremy never mentioned you to me. As for not being informed of his death, the department contacted next of kin. His family."

Her thin eyebrows dipped into a frown. "I don't understand. He has no family. His parents were killed in a plane crash when he was in high school. And he doesn't have any siblings. He only has me and Camille."

The office was so quiet, they could've heard the proverbial pin drop. Anger stirred inside Maxwell, and he gripped the arm of his desk chair. Rarely was he speechless, but he was at a loss of what to say to the woman.

If she was telling the truth, that would mean she was yet another woman who'd been deceived and used by Jeremy. The man was proving over and over again how much of an asshole he really was, but to lie and say his family was dead? That was even more disgusting than some of the other crap he pulled.

"He must have mentioned us. We've been together for over a year and a half. How is that possible? And you're saying that he has a family?" She shook her head. "That can't be right. His parents are dead. He wouldn't have lied to me about something like that. We live together. He…" She stopped abruptly and swallowed. "Or we did live together before…this," she said quietly, her eyes blinking rapidly, trying to keep her emotions in check. "This…none of this makes sense."

On that, Maxwell had to agree. He didn't confirm or deny her claim about the family. For now, he'd let her believe what she wanted to. They couldn't give her any information until they had her checked out, and even then, nothing was guaranteed since she wasn't family.

Rochelle turned her attention to the beautiful baby girl who was stirring, but hadn't awakened. Even in her sleeping state, Maxwell could see the resemblance to Jeremy.

"How old is your daughter?" he asked.

"Three months. She'll be four months next week," she said absently, and looked at Maxwell. "Jeremy told me all about you—you're his best friend. How is it that you didn't know about us…about her? Jeremy was even more excited than me when he found out we were having a baby. It just doesn't make sense that he never mentioned us."

"Rochelle, I'm sorry. Jeremy was a private guy. Maybe that's why he didn't say anything." Maxwell was at a loss, but since they had her there, might as well ask a few questions. "When was the last time you saw him?" he asked.

She played with the earring that was dangling from her left ear, devastation written on her face. "Three days ago. Right before I went to visit my mother in California." She shook her head. "I never thought that would be the last time."

"How was he before you left?"

Her eyebrows pinched together. "What do you mean how was he?"

"Was he upset?" Danny asked. "Distant? Was anything bothering him?"

Maxwell had noticed that, for the most part, Danny and Zeke had been pretty quiet, but they were probably thinking like him. Maybe this woman could tell them something that would help with the case.

Rochelle tilted her head slightly as she thought back. "Not that I know of. Jeremy was pretty easygoing. Nothing seemed to get him down for long." She shrugged. "As far as I know, he was fine…except when he got suspended a couple of weeks ago. That bugged him, which I couldn't really understand. It was one day. I told him he should treat it like a much-needed day off, but he wasn't trying to hear that. He was pissed."

Maxwell exchanged a look with his detectives. Yet another lie that Jeremy had told her. He'd been suspended for three days. "Did he tell you why he was suspended?" he asked.

"Something about him not following procedures during an arrest. To be honest, work was starting to get to him. He didn't actually come out and say that, but all the overtime was starting to be a little too much."

"Was Jeremy having any problems with anyone that you know of?" That question came from Zeke.

The more the woman talked the angrier Maxwell was getting. It was becoming abundantly clear that Jeremy lied to her pretty much about everything. They all did a little overtime, but not more than ten hours a week. So that meant he was using work as an excuse for arriving home late, if at all.

Rochelle gave a half-hearted shrug. "Not as far as I knew, but… Wait." She leaned forward, and her gaze bounced between all of them. "Who would cause him trouble? He was the police. What's going on here?"

They couldn't share anything about the case, but Maxwell didn't want to lie to her. "Just wondering. We want to make sure he was doing okay before…"

She nodded and released a noisy sigh. "This doesn't seem real. It feels like a really bad dream, and nothing's making sense. The news reporter said the name of the fallen officer, and I didn't want to believe that it was *my* Jeremy." Her voice cracked, and she cleared her throat. "I thought it couldn't be, especially since the name of the deceased can't be released until next of kin is notified. But I wasn't called," she said, almost absently. This time she didn't wipe away the tears that slid down her cheeks.

Maxwell reached for the tissue box on the shelf next to him and handed it to her.

"When we first got together, I didn't see him much because of the hours he worked. But right before Camille was born, he proposed and moved in with me. When he wasn't working a shift, doing undercover work or traveling, he was home," she said more to herself than to them in the room.

Again, Maxwell and his detectives exchanged looks. Jeremy didn't do undercover work, and he never traveled out of the state for work. If they kept this woman talking, who knew what else they'd learn. One thing was clear; she didn't know about Amina.

"So his parents aren't dead?" she asked, a hint of anger in her tone.

"I'm sorry, but we can't give out that information," Maxwell said.

"But I'm his fiancée!" she snapped. "There's no way he would lie to me about something like that. He wasn't that type of man. He was a good person, and he said he would always take care of me and Camille."

The hurt and disbelief in her voice tore at Maxwell's heart. If what she was saying was true, especially about how long she'd been with Jeremy, that meant he had stepped out on Amina. And if he wasn't already dead, Maxwell would kill him himself.

Rochelle dropped back against her seat looking defeated. "He said you guys were best friends, and I always wondered why you never came around." She bit down on her bottom lip. "What else don't I know? What else did he lie to me about?"

Maxwell assumed that was a rhetorical question.

She released an exhausted sigh. "I don't know what to do from here. Who do I talk to about our benefits, and is financial help offered for his funeral? I have to start making arrangements and I'm not sure where to begin. These guys," she pointed at Zeke and Danny, "wouldn't even let me see the body."

"Unfortunately, since you're not family—"

"I am his family, dammit!" She pounded on the desk. The baby stirred and started whining before bursting into a full-on cry. "What about his daughter?" Rochelle said as she lifted the infant and started rocking her. "How am I supposed to take care of her by myself?"

Almost instantly the infant quieted, and she opened her eyes. *Jeremy's* eyes.

*Damn.* Maybe she was his, but Maxwell still had no intention of giving the woman information, especially without knowing more about her.

"Rochelle, I'm sorry for your loss and what you must be going through right now. But we can't give you any information about Jeremy or the case. As for his burial, that's being taken care of." He couldn't even tell her that his parents had already started making arrangements for the funeral that would take place in a few days.

"Then what am I supposed to do?" she sobbed.

"Do you have any proof of what you've told us?" Danny asked.

"What type of proof? What do you need? I can get you a copy of the lease agreement for the house we're renting. It has both our names on it. If you want me to have a paternity test for Camille, I'll do it. Just tell me what to do." She swiped at the tears streaming down her cheeks while she continued rocking her baby back to sleep. "I'm not lying, but it seems like Jeremy has lied to me over and over again." The more she talked, the more upset she got.

"I'll tell you what," Maxwell started, "leave your contact information here with Detective Haines," he said of Danny. "And we'll see what we can do to help."

"He told me that he would take care of us, that we would get married this fall. Now he's gone." She sobbed harder and set the sleeping baby back in the stroller, then stood. "I'm sorry. I didn't mean to come here and cry all over everything. I'm just…shocked."

Maxwell went around the desk and shoved his hands into his pants pockets. This whole situation was awkward and at the moment, there wasn't really much they could do for the woman or tell her.

"Come with me," Danny said. "I'll get your information, and we'll see you home."

The moment they walked out the door, Maxwell whirled around and positioned his fist to punch the wall but pulled up short of hitting it.

"That bastard," he said from between gritted teeth. Then turned to Zeke. "I want you to dig into Jeremy's life as if you were searching for a mass murderer. Start with the past six months. I want to know everything from what type of toothpaste he used to who the hell he was with before duty that morning. *Everything*."

"I'm on it, and what about Rochelle? I'll start digging into her life, and I assume you'll want that paternity test done?"

"Absolutely."

After Zeke left, Maxwell stood at the small window and gazed out at the parking lot. He hated this. He hated *all* of this. Now he had to go home and talk to Amina. If Jeremy hadn't already broken her heart, learning that he fathered a child while he was married to her would rip it to shreds.

## Chapter 10

Amina stared up at the popcorn ceiling, listening for any sounds or movement in the house. It was after ten, and she was glad she'd been able to fall asleep once she made it to the guest room hours ago.

An involuntary smile touched her lips and it soon turned into a laugh. How in the world had they ended up in that position? But did it really matter?

She mentally relived the velvety warmth of his mouth during that incredible kiss. Lips connected, bodies entangled...it was everything. No amount of fantasizing could have prepared Amina for waking up on top of Maxwell. For too long she had wondered what it would be like to be in his warm embrace. To feel his strong arms protectively wrapped around her. Now she knew.

She released a noisy yawn and scratched her neck, but winced when her fingers made contact with the bandages. The event that caused her to be there in the first place came to the forefront of her mind and washed over her like a bucket of ice water. Her visit wasn't some type of second chance at love, or a dream fulfilled. Maxwell had come to her when she needed him and given her a place to stay for the night. The last thing she should be doing was thinking it would be anything more than that.

"Let me get up."

She ambled to the attached bathroom, flipped on the light and caught sight of a yellow slip of paper. Removing it, she quickly scanned the messy writing.

Had to go to the station. Be back soon. Don't leave. Make yourself at home. Coffee downstairs. Breakfast when I get back.

Amina smiled and held the paper to her chest. It didn't sound like he regretted the kiss, but how awkward would it be for them when he returned?

"Well, we'll see."

After freshening up, Amina headed downstairs and followed the scent of strong coffee. The only thing Maxwell's note didn't have was what time he planned to return. He mentioned breakfast, but there was no way she was going anywhere in clothes she'd slept in.

"But right now, I need coffee."

She had just taken her first sip when she heard the garage door go up. A few minutes later, Maxwell stomped through the mudroom before entering the kitchen. He pulled up short when he saw her standing at the counter.

"Hey," he said, his gaze, the one that didn't miss anything, slowly sweeping down her body and back up

again. Each time he regarded her with those dark, smoldering eyes, her insides got all tangled.

"Hey, yourself," Amina said, and set the coffee mug
down. She tried not to fidget under his perusal, but it
was no use. There was something about the way he
looked at her. Like she was the most beautiful woman in
the world. It had been a long time since someone made
her feel that way. Unless she counted Dr. McPherson,
but her body didn't come alive the way it did with Maxwell's attention.

"You sleep okay?" he asked, strolling farther into
the house.

Amina's gaze followed every step he took. She didn't
think she would ever get enough of looking at him. He
set his keys and cell phone on the glass kitchen table that
was pushed against the wall near the window.

"I slept great, but I'm thinking we should talk about
what happened last night."

Hopefully, she wasn't making too big of a deal over
it, but Amina wanted to see where his head was at. The
fear of another man hurting her was real, but if she didn't
shoot her shot with Maxwell, she would always wonder if anything could've ever developed between them.

She cleared her throat. "We should discuss the kiss."

"What's there to discuss?" he asked, and poured a
cup of coffee. "We kissed. We liked it. And I hope we
do it again."

Amina stood flabbergasted with her mouth hanging
open. What could she say to that? It was true, but she
had expected him to say it couldn't happen again. That
it was a mistake.

"I will always be straight with you," he continued.

"And I hope that's the case with you. Based on the way you kissed me back, I'd say you felt the same way."

"I do," she said without having to think about her response. No sense in acting as if she wasn't interested. "So where do we go from here?"

"We get to know each other better."

Amina nodded. "I'd like that." She wasn't sure what that would look like, but they would figure it out.

They both stood at the counter sipping their coffee until Maxwell said, "What are your plans for today?"

He was always so confident, but right now, his expression seemed guarded. She wasn't sure what that was all about. Or it could be she was seeing something that wasn't there.

"I don't have much planned. I was hoping you could drop me off to pick up my car. Then I was just going to head home, change clothes and see what I can get into today."

"How about going to Trinity's house for brunch with me?" he said of his sister. "She called me on my way here."

Amina would love to finally meet Trinity and her family. She had heard so much about them, it felt like she already knew them.

"I'd love to, but…" She waved her hand down her body. "Besides the scrubs I had on yesterday, I don't have anything else in my bag to wear. I'm going to have to take a rain check."

"I'll take you home to change, we'll go eat and then once we're done, I'll take you to get your car."

He set his coffee mug down and then braced his hands on the edge of the counter. Something was going on with him.

"What's wrong? Did something happen at the station? Oh, and thanks for leaving the note."

He gave her a small smile that didn't reach his eyes. "I'm glad you saw it."

"And I'm glad you didn't just leave."

This time his smile was genuine and it turned into a chuckle. "I don't usually make the same mistake twice. Trust me—I've learned my lesson." He sobered, and his gaze dropped to the floor.

Amina stood next to him and placed her hand on his back. "Max, what is it?"

The day before, she'd been so caught up in her own situation that she hadn't asked how he was doing. He hadn't really had a chance to grieve because of dealing with her and helping with Jeremy's case.

"Are you feeling all right? Did something happen while you were at work?"

He blew out a breath and draped his arm around her shoulders. God, he smelled so good. His fresh scent with a hint of sandalwood made her want to lean in to him.

How sad was it that she hadn't been with a man in so long that just his scent turned her on?

"Let's sit down," he said, his large hand sliding down to the center of her back. Normally, she loved his touch, but her body stiffened at his words, and she went on alert.

"Why? What happened?" She stood frozen until he gently nudged her to the table and pulled out one of the chairs.

"We need to talk."

"No good ever comes from a conversation that starts with, *we need to talk*," she mumbled.

He chuckled and took the seat across from her. "It's about Jeremy."

"Nope. Don't want to hear it." Amina started to stand, but Maxwell gently grabbed her hand. This time his touch did what it usually did, sent goose bumps racing up her arms.

"Come on. Hear me out. There's something I need to tell you," he said. His tone alone had her body stiffening. And the dire expression on his face had Amina thinking the worst. But what could be worse than Jeremy being gunned down?

"A woman came to the station this morning claiming to be Jeremy's fiancée."

Amina studied him. When he didn't continue, she gave a slight shrug. "I'm not sure what you expect me to say. You know Jay and I have been divorced for over six months. So whatever he did after our marriage, I don't care."

"He was dating this woman while still married to you."

Amina hadn't expected that and tapped down the nauseating despair creeping through her body. Just when she thought she had moved on from the hurt Jeremy had caused, she kept being reminded of her colossal mistake. If only she hadn't married him. Then he wouldn't get to embarrass her even in death.

*He cheated on me,* Amina thought as she continued listening. She really shouldn't be surprised, and if she was honest, there had been signs. It had been months into their marriage during a time when she struggled to care what he did. The late nights at work, hanging out at the neighborhood bar and being emotionally unavailable were signs of the beginning of their troubles.

If she had to pinpoint when their marriage really started crumbling, it was two months in when he accused her of being in love with Maxwell. Amina didn't know where that had come from. She never did anything that she knew of to make him come to that conclusion. She vehemently denied the accusation. When she got married, she really did think she was in love with Jeremy.

But as time went on, Amina came to the conclusion that she'd been in love with the idea of being in love. Yet, she'd been determined to keep her marriage together. She had made a commitment that she wanted to honor. Until the arguing and verbal abuse started, and then he put his hands on her. They'd barely been married four months before she filed for divorce, and it took another four months before Jeremy finally agreed to sign the papers.

Amina folded her arms and held herself tight. She listened to Maxwell tell her the little he knew about Jeremy's other woman.

"Did you know he was cheating on you?" Maxwell asked.

"No," she said, but she should've figured it out. Maybe that was why he had started changing. He had someone else.

"Since Rochelle didn't know about Jeremy's parents or his sister, I don't think she knew he was married. There's something else, Amina," Maxwell said, staring down at their joined hands. "Jeremy has a three-month-old daughter with the woman."

Assailed with a terrible sense of disbelief, Amina tugged her hand away. The words spoken were like a cannonball blasting into her chest, and she dropped back against the chair speechless.

*Jeremy has a baby.*

What the hell was she supposed to do with that information? What was she supposed to think? It wasn't just that he had a child. If the baby was three months, that meant he'd been screwing around with the woman shortly after they'd married.

"We're not a hundred percent sure the child is his, but the woman is willing to have a paternity test done."

Fury and hurt battled within Amina, but she was determined not to take her frustration out on the messenger. "You saw the baby. What do you think?" she asked.

"I think she's his."

Amina nodded. In the big scheme of things, it didn't matter. Nothing about Jeremy mattered to her anymore. Yet...

She stood abruptly, practically knocking the kitchen chair over. She wanted to believe that it didn't matter, that nothing about him mattered, but she'd be lying. She had wanted a baby more than she wanted anything in her life. Jeremy had been willing. As a matter of fact, he'd wanted to get her pregnant even before the wedding, but that had been a solid *no* for her.

"There was nothing I wanted more than a loving husband who I could raise a family with. At first, months after we started dating, I thought Jeremy was that man. As we got closer to getting married, I had a few doubts about him, but I brushed them off. My stupid ass ignored signs."

Maxwell stood, but kept a little distance between them. "Amina, you don't have to—"

"Please, I need to say this," she said quietly, her words almost choking her. "When I found out what he had done to you...to us, I was pissed at him. Yet, I was ignorantly flattered that he did it all to win my heart. More than anything I was ready to be a wife and mother. Almost to the point of obsession."

Amina shook her head, disgusted at her naivete. She wished she could blame her ignorance on being young, but she'd been thirty-one at the time.

"Everyone around me was either married or getting married, which was something I wanted too. And when Jeremy came along, saying the right things and treating me like I was a gift from God, I fell hard for him, and I honestly thought I was in love. Even when I had learned that he had stabbed you in the back, I couldn't see past how sweet and kind he was to me."

"Ahh, babe. I get it," Maxwell said. "We all make decisions based on where we are mentally and emotionally in that moment. Some might be good choices, but many won't be. Don't be so hard on yourself. There's not a person alive who doesn't wish they could have some do-overs."

Amina bit her bottom lip, willing herself to keep it together. She knew he was right, but there was still that lingering disappointment in herself that she wasn't sure she'd ever be rid of.

"I think it was a month or two after we were married. I had a conversation with my mother about Jeremy. There was tension in our relationship, and I needed a sounding board. I told her what he had done to you. I'll never forget her words. She said that wasn't love that made him betray his friend. That was selfish ambition. Do you know what else she said?"

Maxwell shook his head, and the compassion radiating in his eyes was almost Amina's undoing.

"She said that she was concerned for my well-being,

because if he could treat his best friend like that, imagine what he'd do to me."

Amina didn't realize she was crying until Maxwell pulled her into his strong arms. She molded in to his body, holding on tight as she soaked up his strength.

Jeremy had made a fool of her more times than she could count. Sometimes in front of others, but mostly when it was just the two of them. He never respected her. Maybe in the beginning, but… Actually, probably never.

Anger warred inside her along with disappointment and sadness. Those were the emotions that were usually synonymous with thoughts of him. What a fool she had been. How could an educated woman with common sense mess up so bad by choosing him?

Amina tried to pull away from Maxwell, but he didn't let go immediately. He placed a lingering kiss against her temple and held on a little longer before finally releasing her.

"Thank you for telling me," she said, wiping frantically at her wet cheeks. She couldn't bring herself to look at him. She didn't want to see pity in his eyes or imagine him saying *I told you so*. He had never actually spoken those words, but she remembered him claiming a long time ago, when it was just them, that she could do so much better than Jeremy. That she deserved better.

If only she could have a redo of her life. At least the part that started after the party where they all first met. She never would've given in to his charming ways.

"Do you mind taking me home?" Amina asked quietly, still too embarrassed to look at Maxwell.

"I'll take you home, but only for you to change clothes. I still want you to go to brunch with me."

Amina finally met his eyes. "I don't think that's a

good idea. I'll be lousy company, and I'm not sure I can handle being around people right now." She especially didn't want to be around a loving couple with cute kids. If that made her childish, oh well. Her heart just couldn't take it.

"I think family, even if it's mine, is exactly what you need today."

He lightly brushed her bangs to the side then cupped her cheek as he stared into her eyes. "Do it for me. Our time together yesterday was for you. Today, I need you with me."

Amina stood dumbfounded. Maxwell had never asked her for anything.

"Why do you need me with you?"

"Partly because I'm worried about you. Also, because I love spending time with you."

How could she say no to that?

"You don't play fair," she said, struggling to smile.

Maxwell chuckled and pulled her into his arms again. This time he kissed the top of her head. "You are the strongest woman I know, and I'm sure it'll probably take time to process the news about Jeremy, but don't let him steal your joy, Amina."

She nodded against his chest. "You're right. Thanks for reminding me of that. No more wallowing in past mistakes."

"Good. Now can we go eat? I'm starving."

Amina's stomach chose that moment to growl, and she groaned. "How embarrassing."

Maxwell laughed and moved across the kitchen to the pantry. He pulled out a breakfast bar. "Here's a little something to tide you over until we get to my sister's.

## Get up to 4 FREE FABULOUS BOOKS You Love!

To thank you for being a loyal reader we'd like to send you up to 4 FREE BOOKS, absolutely free.

Just write "YES" on the Loyal Reader Voucher and we'll send you up to 4 Free Books and Free Mystery Gifts, altogether worth over $20, as a way of saying thank you for being a loyal reader.

Try **Harlequin® Romantic Suspense** books featuring heart-racing page-turners with unexpected plot twists and irresistible chemistry that will keep you guessing to the very end.

Try **Harlequin Intrigue® Larger-Print** books featuring action-packed stories that will keep you on the edge of your seat. Solve the crime and deliver justice at all costs.

Or **TRY BOTH!**

We are so glad you love the books as much as we do and can't wait to send you great new books.

So don't miss out, return your Loyal Reader Voucher Today!

*Pam Powers*

# LOYAL READER
# FREE BOOKS VOUCHER

**YES! I Love Reading, please send me up to 4 FREE BOOKS and Free Mystery Gifts from the series I select.**

Just write in "YES" on the dotted line below then return this card today and we'll send your free books & gifts asap!

→ YES ←

Which do you prefer?

☐ **Harlequin® Romantic Suspense**
240/340 HDL GRHP

☐ **Harlequin Intrigue® Larger-Print**
199/399 HDL GRHP

☐ **BOTH**
240/340 & 199/399
HDL GRHZ

| | |
|---|---|
| FIRST NAME | LAST NAME |

ADDRESS

| | |
|---|---|
| APT.# | CITY |

| | |
|---|---|
| STATE/PROV. | ZIP/POSTAL CODE |

EMAIL ☐ Please check this box if you would like to receive newsletters and promotional emails from Harlequin Enterprises ULC and its affiliates. You can unsubscribe anytime.

HI/HRS-520-LR21

## \oplus HARLEQUIN® Reader Service —Here's how it works:

**BUSINESS REPLY MAIL**
FIRST-CLASS MAIL    PERMIT NO. 717    BUFFALO, NY

POSTAGE WILL BE PAID BY ADDRESSEE

**HARLEQUIN READER SERVICE**
PO BOX 1341
BUFFALO NY 14240-8571

NO POSTAGE
NECESSARY
IF MAILED
IN THE
UNITED STATES

I wouldn't suggest eating more than that because she usually cooks enough to feed an army."

"Excellent because right now I think I'm hungry enough to eat a tank."

They both laughed and though her heart was heavy, Amina had a feeling it would get lighter as the day went on.

# Chapter 11

"You keep staring at her like that, I'm gonna grab the fire extinguisher and hose you down," Trinity Layton-Brooks said. "I don't think I've ever seen you so taken with a woman. But she's not just any woman, is she?"

"Nope, she's not," Maxwell responded absently, as he watched Amina from the kitchen.

They had arrived an hour ago, and it was as if she'd known his family forever. Not that he expected anything less. But considering how distraught she'd been after their conversation in his kitchen, he hadn't been sure how things would go. Yet, Amina's strength and grace were on full display. She handled the news of Jeremy's infidelity better than most would have. Now she was in the family room playing video games with his four-year-old nephew as if she didn't have a care in the world.

Maxwell smiled when she shrieked. She must've lost,

because she suddenly wrestled Jonah to the floor, sending the kid into a fit of giggles. Clearly, they both were having a good time.

After the conversation about Rochelle, he had taken Amina home to change clothes, hoping she wouldn't try to back out of their plans. She did, claiming she didn't want to have to explain the cut on her neck. Maxwell had refused to let her off the hook. So she opted for a sleeveless red turtleneck that hid the bandages and was still cool enough to survive the Las Vegas heat.

"Max?" Trinity said, sounding exasperated as if she had called his name more than once.

"Yeah," he responded just as she sidled up to him with her hand on her hip.

"I'll admit that she's cute, but quit drooling over the woman and help me clean this kitchen."

He pushed away from the huge center island and moved to the sink. "I think I'm jealous of my nephew. He's been monopolizing all of Amina's time."

"I guess I should've warned you. My son is charming like his father. No woman can resist all of that cuteness."

"Are we talking about Jonah or Gunner?" he asked of her husband.

Trinity grinned and handed him a stack of plates. "Both, but Jonah is your only threat."

He snorted and started putting dishes in the dishwasher. "Don't even play like that. One man already came between her and me. I'm not about to let another one do the same thing."

"Oops, I guess that is a sore subject."

They might've been joking around, but deep down, that was one of Maxwell's sore spots.

Trinity bumped him, practically knocking him over and causing him to splash water.

"Hey!" he yelled.

"Well, move over. You're hogging up all the space."

They both burst out laughing remembering how it used to be when they were kids and washing dishes after dinner. Back then, they didn't have a dishwasher, and like Trinity, his mother loved to prepare huge meals. Sometimes it took them hours to clean the kitchen. Spending so much time together only strengthened their bond. Maxwell might've been two years older than her, but she was one of his best friends.

"How are you holding up in regard to what happened with Jay?"

Maxwell rinsed another plate and handed it to her. The last couple of days, Jeremy hadn't been far from his mind. Between possible drug use and knowing he cheated on his wife, it had been impossible to think of his so-called friend in a good way.

"It still doesn't feel real. My thoughts go between *it could've been me* to *why was my life spared and not his.*"

"I hate what happened to Jeremy," Trinity said. "But I'm glad it wasn't you."

She was another person who wasn't a member of Jeremy's fan club. He had blown his first meeting with her when he walked into her house looking as if he was casing the joint. Trinity had immediately gone on guard. Then Jeremy made a comment about if she ever got tired of Gunner, to give him a call. The visit had gone downhill from there, and she told Maxwell not to ever bring him back to her home.

"I might not have been there, but hearing on the radio that an officer had been killed took a few years off my life. I immediately started praying," she said shaking her head. "And then when you didn't answer your phone, my imagination got the best of me. I think I was holding my breath from then until I got your text saying you were all right."

Years ago, Trinity used to be a police officer, and they had an agreement that whenever there was an officer down or an officer-involved shooting, they would check in with each other within an hour. It was bad enough hearing about cop incidences, but when it was possible it could be your sibling, that took the worry to a different level.

"I'm sorry I scared you. I was just as terrified. It was like something out of a suspense movie, but instead of watching I was right there in it." Maxwell's pulse ratcheted up as his mind took him back to the moment when Jeremy's body jerked and he fell to his knees. "No amount of coursework, police training or even life experiences could have prepared me for witnessing one of our own get shot. It's wild how you always think about what you'd do in various circumstances. You plan it out perfectly in your head, but then when you're smack dab in the middle of that situation, it's never how you envisioned it."

"I can't even imagine how you must have felt...what you're still feeling. I'm glad your training kicked in and you knew what to do. It's just too bad you couldn't save Jeremy, but at least you can help find his killer."

As they worked on the dishes, Maxwell talked a little about the case. He couldn't share much since it was still early in the investigation. Besides that, it wasn't a good idea to discuss pending cases, but he trusted his sister more than any other person on the planet. He often

bounced work situations off her, pleased when she tossed
out ideas or asked questions he hadn't considered.

"Have you talked to a therapist yet?" she asked.

With the suicide rate for police officers rising, their
department implemented a critical-incident policy. If
they were involved in a shooting or some other act of
violence, they were required to talk to a counselor. Maxwell didn't feel he needed to, but to be a good example
to those who reported to him, he planned to soon. And
that's what he told his sister.

"Okay, enough about work. What are your intentions
with Amina?" Trinity whispered.

Considering how loud the video game was in the
other room, it was safe to say that Amina and Jonah
wouldn't hear them talking. Gunner had taken the baby
upstairs to change her diaper. So they probably only had
a few minutes alone to discuss Amina.

"I'm going to shoot my shot and see what happens.
My feelings for her are the same as they were the first
time we met, if not stronger. Which is just mind-blowing.
Until the other day, I hadn't seen her in months, but since
then, it's as if no time has passed between us."

"Sometimes when that special person comes along,
you just know."

The wistfulness in Trinity's tone had Maxwell turning back to the family room. He could admit to having
moments of uncertainty when it came to Amina. Especially knowing she had been with Jeremy. Yet, each
time he looked at her, like now, his heart felt so full he
was afraid it might burst out of his chest. She was the
woman he'd been waiting for even when he didn't realize he was waiting.

Even knowing that, though, he didn't plan to make

another move before he was sure she was ready. Before they both were ready. Yet, when it came to wanting her and wanting to be *with* her, Maxwell couldn't help himself. It was going to be nearly impossible to take things slow.

"There you go staring at her again. Can you just make a move and put us all out of our misery?" Trinity cracked.

Maxwell laughed. "Be quiet."

They both were facing the family room with their backs to the sink when Trinity elbowed him. "On a serious note, though, I like her. I can tell she has a beautiful spirit, and more than that, I can tell she's really feeling you. Oh, and Mom is going to love her, especially since Amina knows how to cook and she wants kids."

Maxwell only grunted at that. Their mother would love anyone he settled down with. She just wanted him to be happy and to add to her number of grandchildren. A widow since they were kids, his mother's life currently revolved around her church. But because of Jonah and Brielle, she was finally warming up to the idea of leaving Los Angeles and moving to Vegas.

"Hey, here comes my precious baby girl," Trinity said as Gunner trotted down the stairs carrying Brielle in the crook of his arm.

"Well, this little one is all cleaned up and ready for family time," Gunner said, and kissed Trinity as if he hadn't just seen her minutes ago.

Even if he had tried, Maxwell couldn't have picked a better man for his sister. He and Gunner had been college roommates and were closer than some brothers. And though Trinity wanted nothing to do with Gunner at first, especially when she'd learned he was a profes-

sional poker player, she eventually warmed up to him.
It was hard not to like him. His brother-in-law might be
a multimillionaire, but he was one of the most down-
to-earth people Maxwell knew.

"All right, break it up. You can do all that kissing and
crap when I'm not around," Maxwell said, and dried his
hands. "Give me my niece so we can do a little bonding."

Gunner handed her over, and Maxwell kissed her
chubby cheek. God, she had to be the cutest kid with
big bright eyes, long eyelashes and a toothless grin that
you couldn't help but smile at. He nuzzled her scented
neck, loving her baby-powder smell as she wiggled in his
arms. Each time he held the little cutie-pie, he imagined
holding his own little girl someday. Thoughts of marriage and kids had been creeping more and more to the
front of his mind even before Amina came back into his
life. It was time to start seriously thinking about a family. At thirty-five, he didn't want to wait too much longer
and end up being too old to run around with his kids.

He strolled into the family room and made a beeline
to the double-wide upholstered chair that was his favorite
piece of furniture in the massive home. It could easily sit
two people and was just as comfortable as a bed.

Once he was settled, he glanced up and his gaze collided with Amina's. God, she was beautiful. Even with
her short hair sticking out in places and her top and
shorts wrinkled from wrestling with Jonah, she was
still gorgeous.

"Hey, Uncle Max!" Jonah yelled as if seeing him for
the first time that day. He darted across the room when
he noticed Brielle. "Hi, Bri Bri," he said in baby talk,
then turned back to Amina. "Do you want to play with
my little sister again?"

Amina turned off the game and ambled toward them. She didn't look as dejected as she had earlier in his kitchen. Still, that spark that usually shone in her eyes had dulled.

"Come sit next to me," Maxwell said to her, and scooted over some. She hesitated for a moment, glancing at Jonah, but the corners of her enticing lips lifted.

"Oh, all right. If you insist," she joked, and settled into his chair.

He loved having her close, especially when she was close enough to kiss, which he did. The quick peck on the lips wasn't nearly enough, but it was what they could sneak in while Jonah was preoccupied with making faces at Brielle.

"You doing okay?" Maxwell asked Amina.

"Yes, and I'm glad you forced me to come to brunch."

He laughed, and this time she flashed a real smile. Some of the tension in her face eased.

"*Forced* seems so harsh."

"Okay, maybe you didn't actually force me, but either way, I'm having a great time. I appreciate you inviting me."

"I'm glad you're here. I like having you around."

She leaned in closer. "I feel the same about you." She gently ran her hand over the baby's curly hair. "Can I hold her again?"

"Of course." He handed Brielle off, and Jonah trotted over to Amina's side of the chair.

As Maxwell watched her interact with the kids, an intense longing filled him. This was what he wanted. Her by his side with a couple of children of their own. He had no doubt she would make an amazing mother, but could they finally get together?

He rested his arm on the back of the chair. "You know your day is coming, right?" The words slipped between his lips before he had a chance to analyze them. "You're going to have everything you've ever wanted," he said with authority.

Amina glanced at him and a faint light glimmered in her beautiful eyes. "I hope you're right, because some days what I want seems impossible to have."

"Don't lose hope. I'm a true believer that anything is possible."

Maxwell didn't know for sure how things would turn out for them. But no matter what, he would do whatever he could to make their time together a positive experience. Soon, the disappointments of their pasts would be a distant memory.

And he couldn't wait.

Hours later, Amina pulled out of the hospital's employee parking lot with Maxwell trailing her in his vehicle. When he dropped her off to pick up her car, she hadn't expected him to stick around then follow her home. Yet, she shouldn't have been surprised. He was the consummate gentleman, always making her feel valued and cared for.

Considering how devastating the day started, it progressed nicely. Spending time with Maxwell and his family had been just what she needed to temporarily take her mind off her problems. It definitely beat sitting around the house alone with her thoughts and wallowing in self-pity. The news about Jeremy's indiscretion probably shouldn't bug her so much, but each time she thought about how he played her for a fool made her want to scream.

Amina's grip tightened on the steering wheel, and she took several cleansing breaths. *Let it go, girl. Let it go.* She had to stop rehashing all that he had done. Especially since there was nothing she could do about it. There had to be a way to stop letting him or his memory continue having control over her. If only it was that easy to shut off that part of her brain.

She glanced in the rearview mirror and smiled knowing that Maxwell was still behind her. It was too dark to truly make out his car, but she knew he was there. Having that type of confidence in a man she wasn't related to was a foreign experience.

"How sad is that?" she murmured.

Her cell phone rang, and Samantha's name showed on the dashboard. Amina answered with Bluetooth.

"Hello."

"I bet you thought I wasn't going to call you today," Samantha's chipper voice boomed through the speakers, and Amina smiled.

"I knew I'd be hearing from you at some point. How's it going?"

"I should be asking you. How's the hottie you walked out of the hospital with yesterday?"

"What? I don't get a—*How are you? Do you feel okay? Did you have nightmares?*"

"Oh, my bad. You know I have a one-track mind. How are you?"

Amina couldn't help but laugh. Samantha was that friend that every woman has at least one of. The one who makes you laugh without really trying.

"I'm fine. Max just dropped me off to pick up my car. Now I'm headed home."

"Glad you're feeling all right. Now start talking. I

want to know every single detail about that gorgeous, tall drink of water. Where'd you meet? How long have you been dating? Does he have a brother?"

Amina shook her head grinning. "First of all, you're married. Why do you want to know if he has a brother?"

"Just in case things don't work out with me and Teddy, I want to have options."

"Oh, please. You guys have been married like forever, and the way you talk about how he puts it on you, I know you're not going anywhere."

"Okay, that's true. He's stuck with me. I actually wanted to know because I'm always trying to play matchmaker. If Max has a brother, I might be able to fix him up with one of the single women I know."

"Well, he only has a sister."

"Okay, answer the other questions and hurry up. My break is almost over."

"Why'd you call me if you have to rush off the phone?"

"Quit stalling and answer the questions."

"We met at a party years ago, and we're not dating."

"Like hell you're not. The way he dropped everything to get to you, nah, I'm not buying that. And don't even get me started on the way you two were eyeing each other. I was about ready to say—get a room! Then I realized you already had one. Talk about three's a crowd."

Amina burst out laughing. Apparently, the feelings she had for Maxwell showed on her face because he definitely made her hot.

"I'm serious, Sam. We're friends, but I'll admit that he's very special to me. Oh, and thank you for being my nosy friend. I'm so glad you answered his phone call last night."

"Yeah, me too. I hated the idea of you going home alone. Did he stay the night?"

Amina bit her bottom lip, trying to hold back a smile even though her friend couldn't see her. "Actually, he took me back to his place."

Silence filled the phone line before her friend squealed. "Yes! It's about time you got some. I was starting to—"

"Wait. Nobody said anything about getting some. I told you we're friends."

"Seriously?" Samantha said, disappointment sounding loud and clear in those syllables. "The man is *hot*. You cannot let all of that testosterone go to waste. Have I not taught you anything? You have to go for it, especially when I know you're interested in him."

"I didn't say that."

"You didn't have to. It was clear by the way you looked at him." Amina started to speak but Samantha cut her off. "Don't even bother trying to deny it because you'd be lying. Besides, I don't have time, but promise me something."

Amina was almost afraid to ask. "What?"

"If he wants to do the horizontal tango, don't say no."

"Sam—"

"Oh, and did I mention that you two would make some pretty babies?"

"Would you knock it off?" Amina said weakly, trying to fight off the sudden pang of melancholy settling around her. She couldn't allow herself to get all weepy every time someone mentioned babies. She was stronger than that. Like Maxwell said, her day would come. At thirty-four, she knew her window of opportunity to birth her own children was slowly starting to close, but there was always adoption. She could still have everything she ever dreamed of.

"Okay, I'll stop. Just remember what I said. Go for it! Now for real, I gotta get back to work. Love you."

"Love you more," Amina said before disconnecting and pulling into her garage. By the time she climbed out of her Camry and grabbed her bag, Maxwell was at the car door.

"You're not staying?" she asked, noticing his vehicle was still running.

"Nah, I'mma get going. I just wanted to make sure you got inside okay."

Disappointment lodged in her chest. Spending the last twenty-four hours with him had given her a chance to see yet another side of him. A man who showed her more compassion than any other man she'd been with and one who adored his family. Amina hated for the day to come to an end.

"You sure you don't want to step in for a drink or something?"

He glanced at the door as if considering the invitation. When he returned his attention to her, she knew why he was saying no.

"Is it always going to be like this, Max?"

He frowned. "Like what?"

"You not wanting to come into my house because it's the place I shared with Jer…with my ex?"

"Yes."

Amina didn't expect him to be so candid, but she had a feeling with Maxwell, he would always be straight with her.

"It's not the same place," she said. "I've done a complete remodel and mostly all new furniture. It looks nothing like it used to."

"Sweetheart, it's not about the way the house looks or the furnishings." Maxwell ran the backs of his fingers gently down her cheek, and the compassion in his eyes almost made her whimper. "It has everything to do with the memories. It's about knowing a man who used to be my best friend lived here with a woman I've always been wild about. It's knowing that he hurt you and verbally abused you more times than I probably know of."

Embarrassment clouded Amina's mind and her gaze dropped to the concrete floor. It was bad enough that she had tolerated Jeremy's behavior. It was another thing to know that her family and friends had witnessed him disrespecting her.

Maxwell lifted her chin with the pad of his finger and forced her to meet his eyes.

"It's imagining all the things he did to you that gives me pause whenever I consider walking across that threshold. I would love nothing more than to spend time with you on your turf, but not yet. Not until I can completely set aside the hate that I had for the man I used to call friend."

Amina nodded. "I totally understand," she said around the lump in her throat. "I wish there was a way to wash away unhappy memories."

"There is, and I'm planning on us creating new memories."

Something akin to relief flooded her body with joy chasing behind it. "I look forward to that."

"I'll let you get inside and get some rest." He moved even closer and the heady scent of his cologne surrounded her like a lover's embrace. "Today has been amazing," he said.

"I agree. Thanks for convincing me to hang out with you and your family. They are wonderful, and I had a great time."

"I'm glad, especially since I'm planning on us spending more time together. That is, if you're all right with that."

A smile spread across Amina's mouth and that joy from a moment ago bubbled inside her. "I'm totally all right with that."

"Good."

Without another word, Maxwell lowered his head and covered her lips with his. The slow, drugging kiss was sweet and tamed at first, but quickly became more demanding when he tenderly gripped the back of her head. His mouth moved over hers. His experienced tongue explored the inner recesses of her mouth and had her moaning with pleasure.

This was what she longed for during her marriage, an unexplainable connection, a passion that made her want to keep coming back for more. Maxwell was ravishing her lips as if his life depended on it. All the while kindling a hunger inside her that had lain dormant for far too long.

When the kiss ended, Maxwell maintained his hold on her and stared into her eyes. Amina ached for him to continue massaging her lips with his. She respected his reasons for not entering her home, but *man* did she want him in her bed. If he was as gifted in other areas as he was in tongue aerobics, she wanted to experience it. All of it.

*In time*, she told herself. *In time.*

# *Chapter 12*

Two days later, anxiousness rumbled inside Amina as the minister delivered final words of the committal service. She didn't like funerals, and creepy cemeteries, even in the early morning hours, made her uncomfortable. Yet, she was standing a few feet from Jeremy's grave site, surrounded by his loved ones.

Staring down at the white rose in her hand, Amina gently fingered one of the soft petals. Attending the funeral had been a last-minute decision, but now she was glad she had. It would give her the closure she didn't realize she needed, and she could finally move on from him in every way.

Amina glanced up just as Jeremy's family moved forward to place their roses on his casket. Sitting in the back pew during the church service kept her from having to face his parents. Now that they were at the cemetery, she wasn't sure what to expect. She hadn't seen or spoken to them since before she and Jeremy separated.

With the back of her hand, she dabbed at the beads of sweat on her forehead. At ten in the morning, it wasn't as hot outside as it could've been. The perspiration could be from the almost eighty-degree weather. Or it could be the satin scarf she had around her neck to camouflage her cut. But most likely, it was partly from nerves.

This was it. This was her final goodbye.

She and Maxwell, who was standing next to her, stepped forward. They watched as those before them paid their last respects. When it was her turn to place her rose on the casket, trees rustled and a warm, gentle breeze kissed her cheek. Maybe it was Jeremy letting her know that he was sorry. Or maybe the sensation was prompting her to release the animosity that she'd been carrying for the past year. It was time to let it all go. That way he could rest in peace, and she could move on with her life.

*I'm sorry for the role I played in the way our relationship ended. Rest in peace.* The words flowed through her mind, and a calm descended on her. She was ready for the next chapter of her life. A better chapter.

Maxwell imitated her moves, placing his flower on the casket and only stopping for a second. Together they turned from the casket and moved away from it.

"I'd better speak to Jeremy's parents since I didn't get a chance to at the funeral," Amina said quietly. She walked gingerly across the grass to keep her high heels from sinking into the soil.

"Okay. I'll go over with you. I saw them before the funeral, but only for a second. They were surrounded by people. Kind of like now."

The church had been packed, especially with fellow police officers. There weren't as many people at the burial, but still, there had been a large turnout. His parents and his sister were about twenty feet away accepting condolences from those in attendance. As Amina and Maxwell fell in line, she couldn't help feeling sorry for Jeremy's parents. It didn't matter how she felt about him, Jeremy had been their only son and his mother's whole world.

Amina repositioned her sunglasses as they moved closer. Jeremy's sister, Elaine, glanced at them and a gentle smile lifted the corners of her lips.

"Amina, Max, thank you both for coming," she said after stepping away from her parents.

"I am so sorry about Jeremy," Amina said into Elaine's ear as they hugged.

"Thank you, and I'm sorry that we all had to come together again like this." They pulled apart and Elaine hugged Maxwell before turning back to Amina. "How have you been?"

"I've been all right. Just trying to get used to my new normal. How about you? How's Seattle?"

"Taking some getting used to." She laughed. "After living in Vegas for much of my life, with sunshine and warm weather, Seattle is…different. I am sooo over the daily rain showers."

They both chuckled, then grew somber.

"It's good seeing you again," Amina said honestly, and squeezed Elaine's arm. It saddened her that another relationship had fallen away because of her and Jeremy's breakup.

"You too. I hope we can keep in touch better," Elaine said.

"Me too," Amina agreed, though she doubted that

would be possible. She was closing the door to everything and everyone related to Jeremy. At least until she was sure she had put the past behind her.

Elaine said her goodbyes to them and went back to stand near her parents, who were still speaking with others. Soon Amina would be face-to-face with her former in-laws.

Her gaze took in Jeremy's mother, a statuesque woman who had on a beautiful black dress that hugged her petite body. She had always been a snazzy dresser, keeping up with the latest styles. Her long salt-and-pepper hair hung in waves around her shoulders beneath a pillbox hat.

When it was her turn to greet them, Amina stepped forward. "Mr. and Mrs. Kelly, I'm so sorry about Jeremy."

"Are you?" Mrs. Kelly snapped, and glared at Amina, then Maxwell. "Are you really sorry?"

The question was posed to Amina, and she was taken off guard by the venom attached to the words.

"Mom, come on. This is not the place," Elaine said, but her mother wasn't listening.

"You two-timing hussy probably couldn't wait until my son was out of the picture before seducing his best friend."

Amina gasped. *"Excuse me?"*

"There's no excuse for you. He loved you and gave you everything, but that wasn't enough for you, was it? He knew you two were fooling around. That's why he left you."

"Hold up. Wait." Maxwell's deep, commanding voice held disbelief as he looked back and forth between the older couple. "I don't know what Jeremy told you, but none of that's true."

"You should both be ashamed of yourselves, especially you, Max," Mrs. Kelly said, tears filling her eyes. "He thought of you as a brother."

"Mrs. Kelly, you have it all wrong," Amina hurried to say. She needed this woman to know the truth. "Max and I have never done anything, and I *never* stepped out on my husband. I would never do anything like that. I was faithful to the end."

"So now you're calling my son a liar?" Mr. Kelly snarled, and stepped toward Amina, but Maxwell stuck his arm out and stopped him.

"That's exactly what I'm calling your son," he growled, his voice low and lethal. His anger was palpable, and she appreciated his presence. "You can believe what you want," he continued. "But I *never* disrespected their marriage, and neither did Amina. Instead of you accusing her of being unfaithful, you need to get your facts straight."

Mr. Kelly never had much to say, but the anger radiating in his eyes let Amina know what he thought of her. Without another word, the couple turned and walked away. Elaine mouthed an *I'm sorry* before following behind her parents.

"Un-frickin-believable," Amina seethed, her fists balled at her sides. Anger gripped her like the leather straps of a straitjacket, squeezing, torturing and practically cutting off her breath. She didn't want to speak ill of the dead, but *damn* Jeremy.

Maxwell cupped her shoulder as if sensing she was about to blow. "Even from the grave, his lies are still going strong. Don't let his parents get inside your head. As long as we know the truth, that's all that matters."

Amina wished it was that simple, but what others thought of her did matter. She didn't want anyone walking around talking about her being some type of hussy.

"I'll try to catch the Kellys before they leave town and make sure they know the truth," Maxwell said.

"Whatever you tell them probably won't make a difference. You don't have to defend me."

"Yeah, I do. You've been through enough with Jeremy without his parents thinking the worst of you."

Amina sighed and pulled her keys from her small purse. "I just can't believe he'd lie and make them think that you and I…that I…"

Why was she still acting surprised by anything that jerk did? By now she should come to expect that he'd do anything to make himself look good or come out on top.

*That brother probably had all types of secrets.* Katrina's words flashed through Amina's mind. Who knew what else he had told his family? At least Elaine didn't seem to believe that nonsense.

"Urgh, I'm so disappointed in his parents," she said, struggling to let their words go. "How could they not know what type of person Jeremy was?"

Heck, she hadn't known either. She might as well face facts. Her ex-husband was scum and every word out of his mouth had probably been a lie.

Amina gasped when her shoe heel sank into the grass and she stumbled. Maxwell grabbed her elbow.

"You all right?" He held on to her until she got her balance.

"Yeah, I'm fine. Just clumsy and pissed."

"Jeremy was a momma's boy," Maxwell explained.

"In her eyes he could do no wrong. Besides, he wasn't the type of guy to admit when he screwed up. Nor would he apologize. Except…"

She glanced at him when he didn't continue. "Except what?"

Maxwell's eyebrows drew together like he was in deep thought. "Except shortly before he died. He said something that I totally forgot about. He said he was sorry about you."

Amina's heart kicked inside her chest. What did that mean? Was he sorry for the way he'd treated her? Sorry for playing with her emotions? Or was he sorry that he screwed around on her and had a baby with another woman?

"Considering he had a lot to apologize for, I'm not sure what he was referring to," Maxwell said as if reading her mind.

His cell phone beeped and he pulled it from his pocket as they walked across the lawn. While he read a text message, a feeling of being watched came over Amina. She looked around then slowed when she noticed a woman staring at them. Seconds ticked by, then the woman slipped on her sunglasses.

"Max, do you know her?" she asked, pointing her thumb over her shoulder before looking back.

"Know who?"

Amina glanced to her left and right, wondering where the woman could've disappeared to that fast. "She was just standing back there near that huge oak tree."

Maxwell followed her line of sight, but the woman was gone. "What about her?"

Amina shrugged. "It's probably nothing. I saw her

staring at me earlier at the church, and again just now. Or maybe she was just checking you out."

Maxwell chuckled. "Yeah, right."

Women loved a man in uniform, and Maxwell looked especially incredible in his dress blues. At over six feet, the garment made him appear taller, broader and like a total badass.

"I'm serious. You look *hot*, and I'm not talking about the temperature," she said, displaying her most seductive expression as her gaze slid slowly down his muscular body and then back up again.

He flashed a sexy grin that sent a frisson of excitement coursing through her body and goose bumps skittering along her bare arm. Jeremy's parents might've been wrong about her cheating on their son, but maybe they could see in her what Samantha saw. Interest. Lust. And probably a host of other words to describe what she felt when it came to Maxwell.

"Why, thank you. I might need to dress like this all the time if it evokes that type of reaction from you."

They both laughed and started back walking.

"I take it Jeremy's parents don't know about their granddaughter," she said.

"The results of the paternity test haven't come back yet. So if they know about the baby, they didn't hear it from me," Maxwell said, and glanced at his phone again. "I'm not sure when or how that information will be handled. Listen, I need to head in to work. How about we meet up later for dinner?"

Amina smiled, thoughts of the Kellys flying from her mind. "That sounds wonderful."

The day after spending time with his family, they had gone for coffee at a café near her house. They had talked for a couple of hours getting to know each other on a different level. She knew quite a bit about Maxwell, but that day she realized there was just as much she didn't know. Like how he had a bachelor's degree in criminology. Or how his father had a gambling problem before he died of cancer when Maxwell was young. Or that his favorite color was purple and that he'd always wanted a dog. A rottweiler.

When Amina realized Maxwell was following her to her vehicle, she stopped. "You don't have to walk me to my car. Let's not give Jay's family anything to talk about." She didn't see them, but wasn't willing to take the chance. Besides, Maxwell's car was in the opposite direction. There was no sense in him having to backtrack to get to it.

"You sure? I don't mind."

"I'm positive. Call or text me later once you know what time you'll be available for dinner and we'll plan from there."

"Sounds good." He didn't move, and a smile crept across his full lips. "I would kiss you if I didn't think you would totally freak out."

Amina grinned. "I would let you if I didn't think daggers would be thrown at me from someplace across the cemetery."

They both laughed.

"All right. Well, let me get out of here. I'll call you in a few hours." He slipped on his sunglasses, which made him look even sexier and dangerous, and walked backward still looking at her. "I'll see you later," he said.

"I look forward to it."

Amina was still smiling when she reached her car. They hadn't put a name to whatever they were doing, but as far as she was concerned, they were dating. That made her grin even harder.

"Excuse me."

Amina jumped and whirled around so fast that she slammed her hip into the car. Her hand flew to her chest as panic engulfed her like an out-of-control California wildfire.

*Not this again.* It was like déjà vu. Everything that happened in the parking lot the other night came rushing back. She gripped her keys in her hand ready to fight.

"I'm sorry—I didn't mean to scare you."

With her heart racing, Amina quickly perused the woman from her long micro braids hanging loose over her shoulders to the black maxi dress she wore. It was the same woman she'd seen moments ago. Except this time, she had a baby carrier in her hand. The infant, dressed in pink and white with a pink barrette in her hair, was gnawing on her little fist.

Amina's heart clenched and her attention went back to the woman. Not just any woman, but who she assumed was Jeremy's fiancée.

"Are you Jeremy's wife?" the pretty woman said.

*"Ex-wife,"* Amina replied forcefully. Seemed his name came up at every turn lately. She might have to leave town to totally rid herself of anything revolving around him.

The woman stared at her for a minute then glanced down at the infant who could've been Jeremy's twin when he was a baby. It was no wonder Maxwell sounded sure about the child's paternity. She had Jeremy's intuitive eyes, his nose and his strong cheekbones.

"Who are you?" Amina asked, though she already

knew. What she didn't know was why this woman had sought her out.

"My name is Rochelle and this is…" She swallowed as her attention went to the baby before returning to Amina. "This is my daughter, Camille. At the funeral, I heard someone say you were his wife. I… I never knew he was married."

Her voice cracked and she cleared her throat, but there were unshed tears hanging from her eyelashes.

"He never said a word. If I had known, there is no way I would've been with him. I'm not a home-wrecker. Please believe me. He said he had no family. That they were killed in a plane crash."

Amina relaxed her shoulders. Her first impression of the woman was very different than she imagined. For some reason, she expected some around-the-way girl, popping gum and having a funky attitude. Maybe that's what she wanted her to be like so that she could feel better about Jeremy stepping out on her. Instead, this woman appeared humbled and truly sorry. And dammit, she was movie-star pretty.

"You weren't a home-wrecker. That was all Jeremy," Amina said, struggling to control the anger that was simmering just below the surface. When would it end? When would Jeremy and everything in his life not touch her?

She opened her car door, debating for a second on whether she should say anything else to Rochelle. Actually, Maxwell and his people could determine what to share with her about Jeremy and his family. Amina felt sorry for her. She knew what it was like being one of her ex-husband's pawns, but she had no plans of befriending the woman.

She spared a glance at Rochelle. "For the record, you're better off without that bastard. I wish you and your baby all the best, but please don't seek me out again."

Amina's attitude might've been cold, but that was all she could muster for the woman. More than anything, she wanted to erase any hint of Jeremy from her life.

# Chapter 13

Maxwell rubbed his chin as he swiveled back and forth in his office chair. His mind was on everything but work. He couldn't stop thinking about Jeremy's parents and how nasty they were toward Amina. Now he hated that he talked her into attending the funeral. Initially, he thought it would be a good way to get closure. Instead, she got ambushed because of more lies.

What the heck would happen when people found they were dating? Or sorta dating? Hell, he wasn't sure what they were doing or what to call it. All he knew was that he wanted her in his life, and he had every intention of seeing where their relationship could go.

*And that asshole Jeremy.*

When had he changed for the worse? When had he become this person that Maxwell didn't recognize? His feelings toward the man were growing darker by the day.

Though he was more than ready to catch his killer, more than anything, he wanted to figure out what had changed Jeremy. He hadn't always been the selfish, coldhearted jerk that he had turned into.

"Hey, boss. You got a minute?" Danny asked from the doorway. "Me and Zeke got something."

"Yeah, come on in."

Both men had attended Jeremy's wake, but because of the urgency of the case, neither attended the funeral.

"What do you have?" he asked as they strolled into the office.

"A headache." Danny dropped into one of the guest chairs in front of the desk. "Talk about not being able to predict the direction a case will go. This one is proving to be tough."

Zeke was still standing, typing something into the electronic tablet in his hands. "We have a video from an owner of one of the town houses across from the apartment building," he said. He moved around the desk and handed Maxwell the device.

The video started, and whatever camera had been used, it had a wide lens that picked up not only the apartment building's door, but part of a backyard of what he assumed was the town house. Every few minutes people walked out of the apartment building through a door that Maxwell hadn't noticed when he was there. It was near where Jeremy had parked the squad car the day they were ambushed, but a little hidden by shrubbery.

"What am I looking for?" he asked.

"Just wait for it. You'll know it when you see it," Zeke said.

Maxwell noted the date of the video in the upper right-hand corner. It was the day of the shooting, and a flicker of apprehension coursed through him. Whatever he was about to see wasn't going to be good, but if it could get them closer to finding Jeremy's killer, he was ready for it.

No sooner than the thought entered his mind, a man burst out of the apartment building. He glanced left and right before going left down the sidewalk, but then Zeke stopped the video. The detective didn't have to say anything. Maxwell sat staring at the frozen screen, taking in every detail. The guy was over six feet tall. They could tell because he was standing near a six-foot wrought-iron fence that he could easily see over. He was also dressed in black from head to toe.

None of that stood out as much as some of the other details about him. Like, why was he wearing a black skullcap pulled low over his forehead and a long-sleeve Henley when it was at least a hundred degrees outside? Maxwell's guess was that without the hat something about his head or hair could be easily identifiable. In addition, he'd be willing to bet the man had tattoos on his arms. More than all of that though, was the long black case hanging from his shoulder—a rifle case.

"If you haven't done so already, take note of the date and time." That came from Danny, who was still sitting on the other side of the desk.

Maxwell did as he said, and it was as if all the air had been sucked out of the room. Nothing was definite, and the guy leaving the apartment building looking like a thief in the night could be a nobody. But what were the chances that he'd be carrying a rifle case and leaving five minutes after Maxwell had called for backup?

"It's safe to say he's probably not a professional since he didn't try to hide the rifle case. Nor would a skilled hit man get caught on video," Maxwell said. "A person like that would've used the roof to get away or at least walk out not looking like a damn crook. But he does move with precision, and we can't forget the accuracy of the gunshot. Maybe military? Do we know who he is?"

Maxwell's voice was calm considering the ferocious storm brewing inside him. His heart rate picked up speed as he pressed Play again and the video continued. He kept watching until the man was out of view then pressed Stop again.

"We're going to have the tech guys see what they can do, but whoever this guy is, he did a good job keeping his face concealed from that particular camera," Zeke said.

Maxwell would love to believe that this was just an ordinary guy minding his own business or heading to the gun range to practice. Yet, the more he thought about that day, the preliminary autopsy report and the little they'd uncovered so far, had him believing that the shooting was indeed a setup. A hit.

"There's more," Danny said grimly, and Zeke reached for the tablet. "The lady who lives in the town house mentioned that she saves thirty days of footage before the recorder resets itself. There are shots of Jay leaving through that same door several times over the last few weeks." Maxwell had remembered Jeremy mentioning that he had been dispatched to the apartment complex several times over the last few months, but when they investigated, they'd run into dead ends. Clearly, they needed to follow up.

Zeke handed the tablet back to Maxwell and said, "We need to figure out who this woman is."

He pointed at the screen just as Jeremy strolled out

of the building laughing and his arm around a scantily clad woman.

*Son of a...*

Maxwell gritted his teeth while irritation churned inside him as he continued watching. It might not have been a big deal seeing Jeremy walk out with the woman, but not only was he in uniform, the time stamp showed that it was during his normal shift. If that wasn't bad enough, he kissed the woman like his tongue was trying to make contact with her tonsils.

Maxwell shook his head and set the tablet down. He propped his elbow on the desk and rubbed his eyes.

*What the hell were you doing, Jay?*

Had Jeremy somehow orchestrated the 911 calls all those times he was dispatched there? How often was he there when he should've been on patrol? And was this person involved in his murder?

Maxwell opened his eyes, and Zeke tapped on the tablet's screen. "We find this woman and I bet we get our killer. Or at least some answers."

Shock and rage warred within Maxwell as he struggled to hold his raw emotions in check.

"Get a still shot of the woman with Jay and see if Aaron recognizes her. I guess his sister and Jeremy were hanging out. I'm not sure when or how long, but find out if that's her."

"Okay, and I'll get in contact with Dispatch to see if we can identify any patterns of times and dates when Jeremy responded to that location," Danny said. "We'll also be scouring the neighborhood for more security cameras. Houses, businesses and even traffic cams in the area might help in determining who the guy is.

Hopefully, one of the cameras will give us a shot of the perimeter of the building and surrounding streets."

"And once we see if we can get a better view of that guy, we'll show his photo around. Someone has to know him or know something," Zeke added, and leaned on the desk. "Also, you told us to dig into Jeremy's life for the last six months. I started and haven't gotten far, but I was surprised by something I found."

Maxwell wasn't sure he wanted any more surprises as they related to Jeremy and this case. Drugs in his system, a fiancée who no one knew about and a possible hit man who might've taken him out. He had a bad feeling that this was just the beginning of something more sinister than any of them could've predicted.

"What did you find?" he asked solemnly.

"We know Jay got divorced like six or seven months ago, and that, according to Rochelle, he was living with her for longer than that. He had time to add her as his emergency contact, and set Camille as his beneficiary. He did neither."

Maxwell frowned and gave a slight shrug, wondering where this was going. "Okay, maybe he just forgot or hadn't gotten around to it. Besides, we don't always remember to stop in at HR and update our information."

"See, that's just it," Danny said. "He did stop in there about a month ago. He wanted to take advantage of the supplemental life insurance that's available. You would think that he would've had at least Camille on the policy, but he didn't. His ex-wife is his sole beneficiary, and it's a nice chunk of change."

Zeke, still standing next to Maxwell, made a sound that was a cross between a grunt and a laugh. "You know what they say in situations when the husband is killed and there's a lot of money to be had. The wife is probably the one who—"

"Don't even *think* about finishing that statement," Maxwell growled. The venom in his voice had his detectives straightening. "There's no way in hell Amina had anything to do with Jay's death. So if that's the route you're going, change directions and keep digging."

Neither man said anything, only looked at Maxwell as if they didn't recognize him. Rarely did he snap, but he couldn't sit there and let them talk about her like she was some type of black widow. There was no way she was involved in Jeremy's murder. That, he would bet his life on.

Maxwell tapped down his annoyance. "You guys are the best detectives on the force, and I know I don't have to tell you how to do your job. But I want no stone unturned on this case, and we need it wrapped up quickly."

"We're on it," Danny said, and stood. "Lieutenant Grayson has been asking where we are on the case. We didn't have the video the last time he asked, but—"

"Be honest with him. Don't hold anything back trying to cover whatever BS Jeremy might've been involved in. You don't want to withhold info and then it comes back on you."

"True. All right, we'll keep digging."

They headed for the door, but Maxwell stopped them. "Sorry about snapping, but I know Amina personally. There's no way she's involved in any of this."

"Okay, if you say so," Zeke said. "But I hope you know that at some point, we might have to bring the former Mrs. Kelly in for questioning."

"Well, you better make damn sure you have a seriously good reason for doing so. Otherwise, your ass is going to have to deal with me."

# Chapter 14

"**Y**ou got mugged and didn't tell anyone?" her sister shrieked through the phone. "And what do you mean that bastard fathered a kid while you two were married? *Oh, my God!* That asshole is so lucky he's dead."

Amina bristled at her sister's tone and glanced around to see if anyone heard her. Katrina had FaceTimed her instead of calling just as Amina was leaving a shoe store at the mall. Her next stop was going to be her favorite boutique, but maybe not.

"I should call you back when I'm not surrounded by people," she said to Katrina.

Actually, maybe it had been a bad idea to leave all of that on a voice mail in the first place. But after leaving the funeral, she'd needed to vent. Overwhelmed by the conversation with Jeremy's parents, then the sudden appearance of Rochelle, and seeing Camille—it was all too much. Her first thought had been to call Maxwell after the encounter, but she dialed her sister instead and got her voice mail.

"I can't remember the last time I was this pissed," her sister said. "I don't know how you can be so calm about all of this."

"I guess I've had a little more time to process everything than you. Trust me—I've been on an emotional roller coaster since hearing about Jeremy's death. Now from one moment to the next, I'm struggling with calling him every rotten name I can think of."

"I'm sure you are."

"Excuse me. Pardon me," Amina said as she wove in and out of foot traffic in the mall. She wasn't sure why there were so many people, considering it was nearing closing time. She eventually stepped into the middle and near a railing that overlooked the first floor.

"Let me see your neck," Katrina said.

Amina moved the phone so her sister could see the scar. She had removed the butterfly bandages after arriving home from the funeral. Though the cut wasn't bleeding, it still stung a little with certain movements and whenever she got it wet.

"Does it hurt?"

"It's not as bad as it looks. I just hate it'll probably leave a scar."

Katrina tsked and shook her head. "Girrrl, Dad's going to pop a vein when he sees your neck."

Amina couldn't help but laugh. She hadn't heard that phrase since they were young. Growing up, Katrina was that kid who always got into trouble. When their dad would be in the middle of reaming her out, she'd tell him to calm down before he popped a vein.

"I should fly there to witness the show."

"Well, I have a week to prepare myself before they come back from vacation. In the meantime, I need to go home and get ready for my date." She tried to sound nonchalant, but inside she was doing a happy dance.

"That's right. I forgot about that part of your voice mail. I practically lost my mind when you mentioned a mugging and a baby. I want to hear all of the details on how and when you and Maxwell hooked up. All you said was that he picked you up from the hospital the other day. By the way, you better call if you ever go through something like that again."

"I was fine, and I didn't want to worry you."

"I get that, but you're my little sister. I will always worry about you."

Amina's heart warmed at Katrina's words. She didn't know what she would do without her family's continuous love and support. They'd been her rock, especially Katrina, during the divorce.

"Now, tell me what's up with you and Maxwell."

"All right, but hang up and let me call you instead of doing FaceTime."

Amina called her back and strolled through the huge mall toward the door that she had come in. It was on the other side of the building. For the next fifteen minutes, she filled her sister in on all things Maxwell. She even told her about the kiss and their time at Trinity and Gunner's house.

"And that's been my life for the last few days. So, what have you been up to?" she asked Katrina, who was uncharacteristically quiet. "Hello?"

Had she hung up? As soon as the question came to mind, Katrina burst out laughing.

"That *dream* kiss, though!" her sister howled.

Amina rolled her eyes, unable to keep from smiling herself. It was funny then and now, and it would be one of those kisses that she would remember for the rest of her life.

"Anyway, enough about…" Amina's words stalled in her throat when she spotted the last person she expected to see. He was walking toward her and gave a little wave. "Hey, sis. Let me call you back." She hung up before her sister could protest.

"Well, this is a pleasant surprise," Dr. McPherson said, shoving his hands into the front pockets of his pants and rocking on his feet. "You come here often?"

Amina laughed at the question that was overused in bars and clubs. "No, can't say that I do. Maybe once a month or so," she said, taking in the doctor's smile that only added to his handsome features. "What about you?"

"I stop in here on occasion for a change of scenery. Especially with all of the hours I put in at the hospital."

Amina nodded. At first when she'd spotted him, she'd had to do a double take. He almost didn't look like himself without his white doctor's coat. Dr. McPherson was a nice-looking man on any given day. Today, though, he was downright fine, casually dressed in a light blue polo shirt and black slacks. He seemed…ordinary…normal. Not that he usually didn't, but as a highly acclaimed doctor, he always seemed larger than life when they were at the hospital.

"You look great," he said.

"Thank you." After the funeral, she had changed into an off-the-shoulder top and a pair of skinny jeans.

"It looks like the cut is healing well."

He leaned in and his hand went toward her neck, and

she stiffened. Noticing her reaction, he stopped short of touching her and shoved his hands back into his pockets.

His eyes traveled the length of her and back up again, lingering on her breasts for a second too long. He had never said or done anything inappropriate, but the way he was looking at her suddenly made her want to fold her arms across her chest. His stare wasn't exactly creepy. It was just... Amina wasn't sure.

"If you're free this evening, how about dinner and a movie?" Dr. McPherson asked.

"About that, I don't think that's a good idea. As a matter of fact, I can't go out with you."

"Because of the guy who picked you up the other day?"

Amina nodded. She and Maxwell still referred to each other as friends, but he meant a lot more than that to her. The doctor didn't need to know any of that, though.

"Is it serious?" he asked, catching her off guard.

She wanted to ask *would it matter*? Instead, she said, "Yes. So, I can't go out with you."

He nodded slowly, studying her in that way that was so him. "I'm disappointed, but I can understand that. I hope your man knows he's a lucky guy."

Amina gave him a slight smile. "Thank you, but I'm the lucky one. Anyway, I'd better get going. It was good seeing you."

He touched her arm and smiled. "You too. Have a good evening." With that, he strolled away, and she headed to the exit.

Why had she been nervous talking to him? Sure, he was a reputable doctor who the other nurses fawned over, but still, he was just a man. *One who was inter-*

*ested in me*, she thought. Even if she wasn't available, it was still nice to get attention from the opposite sex. Now she needed to hurry so that she could spend time with the only man who mattered. Maxwell.

Thirty minutes later, Amina stood in her garage, prancing from one foot to the other, while trying to unlock the door to the house. She should've used the bathroom before leaving the mall but figured she'd wait until she got home. Now she couldn't get in the house fast enough.

Once she finally unlocked the door, she pushed it open and dropped her shopping bags in the mudroom. She didn't bother turning on lights and made a mad dash to the half bath, practically slamming the door when she got in there.

*Made it. Barely.*

"I'm worse than a little kid," she mumbled, and released a relieved sigh as she finished taking care of business. Once she was done, she washed her hands but stopped short of drying them when she thought she heard something.

Amina shut off the water and hurried to dry her hands. Then stood silently at the sink, holding the edge of the counter with a death grip as she listened for any sound.

Seconds ticked by.

Nothing.

Amina whooshed out the breath that she hadn't realized she was holding, and opened the door. After walking back to the mudroom, she flipped on the light near the door that led to the garage and had to laugh at herself. Bags were strewn everywhere.

She glanced at her watch and grimaced. "Crap, I'm going to be late for my first real date in years."

Giddiness bubbled inside her as she looped her purse across her body then picked the items off the floor. *I have a date.* Amina couldn't wait to hang out with Maxwell, but first, she needed to narrow down her options on what to wear. Should she go with the sexy light blue one-shoulder dress that hugged her body and stopped just above her knees? Or the low-cut black dress with spaghetti straps that was a little longer than the other? If she had to guess, Amina would peg Max a leg man since she'd caught him staring at hers the other day when she wore shorts.

*Light blue it is.*

She hurried past the kitchen and toward the attached dining room. "Alexa, turn on the lights," she shouted, and dropped her keys on the table. Seconds later, the rooms were illuminated.

Amina stopped in her tracks. The bags dropped to the hardwood floor. Her heart slammed against her chest as her gaze darted around the living room and the open floor plan.

"What the…"

She took in the slashed sofa cushions and pillows, overturned tables and shattered lamps and glass littering the hardwood floor. The television had been ripped off the wall along with some of her artwork and pictures.

*Ohmigod. Ohmigod. Ohmigod.*

Amina slowly backed up. As she continued taking in the destruction of the rooms, her heart was beating loud enough for the neighbors to hear as her mind raced. She ignored the crunching sound of glass under her feet, that she hadn't noticed before, and snatched her keys from the dining room table. This time, glancing in the kitchen, it was impossible to miss open cabinet doors and food and dishes everywhere. She made a mad dash for the door that led to the backyard and bolted from the house.

"Oh, my God." Heart racing, she ran down the street and smothered a sob with her hand over her mouth. The sun was setting, and it was barely light enough out to see where she was going. She didn't stop until she reached the corner.

*Someone's been in my house.*

*Someone destroyed my things.*

After pulling the cell phone from her purse, Amina's hands shook so badly it took three tries to dial the correct number.

"911, what's your emergency?"

# Chapter 15

Maxwell burst through the front door. "Amina!" he yelled and glanced in the dining room. Where was she? He ignored the police officer who was in the living room and the one in the kitchen. "Amina!"

"Max." Amina ran from the back of the house and straight into his arms. "I was so scared," she sobbed, and buried her face into his chest. Her arms wrapped around his waist and were tight enough to crack a rib.

Maxwell didn't care. All that mattered was that she was safe. "I got you." He held her close and even tighter when she trembled against him.

When she quieted, he unglued her from him and grabbed hold of her shoulders. "Are you all right?" He cupped her face and searched her puffy, red eyes while wiping her wet cheeks with the pads of his thumbs.

Ice had clogged his veins when she called him crying, saying someone had broken in. The anguish and fear in her voice had him making the trip to her place in half the time. All the while his mind conjured up one horrible scenario after another.

"I—I'm okay, but Max…" Her voice shook, and she fidgeted while rubbing her hands up and down her bare arms. "Some—somebody…they destroyed everything." She folded her bottom lip between her teeth, fighting off tears, and then dropped her forehead to his chest. "I think they were here when I got home," she whispered, and Maxwell stiffened.

"Christ," he breathed as anger flared inside him. He leaned back, forcing her to lift her head. "Did you see them?"

"No, I was in the bathroom when I thought I heard someone."

*God…*

As she recounted what happened, Maxwell's hold on her tightened. What if she had walked in while the assholes were tossing her house? What if they had hurt her…or worse?

He kissed the top of her head. "I'm glad you're okay. We're going to get to the bottom of this."

A police officer down the hall caught Maxwell's attention when he stepped out of the bedroom. Normally, it wouldn't be more than two cops roaming around the house after a robbery, but Amina was Chief Hudson's daughter. He might be retired, but his name still carried a lot of weight. The moment he and Amina disconnected their call, he had requested an additional unit be sent to her place.

"Come on. Walk with me while I look around and talk to the officers." He linked his fingers with hers and moved through the house, taking in the damage as they stepped around her belongings that had been trashed.

Funny how a couple of days ago he wouldn't have stepped over the threshold into her home. Now he couldn't imagine being anywhere she wasn't.

"Can you tell what was taken?" he asked her.

"I have no idea. I can't tell. It's such a mess," Amina murmured.

Together, they moved from one room to the next. According to the responding officers, whoever destroyed the place had forced their way in through the back door.

"What about the alarm system? Was it activated?" Maxwell asked Amina.

"No. It hasn't been working right for the last couple of days. So I left it off. I called the alarm company earlier, and they're supposed to send someone out tomorrow between one and three. I've never had any problems in the neighborhood. I didn't expect…this."

Maxwell thought it too much of a coincidence that the alarm system wasn't working the day someone decided to trash the place. He didn't believe in coincidences.

*Has someone been in her house before today?* he wondered. He kept that thought to himself, not wanting to freak her out even more.

With each step, Maxwell felt something was off. He took his time thoroughly inspecting each room. Overturned furniture, slashed mattresses, papers covering the floors, something became abundantly clear. Whoever broke in wasn't looking to rob the place. They were looking for something. But what?

And that stirring in his gut that he felt after the so-called mugging the other night was back. The details on that situation hadn't sat right with him from the moment he'd heard about the attack. What if it hadn't been a random mugging at all? What if it had been something even more sinister? Like an attempted kidnapping. And was it possible that this was somehow related to Jeremy's murder?

Maxwell wrapped an arm around Amina and pulled her close to his side and placed a kiss against her temple. "Sweetheart, pack a bag. You're coming home with me."

An hour and a half later, Maxwell carried two small suitcases into the house with a sullen Amina following behind him. She had barely said two words on the way to his place, and the ride was similar to the one the other day. Except, this time he wasn't anxious or questioning the decision about bringing her home with him.

"I'm going to run these bags upstairs real quick and change out of my uniform. Then we can order some dinner. Actually," he stopped and turned to Amina, "why don't you look through the carryout menus and pick what you want to eat. They're in the kitchen drawer closest to the pantry."

"I'm not really hungry." She strolled into the living room and dropped down on the sofa. "But don't let me stop you from getting something to eat."

Maxwell hadn't noticed that she'd kicked off her shoes at the door until she lifted her knees to her chest and wrapped her arms around her legs. He loved how comfortable she appeared in his home. He just hated that the two times she'd been there lately were because of someone scaring her to death.

Right now, she had every right to be in a funk considering all that she'd been dealing with. Before leaving her house, he'd had new locks installed on all of the exterior doors. As well as contacted one of the managers at his sister's security agency regarding an upgraded alarm system. They were able to install a temporary one for the night. By tomorrow evening, she'd have a state-of-the-art system that no one could get past.

They were going to find out who was harassing her, and yes, that was exactly how he was looking at the attempted mugging and break-in. He didn't have any proof, but he had a feeling they were connected. Now all he had to do was figure out who and why. In the meantime, he'd keep her safe and try to get her spirits up.

Instead of heading upstairs, Maxwell set the bags down and went in search of the take-out menus before going over to her. "Sweetheart, you're going to have to eat something," he said, sitting on the sofa and draping his arm around her shoulders. On the way to his place, he had learned that she hadn't eaten since that morning, and it was almost eight at night. "This is not what I had planned for our first official date, but it's not all bad."

Amina's perfectly arched eyebrows dipped into a frown. "You're thinking this could've been worse? Max, someone was in *my house* and they touched my stuff." She visibly trembled and he pulled her closer to him. "I can't ever remember being that scared…except for maybe the other day in the parking lot. But knowing someone has been in my home, my sanctuary, the place I go where I'm safe from the outside world… There's nothing worse than that."

"I know, but—"

"And they destroyed everything." Her voice cracked, and she laid her head against his shoulder.

Except for when he first arrived at her house, Amina was holding up pretty good. Even now, despite the anguish in her voice and periodic shivers, there were no tears. That, he was grateful for. He hated to see any woman cry, but when that woman was Amina, it tore him up inside.

"All of that's true and I hate this has happened to you," Maxwell said. "But you've forgotten one important fact. You weren't harmed. At least not physically. Everything in that house can be replaced."

"That might be true, but—"

"But you." He kissed the side of her forehead. "Sweetheart, you're irreplaceable, and I'm glad you weren't hurt. Now *that*? That would've made the evening a helluva lot worse. Because if that had happened, I would be out for blood. We wouldn't be sitting here together because I'd be out hunting that bastard. Instead, we have others looking into the situation while you and I are getting ready to try and salvage our date. So how about we start by enjoying an excellent meal?"

After a long beat of silence, Amina sighed dramatically and leaned back to look up at him. A slow smile tugged the corners of her lips. "Well, when you put it that way. I guess I should pick a restaurant, huh?"

He grinned and handed her the menus. "Yes, and I'll take the bags upstairs, then change clothes. When I come back down, we can order." He stood and headed for the stairs again but stopped when she called him. "Yeah?"

"Thanks for coming to the house. It meant a lot to have you there with me even though I know it was the last place you wanted to be."

He studied her for a moment. "That might've been the case at first, but I want to be wherever you are, Amina. And I'll always be here, there or wherever for you. Remember that."

She nodded and he jogged up the stairs with her luggage. If he had any doubts about his intentions for Amina, or for them, they were wiped out tonight. She was it for him. He was going to do everything in his power to build something permanent with her. But first, they had to figure out what the hell was going on.

Forty-five minutes later, the food had arrived and Maxwell held up the bags. "Where would you like to eat? The kitchen, dining room or in front of the TV like we did the other night?"

"Let's do the kitchen. The wings might be a little messy, and it'll probably be better to be close to a sink and paper towels."

"Works for me."

"That smells amazing," Amina said, and set out plates and utensils, while Maxwell unloaded the bags of food. "I'm suddenly a little hungry."

"Good, because I'd hate to eat all of this by myself, but I could. I'm starving." He pulled the last container out and handed it to her. "You might want to start with that."

"Why? What is it?"

"Open it." He grabbed the bottle of chilled wine and a couple of glasses from the cabinet.

"Mmm, brownies. They look delicious."

"Not just any brownies, but killer brownies. I heard the ingredients include German chocolate cake caramel, chopped nuts, chocolate chips and a few other ingredients that I can't remember. According to my sister, they're to die for."

"Ahh, hence the name. In that case, I think I will start with them."

As they ate, Maxwell was glad Amina was feeling

better. It didn't go unnoticed that she didn't bring up Jeremy, the case or the break-in. The more time they spent together, the more they learned about one another. And one thing he knew—she was an overthinker. So just because she hadn't broached the subject didn't mean that it was far from her mind.

"Do you still watch basketball?" Maxwell asked, remembering how they used to discuss the games.

She smacked her lips and looked at him as if he had two heads. "Is LeBron James still the greatest player of his time? *Of course*, I still watch. I rarely miss a game, especially the Lakers. You?"

"Every chance I get. A friend of mine has Laker season tickets, and he usually lets me use them a couple of times in a season. Maybe you and I can fly to LA and attend a game one day."

"Seriously? I definitely wouldn't say no to that."

As they chatted while eating, Maxwell realized sports was one of many things they had in common. Others included—personal values, their love for family, and they both enjoyed traveling. He'd never had as much in common with any other woman as he had with her. Tonight, he had also learned that she didn't like butterflies, and calla lilies were her favorite flowers. He planned to store that bit of information in his memory bank.

Amina held her stomach and groaned. "I don't think I can eat anything else. You were right about the wings. They were the best, but those brownies should come with a warning label. Like—beware, you won't be able to stop at just one. They were so good."

"I'll have to try one later," Maxwell said, placing a few more hot wings and fries on his plate. While he ate, he tried to come up with a good way to discuss the break-in, amongst other things.

"Do you think the break-in is connected to the mugging?" Amina asked.

Maxwell's eyebrows shot up. If he didn't know better, he would've thought she was a mind reader. Earlier, when he considered the two incidences might've been connected, he hadn't planned to say anything to her just yet. But in case they were, he needed to do some digging. What he didn't want to do was scare her, but he also wanted her to be on alert.

"Yes," he said honestly. "It's too much of a coincidence. I'm even wondering if that botched mugging wasn't an attempted kidnapping."

Her hand went to her chest. "If you're trying to scare me, it's working."

"Sweetheart, the last thing I want to do is scare you, but something is going on. Until we figure out what, I think you should stay here. In the meantime, can you think of anything you have that someone might want? A family heirloom? Gold? Bonds? A limited-edition book? Anything?"

"No, nothing like that. I have a pair of diamond earrings that my parents gave me when I graduated from high school."

"I might be way off with this next question, but I have to ask. Do you have anything of Jeremy's?"

She frowned. "Not that I can think of—why?"

"I don't know. I might be way off, but I wonder if any of this has to do with his murder?" Maxwell wiped his hands and grabbed his cell phone off the counter. About a half an hour ago, Danny had texted him a still shot of the suspect.

Maxwell held up his phone to her. "Do you recognize this guy?"

Amina stared at the photo for a few minutes. The quality wasn't great, and much of the man's face was hard to make out, but she might know him.

She eventually shook her head. "He doesn't look familiar. Should I know him? Who is he?"

"The suspected killer."

# Chapter 16

She couldn't sleep.

It had been at least an hour since Amina climbed into bed in the guest room. Her mind wouldn't let her rest. She'd been tossing and turning, trying to find a good sleeping position, but she couldn't shut her brain down.

*The suspected killer.*

Those three words rattled around in her head. It was one thing to see the news and know there were killers lurking the streets of Vegas. It was another thing to realize one could've rummaged through her house, and even worse, could be hunting for her.

Amina trembled at the thought and pulled the comforter up to her chin. Her gaze darted around the dark room as her imagination ran rampant.

What if she had walked in on the person? They could've raped her, tortured her and killed her. And hearing that the break-in could be connected to Jeremy's death was even scarier.

*God, they have to find this person.*

She was a nurse who minded her own business. How had this become her life? How had she gotten wrapped up in this mess?

*Think. Think. Think.*

Amina wanted this over. Was it someone she knew who had broken in? She might not have recognized the person in the picture, but had she missed something during the mugging? At the house? Maxwell had come to the conclusion that whoever had broken in was looking for something. But who? What? And why? One question only led to more.

Then there was the mugging, or attempted mugging as Maxwell called it. Now he was concerned that it might've been an attempted kidnapping. No matter how Amina tried to wrap her brain around that scenario, she couldn't see it.

"'Cause it's a ridiculous idea," she mumbled into the quietness of the bedroom. What could someone possibly want with her? She didn't have anything of value. Her family wasn't wealthy, so it wasn't like a kidnapper could grab her for a ransom.

Amina growled in frustration and flipped onto her stomach, punching the pillow a few times before burying her face in it. She wanted to scream, but what was the point? That wouldn't solve her problems, nor would it change anything that had happened over the last few days. What she needed was a shot of the tequila that she'd seen in the pantry. Or she needed a distraction. Or maybe… *Maxwell.*

Knowing that they were under the same roof again

had her feeling some kind of way. Grateful that he came to her. Happy that she felt safe with him. More than anything though, she was horny.

*Definitely horny.*

"Urgh, just go to sleep already," she groaned with her face still buried in the pillow. *Just close your eyes and stop thinking.*

When talking to herself didn't work, Amina flipped onto her back and stared up at the ceiling. It was no use. She was never gonna get any sleep.

Her mind traveled back to the break-in. Would she ever be able to stay in her house alone again? Probably not. At least not for a long time. But she *had* figured out how to get Maxwell inside.

Amina released a humorless laugh that ended with a whimper. She wanted him in her home because he wanted to be there, not because he was coming to her rescue.

*I really should sell the place.*

She could sell her place and buy a luxury condo near the Las Vegas Strip in a new building she saw going up recently. Something she'd thought about on occasion. Or she could…

*Stop. Just stop thinking*, she berated herself, and climbed out of the bed. Pacing the length of the room, Amina didn't care that the floor was freezing. Maybe if she wore herself out, she'd be able to fall asleep. But if she was honest with herself, it wasn't sleep she wanted. She wanted Maxwell.

Amina ran her hand down the front of the red silk sleepshorts set and strolled across the room. She opened the bedroom door, listened for any sounds of Maxwell then stepped into the hallway. The television on the first floor could be heard, but nothing else as she slowly crept down the stairs. When she reached the second-from-the-bottom step, Amina stopped.

There he was, sitting on the sofa, looking too delicious for his own good in the gray tank top and dark sleep pants. He had the television remote in one hand and a glass with dark liquor in the other. For a second, it didn't seem like he knew she was there staring at him. But then he turned. Their gazes collided. And it was as if the earth stopped moving.

*Good Lord.*

The man was a sight for tired eyes. All Amina wanted to do was climb onto his lap and ride him until they both couldn't walk straight. But she wasn't that bold. Even if at the moment she wanted nothing but him, she couldn't do it. She couldn't risk the chance that he'd reject her. Sure, they'd shared hugs and kisses, and the sexual tension between them was amazingly strong. Yet, that didn't mean that they could go to the next level. Thanks to her history with Jeremy, it might not ever happen.

Maxwell stared at her. Neither of them spoke, but Amina recognized the look in his dark, intense eyes. Desire. Lust. Need. All the things she was feeling. His gaze ate her up while traveling down her body then slowly making its way back. He lingered on her bare legs, the swell of her breasts under the button-up top, before returning to her face.

He set the remote and the glass of liquor on the table, then strolled over to where she stood frozen in place.

"What's wrong?" His husky voice was as sensual as a lover's caress, and Amina's pulse quickened.

"I couldn't sleep," she whispered. They were almost

at eye level and close enough for Amina to cover his mouth with hers. That was if she was bold enough.

So tempting, but a kiss wouldn't be enough. With the energy flowing through her body, it was going to take more than just a peck on the lips to tame it. She wanted all of him, and when her gaze dropped to his broad chest, the desire to touch him was almost overwhelming. Maybe it was time to ask for what she wanted.

"Max…"

He slid one of his arms around her waist, and his heated touch had Amina almost leaping out of her skin. "What can I do to help you go to sleep?" he asked. His gaze held hers then dropped to her lips before meeting her eyes again.

"Make love to me." There, she'd said it. It was out there. The ball was in his court.

He lowered his head and captured her lips. The taste of scotch on his tongue sent her senses reeling, and she moaned into his mouth. Aroused, her body yearned for more, and she stood on tiptoes and slipped her arms around his neck. One of her hands went to the back of his head, and their kiss deepened.

Amina would never tire of kissing him. As a matter of fact, she could see it easily becoming an addiction. This was what she wanted. Maxwell was who she wanted… who she needed.

He suddenly ripped his lips from hers. "Damn, I can't get enough. You sure about this? If not, tell me now. Otherwise, I—"

"I'm more than sure. I'm positive."

No other words were spoken when he lifted her as if she weighed nothing. Amina held on to his neck and her legs went easily around his waist. Heat engulfed her body where her core rubbed up against his hardness.

With each step he took, Amina should've been nervous. She should've been hesitant. But as he carried her up the stairs to his bedroom, a calm wrapped around her.

This was happening. Her… Max… It was really happening.

# Chapter 17

Once they reached his room, Maxwell set Amina on his bed as if she was a piece of fine china. He climbed onto the bed and picked up where he'd left off kissing her on the stairs. She held on to the front of his shirt as his masterful tongue explored the inner recesses of her mouth.

Amina squirmed against him as he trailed kisses over her cheek and down her neck. All the while his nimble fingers quickly undid the three buttons on her shirt. Amina wasn't wearing anything under the pajamas, and when the garment fell open, her breasts were on full display.

Maxwell stared down at her and the appreciative look in his eyes had her self-confidence soaring. Before marrying Jeremy, she had never suffered from low self-esteem or had any doubt about her self-worth. Yet, within a few months of marriage, she questioned everything about herself, especially her appearance. She had assumed her husband no longer found her desirable considering the lack of attention he paid her. Add in his hurtful words and she had turned into an insecure woman who she barely recognized. She had allowed him to get inside her head and soon self-doubt had become an unwelcome companion.

It wasn't until a few months ago that she started feeling like her old self. Positive affirmations and the love and support of her family also helped. She had vowed then that she would never let a man degrade or mistreat her in any way again.

And now, the way Maxwell was regarding her and her body only made Amina feel that much more desirable. She felt beautiful.

"I knew you'd be gorgeous, but you're absolutely breathtaking," he said with awe in his voice.

And that was exactly how he was making her feel. Her body sizzled under his intense perusal. He didn't have to say anything else. The smoldering heat in his eyes said it all.

As his gaze held hers, he dragged a finger down the center her chest, between her breasts, and didn't stop until he reached the waistband of her shorts.

Amina swallowed hard when he broke eye contact and glanced down where his hand cupped her sex. She sucked in a breath and her back arched at the contact.

Goodness. He was only touching her through her shorts and she had practically propelled off the bed at how sensitive her sex was to his touch. No telling what would've happened if the contact had been skin to skin. As it was, her body was on fire.

"Lift your hips," he said, and she did, allowing him to slowly slide her shorts down. He was so gentle with each move he made, not that she expected anything less. She liked that he was taking his time, but it was the way he was looking at her that had her body stirring with anticipation. A tenderness. No one had ever regarded her like this.

Once her shorts were around her ankles, he jerked them free and added them to the floor with her shirt.

"Your turn," she said. The man was fine as hell and built like a Mack truck with clothes on. She couldn't wait to see him naked. "Go slow," she added, and he chuckled.

As he moved from the bed, Maxwell reached behind his shoulder, tugged on the back of the collar of his tank top and pulled the garment over his head. Amina barely noticed him drop it to the floor. His smooth, dark skin and sinewy muscles were on full display, and her gaze ate him up.

"You like what you see?" he asked, not waiting for a response as he pushed the sleep pants down his long legs. That left him only in a pair of gray boxer briefs.

*Good Lord.* The man was packing, and she wasn't talking about his service weapon. The way he filled up the shorts that cupped the bulge between his thighs and hugged his tree-trunk-like thighs was downright sinful. Long, wonderfully thick and hard as granite was the only way to describe his glorious erection.

"I absolutely love what I see," she finally said more breathily than intended, but damn. As she took in all of his beauty, he had the attributes of an African warrior. Huge biceps, muscular pecs and a spectacular six-pack that appeared to be painted on. A sudden urge to lick every inch of the man came over her.

Amina unintentionally swiped her tongue over her lower lip before she realized what she'd done. Her eyes shot up and met his knowing gaze. Heat spread through her cheeks and she hoped he couldn't read minds. Then again, there was no shame in showing him how attracted she was to him, and how much she wanted him.

"I guess our feelings are mutual," he said, his attention on her as he reached into his nightstand and set a couple of condoms next to the lamp.

Amina took a cursory glance around his room, which was dimly lit with moonlight pouring into the space. There was also a night-light in the en suite that offered a bit of light. She was surprised when he pointed his television remote to the television and it came on.

*Who watches TV during sex?*

She was glad she hadn't posed the question out loud because seconds later, she realized he planned to play music through the television. "In Tha Mood," an instrumental by ThaSaint, one of her favorite jazz artists, filled the space and created a sensual ambience. The melody flowed through her like rays of sunshine cutting through the clouds as Maxwell put down the remote.

"You sure about this?" he asked, studying her in that way he did that evoked an excitement she only felt with him. "I want you more than anything in this world, but if you're not ready…"

His body was partially covering hers, but he was careful not to put his full weight on her. Supporting himself with his elbow, he stared down into her eyes. She knew without a doubt that she wanted him. All of him.

"It's been a long time for me," Amina said. "But I'm positive."

No other words were spoken when his mouth returned to hers, and he kissed her with a hunger that rivaled her own. With each sensual stroke of his tongue, her desire increased. She had never wanted a man as much as she wanted this one. Her hands slid up the sides of his torso and she held on for the ride.

As their tongues tangled, he moved on top of her, and Amina's hands moved down his body and she gripped his firm butt. Pressing him closer, she wanted him to know that she was ready for more, but he didn't seem to be in a hurry. Not that she was either, but she was eager to feel him inside her.

Normally, she was a patient person, but it *had* been a long time since she'd been with a man. When her marriage started to fall apart and she realized she had chosen wrong, Maxwell was the person she fantasized about. How many times had she imagined them together? Back then, it was just wishful thinking, but now…now she was going to take all that he was willing to give and not second-guess her decision to be with him.

Her temperature rose as he shifted slightly and his right hand slid down her side, gliding over every curve and dip of her body. He pulled his mouth from hers and a whimper slipped from her before his heated lips made contact with her neck. He quickly figured out that the area just below her ears was an erogenous spot, guaranteed to make her squirm.

"M-Max," Amina stuttered, unable to say more than that as he kissed his way down her body. Her moans blended in with the music, and everywhere his hands and mouth touched, heat crackled along each nerve ending.

When Maxwell palmed one of her breasts and his lips covered a taut nipple, Amina hissed. Damn, every inch of her body was extra sensitive, and Maxwell ignited a passion within her that had her on fire with need.

Amina moaned and gripped the back of his head as he moved to her other breast and paid the same homage to that nipple. Teasing and tweaking, he swirled his tongue around the hardened peak before gently pulling it between his teeth. She couldn't take much more. Her heart pounded erratically as she wiggled beneath him and her nails dug into his arm. He wasn't even inside her yet and already her control was…

"Max," she gasped when he slid his hand between her thighs and touched her intimately. He dipped his finger into the entrance of her core, and on impulse, she squeezed her thighs together, locking his hand in place.

Maxwell wasn't deterred. "Damn. You're so wet." He placed a kiss on one of her knees and her legs quivered under his touch and fell back open.

Her eyes slammed shut. He had her whimpering and panting with the pressure of his thumb on her sensitive pearl. "Ahh, yes. That feels so good." She whimpered and fisted the sheet on either side of her as she lifted her hips and bucked against his hand. Her release was so close as her control continued to diminish. She was barely holding on and still, he hadn't entered her.

Without warning, Maxwell stopped, and Amina's eyes popped open. She was panting with need when she said, "Max!" Frustration roared through her, especially at his soft chuckle. She was ready to inflict bodily harm until she realized he had snatched a condom from the nightstand.

"Why are you torturing me?" she murmured under her breath.

With a wicked grin spreading across his handsome face, Maxwell quickly sheathed himself then hovered above her. He leaned forward with his hands on either side of her head, and touched his lips to hers before saying, "I want to be buried deep inside of you when you come the first time."

"Oh."

Maxwell eased into Amina's sweet heat inch by delicious inch, surprised at how tight she was but loving the way her interior muscles gripped his shaft. He moved slowly, allowing her to adjust to his size. She felt too damn good, and he marveled at how perfectly they fit together. But the intensity of their connection was almost too much for him. He gritted his teeth to keep from exploding before they got started good.

When she came down the stairs looking sexy as hell in the tiny pajama set that showed off her long, shapely legs, he knew he was in trouble. And the lust that had been brimming in her eyes, begging for something from him, hadn't helped his willpower to take things slow with her.

All night, he had tried to tap down the sexual energy vibing between them. He made a vow to himself the other night that he'd follow her lead. But after dinner, all he had wanted to do was carry her upstairs to his room and make mad, passionate love to her. Which was something he'd wanted to do from the moment he met her. Their relationship was complicated at best, but in this moment, all that mattered was that she had come to him willingly.

As Maxwell moved slowly in and out of her, he kissed her with a passion that rivaled anything that they'd shared up to this point. He wanted her to feel how much he adored her and how much she meant to him. His heart was so full of love for her it felt as if it would burst. He had never loved another woman the way he loved Amina. *His woman.*

"Ma-Max," she sputtered, her moves getting more frantic as he increased their pace.

With each thrust, their moans filled the space, even drowning out the music. Maxwell wanted this to last. He wanted to take his time and spend the whole night making love to her, showing her how much he desired her. But as she tightened her grip on his butt, squeezing and pulling him closer, this first round was going to be a quickie whether he wanted it to be or not.

Her frantic moves and the way pressure built inside him made him know that he wouldn't be able to hang on much longer. Especially with how she was rotating her hips, matching him stroke for stroke and pushing him to the edge of no return.

And then she shocked the hell out of him when she wrapped her long, sexy legs around his waist, pulling him deeper into her core. "Damn, baby. You feel so good, I don't know if I can—"

"Maxwell," Amina cried out, and her legs lowered as her body bucked viciously beneath him while she clawed at his arms. Her eyes were tightly closed as her head thrashed back and forth against the pillow.

Watching her come with such reckless abandon had Maxwell driving into her harder and faster until his release gripped him. His world spun out of control like a cyclone and he barely hung on as it careened over the edge. He collapsed on top of her, and Amina wrapped her arms around him.

Maxwell placed a lingering kiss on the side of her head. "I'm too heavy," he managed to say between breaths, and lifted slightly as to not crush her.

Still panting, he eventually rolled onto his back. Amina snuggled up against him, and he put his arm around her and kissed the top of her head. Neither of them spoke as they continued struggling to catch their breaths. Their connection years ago had been immediate, but what he had just experienced with her exceeded even his imagination.

"I'm never letting you go," he mumbled, not intending to say it aloud, but it was too late.

"Good, because I'm not going anywhere."

Maxwell planned to hold her to that. Never in a million years did he ever think that she'd be in his bed lying next to him. But now that he'd had her, there was no way they'd ever be able to go back to being just friends. He wanted them to give their relationship a real chance to see where it could go. In the meantime, he planned to worship her gorgeous body over and over again.

# Chapter 18

The next day, Maxwell strolled into the police station feeling like a new man. His steps were lighter, the day seemed brighter and he couldn't remember the last time he felt like all was well in the world. And he knew it had everything to do with his little vixen.

Spending the night and the early morning hours making love to Amina was literally like a dream come true. He'd be embarrassed to tell anyone how he used to fantasize about her, but imagining them together didn't compare to actually being with her. Their sexual chemistry was more than he could've hoped for, and it had been downright hard to leave her in bed.

After giving her instructions on how his home security system worked, she felt comfortable staying at his place alone. They agreed that she wouldn't venture outside, at least not by herself. Maxwell wasn't sure if she was in danger, but clearly, she had something someone wanted, or they thought she had something.

He'd made arrangements for his friend Trace Halstead, a private investigator and a security specialist, to escort Amina to her house later. The police department could only do so much when it came to home break-ins. Trace would investigate and try to find some leads on who the burglar might be. And instead of having her old security system repaired, Trinity's company, Layton Executive Protection Agency, LEPA, was installing a new system that would include cameras on the exterior.

"Somebody must have had a good night. Nobody walks in here whistling unless they got lu…" Danny's words trailed off, and a stupid grin spread across his face. "*And* you bought pastries? Oh yeah, you got lucky."

Maxwell shook his head but stopped short of smiling even though it was hard not to. It had been a long time since he'd felt this good. But no way would he give his peeps any reason to gossip about him. "Save all of your investigative work for the job, Detective."

"That I can do," Danny said on a laugh. "I can also take those treats off your hands and put them by the new coffee maker if you want."

"Works for me." Maxwell handed over the pastry box and glanced around the bullpen. The day before, one of the guys had cleared a space in a corner and added a microwave stand to hold a large coffee maker. Why no one had thought to do that sooner was a mystery to Max, but it was a needed addition.

"By the way, did you get my message this morning?" Danny asked quietly.

"I did." They had determined that it was Aaron's sister who was in the video with Jeremy exiting the apartment building.

"Zeke and I are going to pick her up shortly and bring her in for questioning."

"Sounds good," Maxwell said, and headed to his office.

He didn't want to believe that one of his guys had anything to do with Jeremy's murder. But with all of the information they'd been uncovering so far, they wouldn't leave any stone unturned. They still didn't have a name for the suspected killer, but Maxwell had a feeling they were getting closer.

He flipped on the light and noticed the large manila envelope on his desk. The day before, he had requested Aaron's complete personnel file. Maxwell had only been at that precinct for four years, but most of the people who reported to him had been at that location their whole careers. He didn't know everyone's background but thought it a good time to learn all he could about Aaron.

As Maxwell sat in his chair, he pulled the file out of the envelope and started scanning the contents. He already knew that Aaron's parents had been killed in a car accident when he was only eighteen. He had just graduated from high school. Aaron was left with the responsibility of raising his brother, who had been sixteen at the time, as well as his sister, who had been fifteen.

Assuming the care of his siblings had earned Aaron a certain level of respect from Maxwell. Over beers one night at a bar that many of the officers hung out at, Aaron had mentioned how hard those first couple of years had been. His parents had left a life-insurance policy that helped with the burial and household expenses for a couple of years. But Aaron and his brother still had to find work wherever they could. Once his brother became an adult, he'd moved to California. That left Aaron to care for just his sister until she was eighteen and decided she wanted to be a Hollywood star.

Aaron joined the military when he was twenty-two and did two tours in Iraq before returning to Vegas and joining the police force. That was over six years ago, and he had a stellar employee record until his fight with Jeremy the other week.

Maxwell rocked in his seat as he sifted through a few more pages, but stopped at the information about Aaron's army days. Seemed he wasn't just a model cop. He had worked his way up to a commissioned officer while in the military. The guy definitely had earned bragging rights. It was interesting that the man rarely discussed his army days.

Honorable discharge. Second Lieutenant. Specialist.

*Specialist in what?* Maxwell thought. And why was Aaron only a patrol cop? With his experience, he could've been at least a sergeant or even a lieutenant with the police department.

Maxwell leaned forward, setting the papers on the desk, and as he continued reading, unease spread through his body. Aaron was a *weapons specialist* and…a sniper.

"What the hell? How the heck did I not know this?"

Granted, none of the information made Aaron a suspect, but when Maxwell added in the fight and the fact that Jeremy was screwing Aaron's sister, it didn't look good. He had motive and that was enough to question him. Which was something Maxwell didn't want to do. He didn't even want to think that one of his cops might've had something to do with the murder.

Would Aaron honestly put his life and career in jeopardy by killing a fellow officer? He might not have pulled the trigger, but had he arranged the murder?

"No way. No frickin' way," Maxwell mumbled. He didn't want to believe that. There was no way Jeremy had angered him enough to kill him.

Maxwell turned to his computer and brought up the screen that would give him information about where his officers were on any given day. As he scanned the information, it showed that Aaron hadn't been on duty at the time of the shooting. Maxwell growled under his breath, but tried to keep an open mind. The guy in the video who was caught leaving the apartment complex minutes after Jeremy had been gunned down wasn't Aaron. But hopefully, he had a good alibi for where he was at the time of the murder.

Thirty minutes later, Maxwell stepped into the interrogation room. Aaron was pacing the length of the small space but stopped and looked up.

"What the hell is going on? My sister is being questioned, and I want to know why. She shouldn't be talking to any damn person without a lawyer!"

"Like I'm sure Danny told you, she said she didn't need a lawyer because she had nothing to hide."

"This is bull," Aaron growled, daggers shooting from his eyes. "How would you feel if your sister was dragged in here...your *innocent* little sister?"

Maxwell met his gaze. "I wouldn't like it, but I would expect her to cooperate. Now have a seat," he said, nodding at one of the chairs. "I have a few questions for you."

Aaron folded his arms across his wide chest. His unwavering expression was like that of stone. "I'll stand."

"Sit. Down," Maxwell said forcefully, and set an envelope, a pad of paper and a pen on the table. He couldn't much blame the guy's attitude. There was nothing worse than walking in and being told to meet in the interrogation room. Especially when you realized that you were the one being questioned.

Aaron glared at him for a long moment, before reluctantly dropping down into one of the chairs. "Why am I here?"

Maxwell sat across from him. "Where were you last Thursday morning?"

Aaron's eyes narrowed, and he tilted his head slightly as if thinking. "Thursday? Why?"

"Answer the question."

Instead of responding, Aaron's mouth dropped open. "Hold up. I *know* you don't think that I had anything to do with Jeremy's murder."

"I didn't say you did. I asked where were you that morning."

"I was at home. Is that why my sister's here? You thinking she had something to do with offing Jay?" he asked incredulously. "Just because she was messing around with him doesn't mean she had anything to do with his death."

"Can anyone vouch for you?"

"Dammit, Sarge! Are you serious right now?" Aaron roared, and Maxwell stared him down, waiting patiently for him to respond. "No. I was home alone. Anything else?"

"Where were you the rest of that day?"

"Seriously? It was my day off. I was running errands. I didn't have anything to do with Jeremy's murder. And I can't believe you think that I did. Sure, he might've been an asshole, but so are half the people here. I didn't kill him!"

Maxwell slid a photo across the table. "Recognize him?"

Aaron stared down at the picture, frowning again. "No, should I? Wait." He picked up the photo and studied it longer. "That looks like my sister's place."

"The other day, I asked you about the beef you had with Jeremy and you mentioned your sister. Why didn't you tell me that she lived at the apartment complex where he was killed?"

"I didn't know it was the same building," he mumbled, not looking at Maxwell.

"Try again. Those details were all over the news. You tellin' me you didn't know?"

Aaron slammed his elbows on the table and ran his hands down his face. "Fine, I knew, but—"

Maxwell pounded his fist on the table. "So your ass gon' sit there and lie to me? Yet, you want me to believe that you had nothing to do with the murder?" he snapped as anger stirred inside him. "You better start talking and tell me *everything* you know about Jeremy and his murder!"

Aaron lifted his hands out in front of him. "I swear, Sarge. I have no idea who killed him. I'll even take a lie detector test if you want me to. It wasn't me or my sister. With Jeremy it could've been anyone. Dude was out of control. Screwing around with different women, drinking too much, and he had a gambling problem. I wouldn't—"

"How do you know that? I mean how do you know he was gambling?" Maxwell asked, trying to remain calm and not show just how much he was getting tired of learning new crap about Jeremy.

"We used to hang out at this one casino downtown. Jay would spend his whole paycheck at the blackjack tables. At first, he was winning, but over the last couple of months, he started losing…big."

"Did those outings…or the two of you hanging out at casinos, have anything to do with the reason you guys were fighting?"

Aaron huffed out a breath. "I already told you that was about my sister."

"When was the last time you saw Jay?" When Aaron didn't answer right away, Maxwell added, "I suggest you tell me the truth because you know we will find out the truth."

"The night before he was killed. I ran into him at the casino and confronted him again about my sister. I'd heard he was still hooking up with her."

"And what happened?"

"We argued and shoved each other around a little until Security threatened to toss our asses out."

Maxwell shook his head and sighed. He wanted to believe Aaron, but his gut told him the man was still holding back. He might not have been behind the murder, but he knew something.

"Was Jay in trouble with any loan sharks, drug dealers, mafia, anybody?"

"Sarge, I honestly don't know. I *do* know that I wouldn't put anything past him. He wasn't the same guy. After his divorce he…he changed. Maybe you should ask his ex. I heard you two are kickin' it now."

Maxwell remained perfectly still. He didn't doubt there were rumors floating around after he had showed up at her house. Then when she left with him, no doubt that really stirred the gossip mill.

Aaron leaned back in his seat with a smug expression and his arms folded across his chest. "She must be one hell of a woman. First, she turns Jay out, now she's screwing around with you. What is she like…making her rounds or something? If that's the case, I want in because clearly what's between her thighs is like—"

Maxwell reached over the table and snatched Aaron by the collar, pulling him out of the seat. The man's eyes were as large as saucers.

"You can be pissed at me all you want," Maxwell said through gritted teeth. His voice was low and lethal as rage coursed through his veins. "But don't you *ever* say anything to disrespect Amina again. Also, if I find out that you've gone anywhere near her, being a suspect in Jeremy's murder case will be the least of your problems."

Aaron shook out of Maxwell's hold and stumbled back as they glared at each other over the table.

*Dammit! What the hell is wrong with me*, Maxwell thought as he also backed away from the table. It hadn't been a week ago when he gave Jeremy a speech about being stupid and risking his job. Now here he was, losing his cool too. No way in hell would he jeopardize his career because of something stupid that Aaron said. Yet, he was powerless to stop himself from hurting anyone who caused Amina harm.

Aaron huffed out a breath. "Listen, I'm sorry. I was way out of line," he said, rubbing the back of his neck. "I shouldn't have taken my frustrations out on you or… Anyway, I can't believe you think I'd actually kill Jay. He might've been an asshole, but killing him ain't worth ruining my life or sacrificing my job. And then when I saw my sister down the hall in the box," he said of one of the interrogation rooms, "I lost it. She's high-strung, but no way she's involved in any of this."

"Have a seat," Maxwell said quietly. His heart rate was still higher than it should be, but at least he no longer wanted to ring Aaron's neck. "I have a few more questions."

He might've had more to ask, but now his mind was filled with thoughts of Amina and their relationship. And yes, it was a relationship because she was his. He'd made that clear the night before. But they hadn't discussed it in great detail, and at some point, everyone would know about them. Maxwell wanted her in his life more than he'd ever wanted anything, but they were going to have to be ready for whatever people said. Mainly those who knew that he and Jeremy were once buddies. Dealing with Jeremy's parents was bad enough. How would he and Amina deal with mutual friends and their reaction about the two of them dating?

The timing for them getting together wasn't the best, but whatever happened between them was no one else's business. Amina was no longer married, and Maxwell didn't give a damn what people thought about him.

At least that was what he was going to keep telling himself.

# Chapter 19

Amina couldn't stop smiling.

She was making up Maxwell's bed and thoughts of their lovemaking had her body heating up all over again. Spending the night with him had been the most exciting, fulfilling time she'd had in years. It didn't hurt that he was an unselfish lover. The man had worshipped her body in a way that still had every part of her tingling. The three orgasms in one night was definitely a first. A first that she wouldn't mind repeating over and over again.

Maybe if Jeremy had…

*Nope. Nope. Nope. Don't even go there*, Amina told herself. She was not going to ruin a perfectly beautiful morning thinking about a man who had hijacked enough of her thoughts. But even if she refused to think about him, her mood was bound to shift. She was scheduled to meet with the home security people within the hour. Thankfully, she didn't have to go alone. Maxwell had arranged for Trace Halstead, one of his best friends, who happened to be a private investigator, to escort her.

Now Amina understood why Maxwell hadn't wanted her to do any cleaning while they were at her house. He had suggested leaving the place as it was. Not only didn't he think she was up to it, he wanted his friend to do a little poking around the house. Maxwell had sounded a hundred percent sure that whoever had broken into her home had been looking for something. Amina couldn't imagine what they'd wanted. She also wasn't sure if they'd found what they were looking for. Which was why she had agreed not to go anyplace alone.

Amina glanced at the digital clock on the nightstand and was surprised at how fast the morning was going. Trace would be there in fifteen minutes. She had hoped to enjoy Maxwell's huge bathtub before going out, but she had slept in instead.

"Oh well, maybe later."

Again, a smile spread across her face. She could turn it into a bubble bath for two because the tub was definitely big enough. First, they'd eat the romantic dinner she had planned. Then they could talk about taking a bath together.

It was going to be a busy day, but it was one she was definitely looking forward to.

Promptly at ten o'clock, the doorbell rang and Amina peeked through the peephole before opening the door.

"Amina?" the tall handsome man with smooth dark skin said.

"Yes, and you're—"

"Trace, Max's friend," he said, and they shook hands.

"It's nice to meet you. Come on in. I just need to grab my bag."

He stepped into the foyer, and he was taller than she first realized. Over six feet like Maxwell, they both had a similar build with wide chests and broad shoulders.

"Would you like something to drink for the road?" she asked.

"No, I'm good, but I do need to make a quick call before we leave."

"Oh, okay. Make yourself comfortable, and I'll be right back."

Thirty minutes later, they were pulling up to Amina's house. From the outside, no one would ever know that the interior was a mess.

"You doing all right?" Trace asked after he parked the car. "Your purse strap is going to be shriveled to pieces if you keep twisting it like that."

Amina glanced down at her lap and laughed. She hadn't realized the death grip she had on the strap. "I guess I'm a little anxious," she said.

"That's understandable, but I hope you know that we're going to do everything we can to figure out what's going on. There will be two guys working on the alarm system. They should be done in a couple of hours."

Amina nodded. "Okay, but I'll probably need more time to do the cleaning."

"About that. Max and I were talking earlier, and we're thinking maybe hold off on putting the place back in order. He thinks that I might be able to uncover some clues that'll help ID the person or people responsible for the break-in."

"Yeah, he mentioned that. I don't see how leaving

the place a mess will help, but you guys know better than I do."

"There's no guarantee that we'll find anything. But I'd like to have at least a day to take my time going through the interior of the house, as well as the exterior."

"Well, I can think of a lot of things I'd rather do than clean," Amina said on a laugh, but if she was honest, she wasn't ready to go back into the house. Knowing that someone had been in her home, touching her stuff while destroying her belongings, had her on edge. She couldn't ever see being comfortable in there again.

"All right, I'll follow your lead. I would like to at least take care of any food items that might've gotten tossed around."

Trace nodded. "Okay. No problem. One of the things I'm going to do is take pictures of practically every inch of the place."

Amina's eyebrows drew together. "Why? That seems like a lot of work."

"Maxwell said that you couldn't tell if anything was taken. I'm hoping with another walk through, you'll be able to tell, but I'm planning to take pictures of the broken items and the debris on the floor. We're hoping that something will jump out at us or you. Something out of the ordinary."

Amina didn't get it, but she remembered her father saying that during an investigation, investigators had different approaches. No one technique worked better than another, but the most important thing was that they find answers.

Trace continued explaining how much of the morning would go, and Amina was just grateful for his help.

"Are you ready to go inside?"

"As ready as I'll ever be."

"Okay, then let's do this."

Once inside, Amina's anxiety amped up. She followed behind Trace, answering his numerous questions. With every step she took, her happy mood dwindled. Something he did that surprised her though was check for listening devices and cameras. The thought that there could be either was unnerving, and her discomfort skyrocketed.

Buying a new place and moving hadn't been a part of her plan, at least no time soon, but there was no way she could stay in her house again. Even if they found the person responsible, Amina just couldn't imagine being comfortable there. Someone had invaded her privacy. There was no way she could forget that.

When they entered her bedroom, her breath caught. "How did I miss this last night?" she said, stooping down next to the dresser where her keepsake box had been tossed.

"You were in shock. That's why Max wanted you to walk through the space again today. And even tomorrow or the next day, you'll probably notice other things."

"Can I touch it?" she asked after he took photos. It wasn't a large container, and held things like birthday cards, letters or notes that she'd wanted to keep, and a few items of her grandmother's.

"Sure. I'm sure everything in there was valuable in some way to you. But was there anything inside there that you think someone would've wanted?"

Amina shook her head as she picked up the contents that were strewn on the floor near where the box had lain. "Max asked me the same thing. I live a pretty simple life. What I have might be valuable to me, but I can't think of anything that would be valuable to someone else."

They continued through the house much the same as they'd done with the bedroom. By the time she had picked up the kitchen some, the alarm installers were done. There was no doubt that it was a better system, but still, Amina planned to move on.

Next up was the garage. It didn't look as if the burglar had made it out there. Trace told her that she had probably interrupted the person's search when she showed up.

They were standing in the living room when someone pounded on the front door. Amina stiffened and glanced at Trace.

"Relax, you're safe with me. Stand over there," he said of the space between the living room and dining room, then he glanced through the peephole before opening the door. "What's up, man?"

"All's well. How's my girl?"

"See for yourself."

Amina's body came alive at the sound of Maxwell's voice. She'd had no idea he'd be there, and she had to control herself from running to the door.

The moment he stepped into the living room their gazes collided. Heat soared through her body, and a huge grin spread across her face at the sight of him in his uniform.

A sexy *badass*.

"Hey, sweetheart," he said as they moved toward each other.

"Hey yourself. How'd you know we were still here?"

He flashed that sexy grin that she adored and gave a slight nod over to Trace. "A little birdie told me."

Trace smiled and saluted her before heading to the garage.

Amina could've hugged him. She'd wanted Maxwell there in the first place and might've mentioned it once… or maybe even three times. She returned her attention to the man who consumed most of her thoughts.

"You're supposed to be at work? What are you doing here?"

Instead of answering, he looped his arm around her waist and crushed her to his hard body. His lips covered hers before she could take her next breath. This was what she needed, what she'd been craving since he left for work.

She moaned and fisted his uniform shirt as their connection deepened. God, she couldn't get enough. Kissing him was like opening a much-anticipated Christmas present only to find out that it was bigger and grander than you expected. This man was addictive and he was hers.

When the kiss ended, Maxwell lowered his forehead to hers and stared into her eyes. "I couldn't stay away."

Though she was more than happy to see him, she hoped he wasn't done working for the day. She had big plans for him later, but she wanted it to be a surprise. If he ended up taking her home and staying, her idea wouldn't work.

"I can't stay," he said, and lifted his head. "I'm on my lunch break, and when Trace told me that you guys were still here—" he shrugged "—I figured I'd stop by for a hot second, kiss my beautiful woman and then head back to work a happy man."

Amina smiled at him and gave him another quick peck on the lips. Relief and a sweet thrill bounced around inside her. She could still set up the surprise she had for him, but more than that, he took time out of his busy schedule to stop by and check on her. The sensual kiss was like a cherry on top.

"I'm glad you're here even if you can't stay. I've missed you, baby." The endearment rolled off her lips as if they'd been together forever. She and Maxwell together felt good. It felt right. For the first time in a while, Amina was looking forward to what the future would bring.

"You missed me, huh?"

"Oh, yes."

He kissed her again and this one was just as mind-blowing as the first. There had been moments last night that hadn't felt real. She'd felt special and cherished. A feeling she'd never experienced with a man before. Would she ever get enough of him? Probably not.

Amina heard footsteps coming from the garage and reluctantly pulled her mouth from Max's. She smiled up at him and with the pad of her thumb wiped lipstick from his mouth.

"Sorry to interrupt, guys, but I think we found something," Trace said, and held up a medium-sized cardboard box. He set it on the shredded sofa and opened the lid. "I think it's safe to say the person was looking for this."

With gloved hands, he lifted out a stack of money, and Amina's mouth dropped open.

*Oh. My. God.*

*Aww, hell.*

Maxwell knew if there was anything to be found, Trace would find it. Growing up together, he had always been curious about everything. And when he didn't know something, he was quick to seek answers. Actually, Trace's brothers were the same way. Which was why Maxwell wasn't surprised when he and his brother Langston, former FBI, started a private investigation business.

"Bills in small denominations that reek of marijuana in a cardboard box," Maxwell said. His mind had conjured up several scenarios of where the money had come from, but he settled on one.

"Drug money," he and Trace said in unison.

Amina's mouth was still hanging open as she stared at the box then darted her eyes at him and Trace. "That's not mine," she said in a rush. "I swear. I have never seen that box before, and I definitely didn't know about the money."

Maxwell had no doubt that she was telling the truth, but how could she have that type of money in her garage and not know?

"Where'd you find it?" he asked Trace.

"Under a large suitcase near the back corner of the garage."

"Max, you have to believe me. That's not mine," Amina insisted, worry swimming in her gorgeous brown eyes.

He reached for her and pulled against his body. Placing a kiss on her temple, he said, "Of course, I believe you, but we need to figure out how it got here. More than that, we need to determine who it belongs to. If Trace and I are right, and I think we are, some drug dealer is probably looking for their money."

"But h-how did it get here and in my garage?"

"That's what I want to know. Did Jeremy still have a key to the house?"

"No, I had the locks changed while we were separated. And the last time I saw him was after the divorce was final and he came to pick up the rest of his stuff. I'm a hundred percent sure he didn't bring anything in with him."

"What about the keypad connected to the garage? Did you have the code changed?" Maxwell asked. He already knew the answer when her eyes grew big and a sick feeling showed on her face.

Amina shook her head then covered her face with her hands and growled. "It never crossed my mind. God, how could I have not thought to do that?"

"Sweetheart, most people probably wouldn't have thought about that." He reached out and rubbed the back of her neck. "Don't be too hard on yourself. Also keep in mind that for all we know, that box could've been there before you guys started having problems."

She looked at him unconvinced, and even he had to admit that scenario was highly unlikely. Jeremy wasn't a saver. He spent money faster than he could make it. Maxwell was actually surprised that the guy hadn't squandered it immediately. He'd bet his paycheck that the cash showed up within the past couple of weeks or maybe even days before Jeremy was killed.

"Do you have more gloves?" he asked Trace.

Maxwell had some in the car but figured he'd ask and save himself a trip out to the vehicle. Trace pulled a pair out of his back pocket and handed them to him.

"I'd guess there's at least a quarter of a mil in there," Trace said nodding at the box. "Pretty safe to say that this is tied to her ex-husband."

"Yeah, I was thinking the same thing." Maxwell dug farther into the box. Assuming that the money was tied to Jeremy, and he was dead, Amina could be in serious danger. "What I can't figure out, though, is why the burglar would leave when he heard Amina enter the house. This is some serious cash. A drug dealer or worse, a mobster, wouldn't just walk away from trying to find where Jay hid this type of money, especially if it was stolen."

"Oh, dear God," Amina murmured, rubbing her hands up and down her folded arms. "Somebody thinks I knowingly have their stolen money?"

"Not necessarily," Trace said. "My guess is that your ex had something to do with stealing the money. Either he'd been working with someone, or someone knows he had this type of cash stashed somewhere."

Maxwell immediately thought of Aaron. "Yeah, I'm thinking whoever the money belongs to was here looking for it. We just need to figure out the who, when, where and why. My guess is Jay took it from someone, but I wouldn't swear to that. At least not until I know more. But it's safe to say that someone else knows he had it."

"And you think you know who that someone is," Amina said as a statement rather than a question. Her unwavering gaze held his, looking deep into his eyes as if already knowing the answer.

Beautiful and smart. Only two of the reasons why he was falling for her.

"Maybe, but I don't have any proof. So I don't want to say. But I plan to find out. In the meantime, I want us to keep this quiet," he said glancing from her to Trace.

He already knew Trace wouldn't say a word to anyone, but he wanted to make sure Amina kept it quiet. Not that he didn't trust her, he did. He just wasn't sure who else they could trust. Maxwell had a bad feeling someone on the police force was involved. If not Aaron, possibly someone else. There were only a handful of his guys he trusted unconditionally, meaning it might not be a good idea to turn the money over just yet. So far, those involved didn't know that it had been found, and Maxwell wanted to keep it that way. At least for a little while. They could possibly use it to draw out the person who had trashed Amina's home.

Maxwell stared down at the cash. At least now he knew why Jeremy had been killed, but even that didn't make total sense. Why would someone kill him before getting their money?

Maxwell huffed out a sigh and put the cash back in the box. This was a delicate situation, and he wanted to make sure he thought it through before taking next steps. In the meantime, he'd store the money at the station. What he'd do after that...he wasn't sure.

# Chapter 20

Hours later, Amina stood over Maxwell's stainless-steel stove frying bacon. Preparing shrimp and grits for dinner, one of Maxwell's favorites, was bringing her some much-needed peace and normalcy. Her life over the past week seemed like something out of a mystery novel, and she wanted to go back to her quiet, drama-free world.

Amina glanced at the clock. She had to hurry because Maxwell mentioned being home by seven, and she wanted to have everything done by then. But like much of the day, the time was flying. It didn't help that she couldn't stop thinking about the money Trace had found.

"Damn you, Jeremy." The best thing she'd ever done was divorce him. If only she hadn't married him in the first place, then she wouldn't be going through this nonsense. "And maybe me and Max would've been married and living happily-ever-after," she mumbled while sautéing scallions and garlic.

*Woulda, shoulda, coulda.*

There was nothing she could do about the past. All she could do was enjoy the present and wait and see what the future held. Amina just hoped it included Maxwell.

Her phone, sitting on the granite countertop, dinged, signaling a text. She wiped her hands on a dish towel and glanced at the screen of the phone. It was a text from Trace letting her know that he had emailed her copies of the photos he had taken earlier. He and Max wanted her to go through them and see if she noticed anything unusual. Considering all that they were doing to help her and keep her safe, it was the least she could do.

She glanced at the clock noting that it was twenty minutes to seven. She had just enough time to change into the outfit she had planned to wear on their date. After turning off the stove, Amina hurried up the stairs.

Once she had changed clothes, she slipped into the high-heel sandals that matched the outfit. As she took one last look in the mirror, a smile kicked up the corners of her mouth. Maxwell wasn't going to know what hit him when he saw her in the one-shoulder dress. It showed off her best assets while still leaving a little something for the imagination.

"All right, let's do this," she said, eagerness swelling inside her as she made it back to the kitchen.

She wouldn't have been able to pull off her surprise without Trace. He had taken her to the store to get everything she needed and followed her around as she shopped. His wife was one lucky lady. He was one of the most patient men she'd ever met. She had learned that he was a newlywed and he and his wife, Connie, were expecting their first child. The baby wasn't due for another five months, but already they'd finished the nursery.

There had been a time when Amina would've been hit with a wave of jealousy, but not this time. This time she could envision herself in that position in a year or two. Sure, she might be thinking too far in advance, but a girl could hope.

She glanced around. The food was almost done. The dining table was set. All that was left was for her to light the candles. After lighting the last one, the house alarm chirped several times before it went off. She went back into the kitchen and stopped near the center island.

"Honey, I'm home," Maxwell called out from the mudroom, and Amina laughed.

"Welcome home, dear," she said.

When he stepped into the kitchen, he stopped short at the sight of her. His gaze did a slow crawl down her body and eased back up, lingering on her legs and then her breasts. Heat rushed to Amina's face at the way his eyes drank her in while perusing her body. Now she was really glad that she had decided on the light blue outfit. And he brought her flowers. Seeing the vase of calla lilies in his hands almost made her cry.

"How was your day?" she said, trying to break the awkwardness of them both just staring at each other.

"Damn, baby. You're absolutely breathtaking." He strolled toward her. "I don't know what the occasion is, but I'm glad to be a part of it."

His free arm slipped around her waist and he kissed her with a hunger that rivaled their most intimate kiss. God, the man had skills, able to will his tongue with just the right touch to make her entire body tingle with need.

When the kiss finally ended, Amina was breathless and slowly opened her eyes to find him staring down at her.

"I can get used to being greeted like that," she said wistfully.

"And I could get used to coming home to my gorgeous woman."

Her heart flipped inside her chest. *Dang, this man.* He always knew just the right things to say to make her feel so desired.

"I have something for you," he said, and she laughed when he presented the flowers to her as if she hadn't already seen them.

"They are beautiful," she said, accepting the heavy crystal vase. "And you remembered that they're my favorite."

"I remember everything about you."

That made her smile harder. Amina almost started to tell him that while she was married, she had never received flowers, but she didn't. Jeremy did enough to get her, but once she said *I do*, things started changing. Amina kept all of that to herself. She and Maxwell had to get to a point where her ex-husband's name didn't always filter into their conversations.

"I hope you're hungry," she said, and set the vase of flowers in the center of the table.

"I'm starving and whatever you cooked smells amazing." He glanced at the dishes. "And I see you made one of my favorites, shrimp and grits. I can't remember the last time I had some."

During one of their many conversations, he had mentioned how much he loved the dish. She guessed they both were listening, recalling their favorite things.

After sending Maxwell upstairs to change, Amina placed the food on the table, as well as the wine she had picked up. Music was next and she dimmed the lights. By the time he returned, the downstairs looked almost magical.

"Sweetheart, you outdid yourself," Maxwell said as he pulled the dining chair out for her.

"You haven't even tried the food yet," she said.

"Well, if it's as good as it looks, I know I'm going to enjoy it."

As they ate, they discussed their day, but neither mentioned the money that was found. Amina wished she could just forget about it. Actually, she wished she could turn back time and change a few things that had taken place over the past week. Although, had those instances not occurred, she and Maxwell might not have found their way back to each other.

"Damn, girl, you can burn in the kitchen."

Amina laughed. "Now that's an expression I haven't heard in a long time. My dad used to tell my mom that all the time when we were growing up. Instead of being an account exec, she should've opened a restaurant. Man, now that's someone who can throw down in the kitchen."

"So, you picked up your culinary skills from her?"

Amina speared a shrimp and nodded before eating the delectable seafood. "Yup, my mother told me and my sisters that we couldn't move out of the house unless we knew how to cook. The threat paid off. We all enjoy cooking." She actually loved it, but it wasn't always fun preparing meals for one. Now that Maxwell was in her life, it was going to be a blast cooking for her man.

*My man*, she thought, and struggled to keep from

grinning like an idiot. The last few days had been an emotional roller coaster, but every minute she spent with Maxwell was like sunshine on a cloudy day. He filled a void within her that had been vacant for far too long, and she hoped he meant what he'd said the night before. That she was his and that what they were doing wasn't just a fling for him. They might've come together under horrible circumstances, but Amina was glad they'd found their way back to each other.

"So how did things go after I left you and Trace this afternoon? Are you satisfied with the new alarm system?"

"I am, and it's pretty sophisticated. But for the last twenty-four hours, I've been thinking a lot about selling the place. I can't stay there anymore."

Maxwell's eyes widened and his fork stopped inches from his mouth. "Just because someone broke in?" He said it as if it wasn't that big of a deal, though she knew he didn't mean it that way.

"Uh, *yeah.* I know you probably see stuff like that every day or worse, but even having Trace at the house with me, I was so uncomfortable, Max. I'm normally not a scared person, but between the mugging, or as you call it, *attempted mugging*, and someone ransacking my house, I'm afraid. What if the person returned? What if this ends up being a case you guys can't solve? There's no way I'd be able to live in that house by myself again, and I hate feeling like that."

"And I hate that you've gone through so much these last few days. How did you feel being here?"

"For the most part, fine. This morning, I kept thinking about all that's happened, but I wasn't as jumpy as I was last night."

And after Trace dropped her back off at Maxwell's place, the first thing she did was set the alarm. Once she started planning and cooking dinner, the tension she'd been walking around with for much of the afternoon started to ease. Still, every now and then, she'd think about how someone had gotten into her home and destroyed her belongings. Learning that Jeremy might've been a part of something shady didn't help, and even worse, he might've inadvertently involved her.

"I'll position someone outside whenever I'm not here."

"Max, I can't ask you to do that."

"You didn't ask. I want you to feel comfortable in my home, and I know I can't be here with you all day. Besides, it'll just be until we find out who's behind all of this, and I have no doubt we will. When do you return to work?"

"I requested a few more days off. So I don't go back until next week."

He nodded. "Good. That gives us more time to find this creep, and if we don't find him before you return to work, we'll figure out logistics on how to keep you safe while you're there." He reached over and placed his hand at the back of her neck, then gently pulled her closer. "I'm not going to let anything happen to you," he said quietly, and kissed her sweetly.

Amina knew it was too early to think about being in love, but Maxwell had a way of making her feel like the most important person in the world. Then again, hadn't it been like that with Jeremy in the beginning? He had her believing that they were destined to be together and look how that turned out. In her heart she knew Maxwell was different, but what if he wasn't? What if in a few months he tired of her and then moved on to the next woman? Was she opening her heart to him only to have him shatter it the way Jeremy had done?

*God, I hope not.* Her heart couldn't handle being crushed again.

"What?" Maxwell asked when he caught her staring at him. "Do I have something on my mouth?"

Amina shook her head. "No, I was just admiring your handsomeness."

He laughed and she joined in. It was okay for her to be concerned about where their relationship was going, but she couldn't let her past experiences dictate her future. Jeremy had been a mistake that it seemed she was still paying for, but Maxwell wasn't him. They were two very different people, and as long as Amina remembered that, she'd be all right.

Maxwell patted his flat stomach. "Dinner was amazing. Seeing that I can barely boil water, feel free to use your culinary skills on me anytime."

"I plan to. It's nice to have someone to cook for. You'll have to tell me what other dishes you enjoy."

"I'm not picky. I'll eat anything. I have a feeling I'm going to enjoy anything you prepare. But right now, I have a surprise for you." He wiped his mouth and hands with the cloth napkin and stood. "I'll be right back."

While he headed to the garage, Amina started clearing the table. She had made an apple pie for dessert, but maybe they could eat it as a midnight snack.

"Ta-da," Maxwell said, and Amina turned from the sink to face him. In one hand was a bottle of champagne. The other hand held a beautifully woven picnic-type basket. He was holding it up too high for her to see what was inside.

What had her laughing, though, was the boyish grin

that was spread across his handsome face. Whatever he was up to had him feeling pretty proud of himself.

"So what's in the basket?" she asked.

"It's a surprise. I'll show you when we go upstairs." He wiggled his eyebrows up and down and she cracked up laughing.

"I happen to love surprises. Let me clean the kitchen and we can head up."

"Or you can leave all of that, and I'll take care of it later or in the morning."

Amina glanced around the large space. She always washed dishes or loaded them in the dishwasher while she cooked. Outside their dinner plates and glasses, there really wasn't much to clean except for wiping down the stove and countertops.

"You know what? It won't take me long in here. Give me fifteen minutes, then I'll meet you upstairs."

"That's perfect. It'll take me that long to set everything up."

"Okaaay. Should I bring anything with me?" she asked in her most seductive voice, and Maxwell's grin widened.

"In fifteen minutes, be upstairs and only bring your birthday suit."

Amina's mouth dropped open, and then she burst out laughing. Not that he saw it, though. The moment the words were out of his mouth, he turned and jogged up the stairs. She didn't know what she had expected him to say, but it hadn't been that.

*Oh, this should be fun.*

"When you said you had a surprise for me, I never imagined it would be a bubble bath for two. Especially since this morning I had actually thought about us doing something like this."

"Great minds think alike," Maxwell said as Amina settled back against him. The bathtub was huge and could easily accommodate them both, but he hadn't taken into consideration how good her perfectly round butt would feel against his shaft. He wrapped his arms around her and held her close. "Last night, I saw you admiring the tub and figured you might be interested in experiencing it."

"You figured right."

Maxwell had always been a bath guy, and the large master bathroom and tub were what sold him on the house. Add that with dual vanities, travertine floors and a huge walk-in shower, and he'd been sold. Now to share his favorite pastime with the woman who owned his heart was sweeter than the chocolate-covered strawberries he had picked up on the way home. He had to stop by three stores before he found the ones he wanted and another store for the basket and candles. The shocked expression on Amina's face and her slamming naked body when she walked into the bathroom made his efforts worthwhile.

He never considered himself a romantic, but Amina made him want to go the extra mile for her. It wasn't just because she'd had a rough couple of days. No, it had everything to do with the way she made him feel. Alive. Needed. Desired. Maxwell couldn't remember the last time any woman had had that type of effect on him. Then again, she was the *only* woman who ever made him want more. More of what life had to offer. Like a forever love, marriage and children.

Amina turned slightly, her head brushing against his

chest when she glanced up at him. God, he was crazy about this woman. Her beautiful, bright eyes held a happiness that he wanted to see all the time.

"This is the best surprise I've had in a *very* long time. The candles. Chocolate-covered strawberries. Music. Max…" she started, but stopped and bit down on her bottom lip before continuing. "Thank you. Thanks for being so thoughtful. I really needed this."

"Anything for you, baby," he crooned, and lowered his head to cover her mouth with his. Her body was at an odd angle, but he couldn't resist kissing her. Going forward, he planned to do everything he could to keep her happy.

When the kiss ended, Amina settled back against him. Maxwell let his hands wander into the water as Teddy Pendergrass's "Turn Off the Lights" flowed through the speaker.

"This is perfect," Amina said wistfully.

"You're perfect…for me," Maxwell said close to her ear as he placed feathery kisses down the column of her scented neck.

The bubbles tickled his nose, but that didn't stop him from nibbling on her soft skin. He slid his hand over and cupped her more-than-a-handful breast, squeezing and loving the way she moaned and moved against him. The pad of his thumb brushed over her pert nipple and the erotic sounds she was making had him growing hard.

"Damn, you feel good," he murmured against her neck.

"Mmm, I love being hugged up against you like this," she said on a breath. "But if you keep touching me like this, this bath is not going to last very long. I'm going to want you to do something else."

"If that something else involves me drying you off, carrying you to the bedroom and burying myself deep inside of you... I'm all for it."

"That's exactly what I was thinking."

Maxwell learned the night before that her sexual appetite matched his, and he wanted nothing more than to get her back in his bed. But their relationship was more than just sex, and he wanted to make sure there was no mistaking that. Right now, they'd enjoy their bath, talk, and then they'd see where that led.

"We've agreed to date," Maxwell started, "but there's something we haven't discussed."

Amina started to sit up and turn again, but Maxwell held her in place, loving the way she felt against him.

Once she settled back down, she asked, "What haven't we discussed?"

"How do we want to handle those who know me, you and Jeremy?"

Seconds ticked by before she responded. "I have no idea. I would like to believe that I don't care what people think, but deep down, Max, I do. I don't want to be accused of..."

"Of what?"

"Of hopping from one friend to another. That's not who I am. This is not something I go around doing. It's just—"

"Sweetheart, you don't have to explain it to me. I know who you are. You're one of the most virtuous people I know." Maxwell kissed the side of her head. "How about we just wing it?"

"Like we did with Jeremy's parents?" she murmured.

Before the Kellys left town, Maxwell had tried talking to them, wanting to defend Amina and let them know that they were wrong about her. He talked to them, but no matter how he tried to explain that Jeremy had lied, they didn't want to hear it. They believed their son as most parents would. Maxwell was glad they didn't live in town but wondered if that would change once they learned they had a granddaughter.

That was another issue. He had received word that Jeremy was indeed Camille's father. Not that Maxwell was surprised. The kid looked just like him. His only concern was Amina. Though he didn't plan on making it a habit of keeping secrets from her, he wouldn't share that bit of info unless she asked.

"You're mine, baby, and I'm yours. Anyone who has a problem with that can kick rocks," Maxwell said.

Amina sputtered a laugh. "Wow, so eloquently phrased, but it works for me. I'm a grown-ass woman. I don't have to answer to anyone. Thanks for reminding me of that."

"Anytime."

"And for the record," she continued, "my family is going to be thrilled to know that you and I are seeing each other."

"Good, because I'm playing for keeps."

She squeezed his thigh. "Me too."

Silence fell between them as they each got lost in their thoughts. Maxwell never imagined that he'd get a second chance with her, and he wasn't going to blow it. They should've been together from the start, but like the saying went, better late than never.

"How could I have been so wrong about Jeremy?" Amina said out of the blue. "I just don't understand how I could've chosen a man capable of cheating, stealing, and someone who just didn't give a damn about others."

Maxwell didn't know where this was coming from

or what to tell her. Jeremy had changed so much. He was nothing like the person he'd been when they went through the police academy. If anyone would've told Maxwell that Jeremy could be capable of half the things that were turning up, he would've laughed them out of the room. Some of it didn't even make sense, like the cheating.

He placed a lingering kiss on Amina's cheek. *How could anyone mistreat this woman?* She was by far the sweetest, most thoughtful and compassionate woman he'd ever been with. She was the type of person you wanted to make smile, keep happy and, more than anything, protect. Which was what he planned to always do.

"I know I should let it go and move on, but I can't believe he would intentionally put my life at risk," Amina said. "Drug money? He stole drug money," she snapped.

"We don't know that for sure," Maxwell said weakly. They might not have the proof, but he was pretty sure that was exactly what Jeremy had done. Now all they needed to figure out was where it came from and who wanted it back.

"I don't know why I keep acting surprised. I just can't believe I messed up so bad, and for what? To get married? To have a family? If only I had listened to those around me. If only I had heeded the signs."

"I think you're being too hard on yourself," Maxwell said, keeping his arms wrapped around her. He hoped to provide her with some comfort and wanted her to feel how much he adored her. "Jeremy wasn't always like that. Me and the detectives on his case are still trying to piece everything together, but it's clear none of us knew him as well as we thought we did."

"That's for sure. My sister Katrina said something

the day Jeremy was killed. She never liked him and said that she wouldn't be surprised if secrets were revealed now that he's dead."

"Well, she called it because there's been one shocker after another where he's concerned."

Maxwell hated the way his friend's life ended, and he wished he could've done something to get the guy back on the right path. But had he known what was going on before Jay was murdered, Maxwell wasn't sure if he would've been able to make a difference. Especially not after the way Jeremy had betrayed him. That had been hard to forgive…but maybe not impossible.

Maxwell slid one of his hands down the center of Amina's body. He could hear her uneven breathing increase when his hand stopped at the center of her core and he slipped a finger into her sweet heat.

"Ohhh," she moaned, and her legs fell open, giving him more room, but it wasn't enough for him.

"What do you say we move this party to the bedroom?" he suggested.

"I'd say yes…*oh*, yes."

Maxwell wasn't sure what the future held, but one thing he knew—he was never letting Amina go.

# Chapter 21

"Amina?"

"Hmm…" she said, her face buried in the pillow as she struggled to wake up. It felt as if she had just fallen asleep. After their bubble bath, she and Maxwell had made love for much of the night. And though she was basking in the afterglow, she felt like a limp noodle. There was no part of her skin that his hands and mouth hadn't touched, and Amina enjoyed every minute of his exploration.

The side of the bed dipped slightly. "Sweetheart, I'm getting ready to leave." Maxwell's deep voice penetrated her sleep-fogged brain, and heat rushed through her body where his hand suddenly rested on her back. His fresh scent reached her nostrils, and her body stirred with his nearness. Memories of their bath and their lovemaking flooded through her mind. Even though he had worn her out the night before, she craved more of him.

"Do you really have to leave?" she murmured into the pillow. "I was getting used to your hot, muscular body hugged up against me."

He chuckled and nibbled on the side of her neck, which made her squirm. "I would love nothing more than to stay in bed with you for the rest of the day. But duty calls."

Amina didn't want him to leave, but she understood he had a job to get to. She slowly turned onto her back. When she did, her heart swelled at seeing the love brimming in Maxwell's eyes. Sure, it was probably too soon to call what they were feeling for each other love, but that's what she saw when he looked at her.

"Hey, beautiful," he said, and lowered his head and kissed her sweetly.

*God, I could get used to this.*

Never had a man made her feel so adored. She'd been so starved for affection over the last couple of years, it was a little weird to suddenly be the center of a man's attention. But she liked it…a lot.

When the kiss ended, Amina cupped Maxwell's cheek, his light stubble tickling her palm. "Good morning, handsome. I love the way you wake me up."

"Not as much as I love doing it."

His mouth covered hers again and the slow, drugging kiss made her toes curl. Even more so when his hand slipped under the covers, and her body shivered despite the ferocious heat singeing her skin from his powerful touch. With each lap of his tongue, desire sung through Amina's veins making her want him all over again. She knew their relationship was in the early stages, but what she wouldn't give to wake up to him every morning.

"Mmm, you make it hard to leave," Maxwell said when he lifted his head.

"Are you sure you have to head into work?"

"Only for a few hours. Then I'll be back. I was thinking that maybe we can go out and have a late lunch and catch a movie. Are you available?" he asked.

"For you? Definitely. And that sounds like fun. I haven't been to the movies in a while."

"Cool, check the movie listings and decide on what you want to see."

"What if I pick a chick flick?"

"Whatever you want. I'm game."

He stood from the bed and pocketed his wallet and cell phone, then grabbed his keys. He wasn't dressed in his uniform. Instead he had on a gray dress shirt, a dark tie with silver specks and navy blue pants.

"Oh, before I forget to tell you, I have a uniform sitting outside in front of the house," he said of a police officer.

"Wait. What?" Amina pulled the sheet up over her bare breasts and adjusted the pillows behind her. "Why do I need a cop outside? Did something else happen? Am I in more danger than you're letting on?"

"Nothin's happened. I just want to be on the safe side, especially since we don't know who or what we're dealing with. The officer, Ted, will be here until I get back."

"So this is only for today?"

"No, it's until we find the bastard who's been harassing you."

He didn't say whether that *bastard* was the guy who

killed Jeremy, but he'd once said that he thought the incidents were connected.

"I hope you find this person soon," Amina said, tightening her hold on the sheet covering her body. It wasn't that she was afraid, but Amina didn't want to always be looking over her shoulder. "I'm ready for my life to go back to normal."

"I know, baby," he said softly, and brushed her bangs away from her face. Amina's heart kicked inside her chest at the tenderness of his touch. "I'm going to do whatever I can to make that happen. Especially since I'm looking forward to us spending more time together without this mess hanging over our heads."

Amina smiled and reached for his hand. "Me too. Thanks for everything you've done for me. I hate that we had to reconnect under these circumstances, but you're the highlight of this whole ordeal."

Maxwell braced his hand on the headboard and the other on the bed as he lowered his head. He kissed her again and this one was as sweet as the ones before. She felt so cherished and…loved. They might not be at that point yet, but she felt it with every kiss of his lips, every touch of his hand and in the way he looked at her.

*I'm playing for keeps*, he'd said the night before, and Amina planned to hold him to that. She believed in her heart that they were destined to be together, and she couldn't wait to see what the future held for them.

When the kiss ended, Maxwell stared into her eyes. "I'll never be able to get enough of you."

There was so much conviction in his voice with each word he spoke. And the intensity in his eyes made her want to scream to the world that he was hers. Soon. Soon, she'd be comfortable letting everyone know that they were together. First, she wanted everything about Jeremy to be a thing of the past.

"I have to get going. Don't forget to go through the photos Trace took. Shoot me a text if you spot anything out of the norm. There might not be anything in the pictures, but this is a method that Trace has used in the past. And it's helped with a couple of his cases."

"Okay, I'll look through them first thing."

After Maxwell left, Amina lounged in bed for a little longer. Would it always be like this when she woke up next to him? The kissing, the talking, the just being together? It felt so foreign. Yet, she knew that was how it should've been with the man she married. At least that's how it was with her parents and her sisters' marriages. Granted, she was seeing their relationships from the outside looking in, but they all had something she and Jeremy never had—good communication…and mutual respect.

She and Jeremy never had that type of connection. Amina could see it clearly now, but back then, she'd been clueless to what all was missing in their relationship. The two of them also hadn't been friends before getting together, and that was the difference with Maxwell. The last couple of years they'd bonded and a friendship developed. Add that to the mutual respect between them and they had something to build upon. Something that was never a part of her marriage.

Amina growled under her breath then released a frustrated sigh. *I have to stop this.* She had to stop comparing her past with her present. Maybe once Jeremy's case was closed and there was some normalcy in her life, she'd be able to move on without looking back. At least that's what she hoped. Right now, though, she needed to look through those photos and help catch a thief.

Maxwell had a morning full of meetings and had arrived to work a little earlier to do some digging. So far, he learned that a drug stash house had been burned down a month ago. It hadn't been in their jurisdiction, and he'd been at a leadership conference in Orlando when it happened. According to the information he'd been able to obtain, the fire had initially been deemed suspicious, but now the case was closed and listed as an electrical-fire accident. Remnants of money and product were found, and sadly several lives had been lost.

"Accident my ass," Maxwell mumbled, as he tapped his fingers on the desktop.

The case might've been closed, but he doubted it was an accident. He wouldn't be surprised if it was arson covered up to look like an electrical fire. Only a drug dealer would be broken up about losing the place. While those in the neighborhood were probably glad to see the house gone. But nothing Maxwell found so far helped him in the case of the stolen money or Jeremy's murder. That, he still needed information about, which was why he was waiting to hear back from Danny.

Maxwell had met with the detective a few minutes ago, wanting him to check on a few things for him. Danny was one of the few guys who reported to him who Maxwell trusted unconditionally. After Maxwell filled him in on the break-in, the money and the little he knew about the one stash house that had been hit lately, Danny left to check in with one of his CIs. This particular confidential informant had come through for them countless times.

Maxwell's main concern was keeping the stolen-money situation quiet for the time being. Right now, the fewer people who knew about them finding the cash at Amina's place, the better. He needed to determine whether or not it was one of their own who had broken into her house.

The thought sickened him, and Maxwell ran his hands down his face. Even if he didn't want to believe that one of his cops could stoop that low, he had to consider the possibility. They had the means and the opportunity to steal from a stash house, or the money could be a payoff for a favor done. There were any number of scenarios that could fit, and each one of them made him sick. Though most of the officers who reported to him were on the up-and-up, there was always a chance that he had a few bad cops on the payroll. Jeremy could've easily been one of them.

But did the money have anything to do with his murder? That was the question that had been plaguing Maxwell. They needed to find the killer whether it did or not, but even more so now that Amina might be in danger. The unknowns were what prompted him to have someone sit on his house. He didn't want to take any chances with her life.

"Hey, Sarge, you got a minute?"

Maxwell glanced up to find Zeke in the doorway. "Yeah, come on in. Have a seat. What's up?"

"I've been going through Jeremy's cell phone records. Over the last couple of months, most of the calls were to his fiancée, Aaron and Aaron's sister Valerie. But over the last couple of weeks, there was a cell phone number that popped up several times a day. Of course, it's no longer in service. I have tech support trying to figure out when and where the phone was purchased."

Maxwell nodded. "That's a good idea. We find that information, then maybe we can look through the store's security footage and identify the person who purchased it."

"Yep, and then maybe we'll find our killer."

In the past, their tech-support team had been successful in getting that type of information. Not only the store where the phones were purchased, but also the day and time. Maxwell needed them to have that same level of success for this case too.

"Any other leads? Lieutenant Grayson has been asking about the status of the case. The sooner we bring it to a close, the better."

"Yeah, we're trying. We still haven't had any luck in identifying the guy in the video," Zeke said, and stood. "The murderer covered his tracks good, but I'm not giving up. Who knows—he might be the one who purchased the burner phone. Either way, he or *she* will be found," he said, and strolled out of the office.

Maxwell rocked back in his seat as he mulled over what they knew so far, but part of his conversation with Aaron the other day kept playing through his mind. He had no doubt that Aaron's parting words were a shot at him for coming to Amina's defense. There was no way she had anything to do with the murder. Technically, though, their department had an obligation to question any and everyone who had motive or opportunity. He could think of at least ten reasons off the top of his head on why Amina could've wanted Jeremy dead. They all would be good ones.

Hell, based on their precinct's departmental procedures, any one of them could've been questioned, including Maxwell. He, along with others, had bumped heads with Jeremy regarding cases, procedures and any number of things. Did anyone in the precinct hate him enough to have him killed?

"God, I hope not," Maxwell murmured, and headed for the door.

*But we'll find out soon enough.*

# Chapter 22

After eating a light breakfast, Amina sat at the dining room table with her laptop and a huge mug of black coffee. With each photo she looked at, depression seeped in. The objects in her house that had been destroyed might've been just things to an outsider, but to her, they were a part of her life's story.

She swiped left and a photo of the glass-and-steel baker's rack that was in the dining room showed on the screen. It had survived destruction, but the contents that were once on the shelf were now shattered in a heap on the floor near it. That included the vase her sister Sabrina had brought her back from Spain after her honeymoon. Then there was the eight-by-ten photo of her, her mother and grandmother. The crystal frame had been a gift from her mom and was now shards of glass.

Amina inhaled deeply, then released the breath slowly

and reminded herself of something Maxwell said the other night. At least she hadn't been physically injured. That could've easily been a possibility considering she had heard someone in the house when she arrived. Luckily, the situation hadn't been any worse.

*Everything will be okay. I'm going to be fine.*

She brought the coffee mug up to her mouth, and the hazelnut aroma calmed her some as she took a tentative sip of the steaming liquid. Amina went through another ten photos before stopping and studying a picture. It was of a closet near the back door. The burglar had pulled everything out, littering the floor with mostly jackets and a couple of sweaters. But when she enlarged the photo, Amina noticed something else. It appeared to be a gold key chain with the letter *A* hanging from it, but because part of it was covered by a small box, she couldn't be sure.

How had she missed that when they walked through? Whatever it was, it wasn't hers and she hadn't seen it before. Trace had mentioned more than once that if she spotted anything unusual in the photos to let him or Maxwell know.

Amina grabbed her phone. Trace had copied Max on the email, and hopefully she could explain the photo enough for him to know which one she was referring to. She typed out a text to Maxwell.

Photo #48. See the jewelry under the box on the left of the picture? That's not mine. Looks like a key chain, but I'm not sure.

Amina set the phone down. She had a few more photos to get through, but seeing the key chain was disturbing. It could easily belong to the person who broke into her house. The same person who had touched her personal belongings and thought it was okay to destroy her things. That was creepy on so many levels. What if that hadn't been the first time they'd gone through her stuff? Someone could've been there before and she not known.

She trembled at the thought. That particular photo was enough to support her decision to sell the place and move on. No way could she stay there and not be afraid. Granted she had the new security system, but that wasn't enough to change her mind. Even knowing that it was top-of-the-line equipment couldn't wipe out the horror of arriving home and finding the place a wreck. Nor could it erase the images she was currently looking at.

No, Amina was a hundred percent sure she was ready for a change in her life. And what a perfect time for that since she and Maxwell were dating. She was getting that second chance with him and so far, personally, they were off to a great start. If only they didn't have to deal with a murder, a home break-in and now stolen money.

*When did this become my life?* she thought as she scrolled through more photos.

An hour later, Amina was in Maxwell's home gym running on the treadmill. She bumped up the speed, determined to get a good cardio workout that would make her too exhausted to think. She had never looked at so many pictures in all of her life. It wouldn't have been so bad if they were photos of an island or something equally pleasant.

She also hadn't heard from Maxwell. Just in case he was totally swamped, she had also texted the photo with a note to Trace. The more she thought about the key chain, the more she wondered if it was hers. Had someone given it to her, like a souvenir from someplace and she just couldn't remember?

"Nah, I would've remembered."

Amina increased her running pace hoping to drown out the thoughts in her head. She normally ran in the early mornings three or four days a week but had missed the last few days. Running outside was her preference, but Maxwell had a nice gym that would serve her purposes.

He had converted his first-floor bedroom, and the space included everything from free weights to resistance bands and a yoga mat. Next to the treadmill was a recumbent bike and in front of her were floor-to-ceiling mirrors that covered the whole wall. That, along with the tall ceilings, made the room appear larger than it actually was.

Her cell phone vibrated in the cup holder and Amina smiled, hoping it was Maxwell calling. Not only did she want to hear his voice, but she had forgotten to ask him what time he wanted to go to the movies.

She decreased her speed down to a jog then grabbed the cell phone. *Crap*, it was Katrina. Amina had purposely been avoiding calling, not wanting to risk the chance of telling her about the break-in. At least not yet. She could just not answer, but Katrina was impossible to ignore. Her sister would keep calling. Or worse, hop on the next plane and show up on her doorstep.

Amina pressed the speaker button. "Hello?"

"Hey, sis. What's going on?"

"Not much. Just getting in a run. How's it going with you, and since when did you start calling in the middle of a workday?"

"I was taking a quick break and was wondering why

you hadn't called to tell me about your hot date. Wait, why are you huffing and puffing, and what's that pounding noise?"

"I'm running on a treadmill. I didn't get a chance to get out earlier for my run."

"It's probably too hot out there anyway, but on to important things. Since you haven't said anything, I assume your date with the Max-man was a bust."

Amina smiled and wiped sweat from her brow with her forearm. Katrina was always ready with a nickname for someone. "Oh, on the contrary. Our date was amazing." Which wasn't a complete lie. Their date might've started off shaky, but their night had ended with a bang.

She had actually wanted to call Katrina right after the break-in but was concerned that her sister would sense something was wrong. She had the uncanny ability to know when Amina wasn't being completely honest.

"Oh really? Do tell," Katrina said on a laugh.

"Let's just say that the date exceeded my expectations, and I've spent the last two nights with Maxwell." None of that was a lie and based on her sister's screech, it was just enough for Katrina to not get suspicious.

"Oh, my God! Well, it's about time. If you're still there, I guess I don't have to ask if he got to second base. I'll just ask—how was he?"

Amina laughed. She couldn't help herself. She couldn't think of any words that would do her experience with Maxwell justice. He was everything she had hoped and more than she had expected. And for the next few minutes, she gave her sister the highlights. That included the dinner she had prepared last night, as well as the bubble bath, strawberries and champagne he had surprised her with.

"He's such a sweetheart," Amina gushed. "He even bought me red-and-white calla lilies."

"Aww, that is sweet. Did he know those are your favorite?"

"Yeah, it came up in one of our conversations, but the fact that he remembered meant everything. It's nice to be with a man who cares enough to do those little things like buy your favorite flower."

"I agree, but what does this mean? Are you guys just hanging out, or are you officially dating?"

"We're dating."

"Wow, that's cool…and quick." Her sister chuckled. "What about your concern about dating your ex's best friend? Just a week ago, you were worried about what people would think."

Amina decreased the speed on the treadmill to a brisk walk and wiped her face with the towel she'd laid across the handle. She blew out a tired breath before saying, "I don't care what anyone thinks. I want the experience of being with someone who really cares about me."

"And you think that's Max?" Katrina asked, the sound of doubt dangling from her words.

"I do, but why do you sound like that's a bad idea? You were the one telling me to give him a chance. Now you make it seem like I'm making a mistake."

"Oh no. I love the idea of you with Max. You already know I liked him the moment I met him, and I think you guys will be great together. However, I hope you're going into this relationship with your eyes open. Though Mom, Dad and Sabrina will be happy, everyone won't be wishing you two well. Mainly those who know that you were married to Max's friend."

Amina immediately thought about Jeremy's parents

and their accusations. She didn't want to care what they thought, but deep down she did. No woman ever wanted to be accused of cheating on her husband when that was the furthest from the truth. And because of the timing, those who knew her, Jeremy and Maxwell might think the worst of her too. Yet, the three of them knew the truth.

"I'll be fine," Amina told her sister.

As long as she and Maxwell stuck together, no one could ever tear them apart.

"Yes, sir. I met with the task force a few minutes ago and we've gone through the report," Maxwell said into the telephone. He was finally back at his desk. Between meetings and completing reports, the morning had gotten away from him. "Yes, I agree with their findings regarding the training deficiencies. I'll be putting together a comprehensive proposal on how we can correct those problem areas."

"Good to know," Lieutenant Grayson said. "I knew you'd be the perfect addition to the task force. Let me know if I can be of any assistance."

"Will do," Maxwell said before disconnecting the call.

He sat back in his chair and rubbed his eyes while yawning. Now that his meetings were done, he could head home, but he had hoped to hear back from Danny first. He'd give him a couple of more minutes before heading out.

Knowing there was a beautiful woman at home waiting for him, Maxwell was ready to get out of there. Not just because he had promised Amina lunch and a movie, but also because after feasting on her for much of the night, he needed a nap. The woman had worn him out.

That thought brought a smile to his face. Maybe if he was lucky, he could convince her to take a nap with him before they went out. And by *nap* he meant enjoying her body all over again.

Maxwell's desk phone rang, and he glanced at his watch. *Twelve o'clock.* Definitely time for him to get going.

"Sergeant Layton," he said, answering the phone.

"Max, why aren't you answering your cell phone?" Trace's voice boomed.

"I've been in meetings most of the morning. Why? What's up?" he asked, opening the top drawer and pulling out his cell phone that he had left in there before his first meeting.

"Because Amina found something in one of the photos. You're going to want to take a look at the picture. There's a—"

"Sarge!"

Maxwell's head jerked up when Danny burst into the office.

"We have a situation," he said in a rush, and closed the door.

"Trace, let me call you back." Maxwell disconnected the call before his friend had a chance to say anything else. "What happened?" he asked Danny.

"One of my informants enlightened me a little more on that stash house that caught fire a few weeks ago. At the time, there had been one critically injured, who died on the way to the hospital, and three pronounced dead on the scene.

"But here's where it gets a little dicey. I was able

to talk to the sister of one of the men who died on the scene. She refuses to make a formal statement but said that her brother mentioned two cops had been hanging around at the stash house."

"What?"

"Yeah." Danny dropped down in one of the chairs. "Weeks before the fire, the cops were supposedly doing some moonlighting by providing security. They had some type of connection to the dealer, but she wasn't sure of the details."

"Connections?" Maxwell spat. "When the hell did our guys start having some damn connections with known drug dealers?"

Danny held his hands up to stop Maxwell from going off track. "Keep in mind, we're not a hundred percent sure if this woman's story is on the up-and-up. Nor do we know if these are our guys she's talking about. However, there's more. She wasn't sure if they were there the night of the fire, but get this. The house was a temporary holding spot. According to her, the fire happened the night before everything was to be moved. Coincidence?"

Maxwell ran his hand over his head. "I think not. Tell me she gave you a name, or a description or, hell, something."

"She wasn't positive, but she said one of them went by some initials like D.J. or C.J."

"Or maybe, A.J. As in Aaron McCallum Jr.," Maxwell added. He didn't want to accuse Aaron of anything until they had proof. Yet, his gut was screaming that the guy knew more than he was letting on.

"That was my first thought, especially when she said her brother referred to him a couple of times as *that 'redbone' guy.*"

A growl bubbled deep inside Maxwell's chest. This was *too* much of a coincidence not to mean something. First the initials, then the redbone comment, which Aaron had been described as on more than one occasion. His fair, multirace complexion had red undertones, and some of the guys even called him Red, which he responded to.

Still, Maxwell didn't want to assume that the two cops this woman claimed hung out at the stash house were Aaron and Jeremy.

"She thinks the cops set the fire, but she doesn't have any proof. Besides that, she said who would believe her?"

Maxwell logged in to his computer, planning to pull up the schedule.

"If you're looking for Aaron, I already checked to see if he was on duty," Danny said.

Maxwell stopped typing and his fingers hovered over the computer keyboard. "And?"

Danny stood. "He is, but he's not answering his cell. He could be getting lunch or something. But I have Dispatch trying to reach him now. We're also tracing his phone and looking for his squad car."

*Dammit.* Due to budget cuts, some officers on the day shifts patrolled alone and called for backup during an arrest or if they needed any other assistance. If Aaron was with a partner, they'd be able to track him that way.

"Keep trying to locate him. If no one finds him or he doesn't check in within the next fifteen minutes, put an APB out on his ass," Maxwell said, and picked up his cell phone. He had never put an all-points bulletin out on a fellow officer, but he'd had many firsts these last couple of days. Hopefully, it wouldn't come to that if Aaron checked in soon.

Maxwell glanced at his watch. Amina was probably wondering where he was, which reminded him of Trace's call. Maxwell picked up his phone, thinking that what he didn't want to do was cancel his and Amina's date, but he might have to postpone it until later. Catching the person who broke into her place was a priority, and he was hoping Aaron knew something. Amina would understand. She wanted the people or persons involved to be caught more than he did.

Looking at the phone screen, he noted that he had missed two calls from Trace and a text from Amina. He read her text. Then he enlarged the photo that was attached, and unease clawed through his veins.

*"Oh, hell..."*

*The key chain.* It was just like the ones he had given his guys for Christmas the year before, and there had only been one *A.*

*Aaron.*

"Danny!" Maxwell yelled, and within seconds, Danny was in the doorway.

"Yeah, Sarge."

"Put out an APB on Aaron, *now.*" The broadcast alert would notify all police stations to be on the lookout for him. "If asked, he's a person of interest for the murder of fellow police officer Jeremy Kelly."

Danny stared at him, probably surprised that a moment ago Maxwell had only wanted to talk to the guy. But murder? "You got it, boss," was all Danny said before disappearing.

Maxwell called Amina, frustrated that the call went

to voice mail. "Hey, sweetheart. I got your text. I think I know who broke into your place. I'll tell you about it when I get home. I'll be there in fifteen minutes."

# Chapter 23

Amina showered and had just finished dressing when she heard the doorbell ring.

"Coming," she called out, and slipped into a pair of sandals. Seeing that she was upstairs in the master bedroom, it was safe to say whoever was outside couldn't hear her.

She hurried down the stairs and went to the tall, slender window that was to the left of the front door. Glancing outside, she noticed that the squad car was still in front of the house, but the police officer was standing on the front stoop. He gave her a little wave.

Disarming the alarm, Amina cracked the door open. "Hi, can I help you?"

"Hey, Mrs. Kelly. I'm sorry to bother you. I assume Sarge told you I'll be sitting on the house. But do you mind if I use the bathroom? I overdid it with all the coffee this morning," he said, looking sheepish as he rocked from one foot to the other.

Amina chuckled, thinking about the other day when she barely made it to the bathroom herself. "I totally understand. Come on in." Once he stepped inside, she closed and locked the door and immediately a wave of déjà vu washed over her. Cigarettes. The scent was so strong, she brought her finger up to her nose.

"I'm sorry, but what's your name?" she asked. Maxwell had told her, but for some reason she couldn't remember. Did it start with a *C*? Or maybe an *L*.

"It's Ted," the officer said, still looking uncomfortable as he bounced from one foot to the other.

*Ted.* She'd been way off. She tried not to stare, but there was something familiar about him. Amina couldn't put her finger on it.

"Oh, I'm sorry, Ted." She pointed down the hallway that also led to the gym. "The bathroom is the first door on the left."

"Thanks, and sorry about the intrusion. I'll be out of here in a minute," he said over his shoulder before hurrying away.

Amina stared after him. She had a sensitive nose, especially when it came to cigarette smoke, and the guy smelled as if he had smoked a couple of packs already. She started to move away from the front door but stopped when an eerie feeling sent tingles scurrying over her skin.

*Cigarette smoke.*

*Mugging.*

She glanced down the hallway again. *It couldn't be. There was no way.*

She gave herself a little shake as if that would rid her

of the memory of being attacked days ago. Sure, this guy smelled of cigarettes, but the man from the hospital parking lot reeked so bad. It was as if he had bathed in tobacco.

No way could it be the same person. She was letting her imagination get the best of her. So what if the officer was a big smoker. His scent wasn't as offensive. And sitting in a car all day guarding the house was like watching paint dry. The man was probably bored out of his mind, prompting him to smoke even more.

Amina stayed near the front door so she could lock up once the officer left. Just then, Ted stepped out of the bathroom with his cell phone plastered to his ear. He slowed and nodded at whatever the caller was saying on the other end of the line.

"Yes, sir. Okay. Will do," he said before disconnecting and shoving the phone into his pocket. "Mrs. Kelly—"

"Amina," she insisted. Hearing Jeremy's last name fall from the man's lips was like getting doused with a bucket of ice water. It was just enough of a kick in the pants she needed to remember to reclaim her maiden name as soon as her life was back to normal. That would seal the last of her connection to her ex-husband. She didn't know why she hadn't done it the day after the divorce was final.

"Amina it is. Anyway, that was Sarge. He's still at work and asked that I bring you to the station."

Amina frowned wondering why. Maxwell had already told her that they'd go out after he finished work. It wasn't like she was in a hurry or that they had to be anywhere by a certain time. They could easily catch a later movie. But still, she didn't want to ride in a squad car like some type of criminal.

"Why'd he tell you instead of me?" she asked, but then patted the back pocket of her blue jeans and realized she had left her phone upstairs.

Ted looked at her knowingly with a smirk on his face. "He said you didn't answer your phone."

Amina nodded. Still, sending word for her to go with the officer didn't make sense to her. "I'll just call him and let him know that... I'm sorry, but have we met before?" Not knowing where she knew him from was gnawing at her. "You seem so familiar. Were you ever partnered with my ex-husband?"

"Yeah, we worked together a few times. I think I met you once or twice. Maybe at one of the department's Christmas parties."

That probably wasn't it since she never attended with Jeremy. She had gone to one with her parents many years ago, though, before her father retired.

"And my condolences for your loss. Jeremy was a good man and a great police officer. We all were sorry about what happened to him."

"Yeah, thanks," Amina said around the bile in her throat. It was on the tip of her tongue to tell him what her ex was really like. Instead she said, "Okay, let me contact Max to let him know that I'll be staying here. But do you mind stepping back outside?"

Amina couldn't shake the creepy feeling that surrounded her with his nearness. Between that and trying to figure out if she'd met him before, she was ready to have him out of the house.

Ted hesitated and glanced around before saying, "Sure, no problem, but I don't mind dropping you off. My shift ends soon, and—"

"Oh." Amina tapped the side of her forehead with

her finger. "I wasn't even thinking. You're probably sick of just sitting out there. I'll let Max know that I'm fine here. I'm sure he won't mind you taking off. I'll have him contact you after we talk."

Again, there was a hesitation. "Um, all right. I'll get out of your hair," Ted said as he strolled to the door.

Amina followed behind him but pulled up short and gasped when he turned suddenly and grabbed her arm, catching her totally off guard.

"Wh-what are you doing?" Her pulse pounded in an alarming rhythm as she tried twisting out of his hold, but his grip tightened. "I don't know what this is about, but—"

"I don't want to hurt you," he said, and pulled her closer. His strong odor was assaulting her senses, but that wasn't what had her trembling. It was his voice... and his words.

That creepy sensation that had clawed over her skin moments ago had turned into full-blown panic now.

*It's him. The mugger.*

But how? How was that possible? This guy was a cop. No way could he... Amina swallowed. Same height. Same build. And then there was...the cigarette smell. Her eyes grew round.

*Ohmigod. Ohmigod.*

"I take it that you remember me," he said with a mocking smile.

"I don't know what you want, but please, just let me go," Amina said, still struggling against his hold on her. Her mind raced as she tried to form a plan to get free. But knowing the man had a gun in his holster scared her to death.

"Just give me my money, and I'll be on my way."

*Give me my money.* The words played inside her head as realization dawned on her. "Wh-what money?" She tried acting surprised while continuing to struggle against the vise-grip-like hold he had on her upper arm. He had her temporarily immobile as he moved her left and right, keeping her off-balance and making it impossible for her to use some of the self-defense techniques she'd learned.

"My portion of the money Jeremy stole from me. I know you have it, and I want it back. So we're going to go and get it."

Amina shook her head. Fear that was a hundred times more intense than that night in the hospital parking lot slithered through her body.

*Think. Think.* She had to think fast.

"It's here," she blurted before she could stop herself. "Let me go, and I'll get it for you."

Ted, if that was even his name, jerked her hard, and Amina screamed when the front of her body slammed into his. Face-to-face, he had a hold of both her arms, and she winced at the way his fingers were digging into her skin.

He narrowed his eyes. "You have the money…here? If you're lying, I'm going to kill you."

"I'm—I'm not lying. It's here. I'll go and get it."

"I'll go with you."

"No! I mean, that's not necessary. It's down the hall. I'll—"

"Let's go." He pulled his gun and waved it in front of her face. "I meant what I said. If you're playing some type of game and don't take me to my money right now, I *will* kill you."

Amina swallowed hard and nodded. She had to think

of something fast. More than anything, she needed a weapon.

Now, Ted was holding tight to one of her arms as he led her toward the hallway. Amina zoned in on a silver candleholder that she had used for dinner the other night. All she had to do was grab it as they walked past the table.

*Just a few more steps…*

The moment they were close enough, she snatched it off the table. Amina wielded the candleholder like a sword and aimed for the man's head; he dodged left and it made contact with his shoulder. But it was still enough to throw him off-balance, giving her just enough time to make a run for the gym.

"Why you little…" He snatched the back of her shirt and jerked hard enough to send her crashing to the floor.

"No!" Amina screamed, kicking out her legs, hoping to make contact with any part of his body. Hollering for help, she squirmed around, trying to make it hard for him to keep a grasp on her. It wasn't until she heard his gun cock did she freeze.

"I thought that would get your attention. Get your ass up," he said, pulling her to her feet then pressing the gun to her temple. "It's safe to say the money isn't here. I guess you played me. So we're going for a ride."

With his large hand gripping the back of Amina's neck and the gun pointed at her temple, he led her toward the front door. Tears blurred her eyes, and she struggled to keep it together. One wrong move and she was dead.

"Wh-where are you ta-taking me?" she stammered, trying to walk as slowly as possible.

She needed them to stay in the house because she

had no intention of getting in the car with him. Even if that meant getting shot.

*If you let them put you in the car, you're as good as dead.* Her father's words pierced her mind.

"We're going to your house. I know the money is there somewhere, and you're going to help me find it," the officer said from between gritted teeth. "But if you try any more funny stuff, I won't hesitate to shoot you. I won't shoot to kill. No, I'm going to make you suf—"

"Drop your weapon!"

Amina gasped at the sound of Maxwell's booming voice behind them, and she screamed when the cop jerked her around. He had a death grip around her neck, and the cold metal of his gun rested against her temple.

They were now facing Maxwell, and she trembled as her heart worked harder than it should, pounding fast enough to beat right out of her chest. She couldn't stop the tears from sliding down her cheeks. Part of her was relieved to see Max, but the other part of her was afraid the guy holding her would shoot her anyway.

"It's over, Aaron," Maxwell said calmly.

*Aaron. His name was Aaron, not Ted.*

"You already had Jeremy killed," Maxwell continued, and Amina's heart stopped at the revelation. "You don't want to add another murder char—"

"What?" Aaron roared. "How many times do I have to tell you? I did *not* kill Jeremy! I had nothing to do with his murder. All I wanted was my share of the money. But no, the asshole had to go and get himself killed before telling me where it was!"

Amina struggled to take a breath and pulled down on the man's arm that was now choking her. "I can't… breathe," she wheezed. "Hel-help."

"Okay, okay, Aaron," Maxwell said, noticing her distress. "So you didn't kill Jay. Right now, though, I need you to let Amina go. You're hurting her and she has nothing to do with any of this."

Aaron's grip loosened slightly, and Amina inhaled deeply, trying to get air into her lungs.

"All you're looking at right now is reckless endangerment and kidnapping charges," Maxwell told the officer. "Do you really want to add murder or attempted murder to the list? Now put down your weapon and let her go."

Aaron cursed under his breath and was clearly agitated as he rocked back and forth. But he kept his arm securely in place and the gun steady against Amina's temple.

Sweat beaded around the edges of her hair as the temperature in the house seemed to go from seventy to a hundred in a heartbeat.

"None of this was supposed to happen," Aaron said. His voice was low as if talking to himself. "No one was supposed to get hurt in that fire. Take the money and lay low. That was the plan, but no, Jeremy wanted to make sure our tracks were covered. He shot the guys then set the fire. I swear, Sarge. I didn't kill anyone."

"If that's the case, lower your weapon and let her go."

Aaron tightened his hold. "No, because if I let her go, what's to stop you from killing me?"

"I'll do everything I can to help. You have my word," Maxwell said with authority. "But you have to put down the gun. *Now.* This place will be swarming with cops soon. Once that happens, there's nothing I can do for you."

Amina's heartbeat grew louder as seconds ticked by. At first it didn't seem as if Aaron would release her, but then he did. Amina hurried away from him, and he got to his knees with his hands raised.

"Set the weapon down slowly and slide it away," Maxwell instructed, and Aaron did as he was told then linked his fingers behind his head.

A sob slipped through Amina's lips, and she covered her mouth with her hands. Then she dropped down onto the sofa like a sack of bricks and cried outright.

That was too close. She could've died, and for what? Over some stupid money? Listening to Aaron talk so callously about what he and Jeremy had done made her sick to her stomach. All they'd been thinking about were themselves, and everyone else be damned. God only knew what else they'd done while they were supposed to be protecting the public.

Once Aaron was handcuffed and the arrest called in, Maxwell stood in front of her. A whole new wave of tears filled her eyes. He had saved her life. What if he hadn't come home when he did? There was no telling what could've happened.

He pulled her up and into his arms. "Shh, baby, it's okay," he said near her ear, and wrapped her in his warm embrace. "You're safe now."

# Chapter 24

"If he didn't kill Jeremy, then who did?" Maxwell mumbled to himself.

While Amina was giving her statement to another officer, he stood in the observation room watching Danny interrogate Aaron. They'd been at it for the past thirty minutes.

Aaron admitted to everything from witnessing Jeremy kill several people at the stash house to helping set fire to the place. It was scary how well they covered their tracks. Or maybe the detectives who'd been on that case only saw what they wanted to see.

The one thing Aaron was continuing to claim, though, was that he had nothing to do with Jeremy's murder and he didn't know who pulled the trigger. He insisted that the fight that he and Jeremy had weeks ago had been about Valerie, Aaron's sister. He admitted that it was also about the stolen money. Aaron had wanted his cut, but Jeremy kept insisting that it was too soon. As for the drug dealer, whose money they'd stolen, he was under the impression that his product and money went up in flames.

Maxwell stared through the one-way mirror at Aaron. It was disturbing to know that people who reported to him, people Maxwell thought he knew well, could do something so heinous. And the fact that Jeremy put Amina's life in danger by storing that money at her house was unforgivable. She could've been killed.

Maxwell shook his head, not even wanting his mind to go down that route of thinking. The day definitely hadn't turned out the way he'd planned. They'd known Aaron was involved in some way with the money, but Maxwell hadn't known the extent of his illegal activity.

When he had arrived home and found Ted, the officer assigned to watch his house, unconscious in his squad car, Max almost lost his mind. He knew immediately that Aaron had Amina and was probably in the house. But Maxwell's heart nearly stopped when he saw that Aaron had a gun to her head. If he had been five minutes later, there was no telling where the man would've taken her or what he would've done.

On the way to the police station, Amina had told him how Aaron had gotten in. Maxwell was glad she'd been suspicious. Hopefully, they'd never be in this position again, but they both agreed that if they had plans and something changed, they'd call each other directly.

Aaron had lied to her about Maxwell calling. As a matter of fact, his cell phone had been off. He'd made up the whole story and pretended to be Ted in an effort to get her out of the house. His squad car had been around the corner, and Ted hadn't seen him coming until he had climbed into the car. Ted was going to be fine, but knowing how horrible that situation could've turned out made Maxwell angry all over again.

"Man, what the hell were you thinking?" Danny snapped, pulling Maxwell's attention back to the interrogation. "Why would you risk everything for—"

Aaron pounded on the metal table, the handcuffs clanging with each move. "How you gon' sit there and judge me? You don't know what the hell I've been through. And the chump change that the police department pays in salary is laughable. We risk our damn lives out there every day, and for what? A few measly dollars? Don't sit there and act all self-righteous with me. You would've done the same thing if the opportunity presented itself."

"Man, you're a disgrace to the badge. I hope they put your ass with general population," Danny said with disgust, and slapped a yellow legal pad on the table along with a pen. "Write it all down," he told Aaron before stomping out of the room.

Maxwell was just as appalled and met Danny in the hallway. "You all right? For a minute there, I thought you were going to strangle the guy."

"Cops like him make the rest of us look bad. I'm busting my butt trying to make a difference, and he's out there robbing and kidnapping people. I hope they lock his ass up and shred the key."

"I feel you, man, but don't let him get to you. We still have Jay's killer to catch."

"Yes, we do. I just got a text that I'm hoping will be the break we've been needing. I'll be back. Hopefully, with some good news."

* * *

"I want a lawyer!" Amina yelled, and bolted out of her seat.

Her fists were balled at her sides as she glared across the table at Detective Zeke something or another. Whatever the heck his name was, she was ready to commit bodily harm because of the way he'd tricked her.

One minute she'd been giving a statement to another officer about what happened at Maxwell's house. The next thing she knew, she was being led to the interrogation room. He was questioning her about Jeremy. Talking to her as if she had something to do with his murder. This had already been a horrible day, and it just got worse.

"All I'm asking is were you aware that Jeremy had not only bumped up the amount of life insurance he had but that he also made you the sole beneficiary? Why do you think that is?"

"Why don't you go to hell and ask him," Amina snapped.

It normally took a lot to make her mad, and rarely did she blatantly disrespect someone, but she didn't like this guy. He was treating her as if she was some low-life criminal asking her questions like, *Where were you the day Jeremy was gunned down? Have you ever hired a hit man? When was the last time you saw Jeremy?*

She had answered a few of his questions, but now she was done. "Either get me a lawyer or I'm out of here! Better yet, give me a phone. I'll call my sister who's a lawyer, and let me tell you, by the time she's done with you, you'll be begging us to leave!"

"If you're innocent, why do you need a lawyer?"

The door banged open, and Amina jumped but settled down when Maxwell stormed in.

"What the hell's going on here?" His eyebrows were bunched together as he glanced from her to Detective Zeke. "Why is she in here?"

"Sarge, you know one of us had to bring her in for questioning. Since you—"

"Wait," Amina shouted, and stomped toward Maxwell. "You knew about this? You think I had something to do with Jeremy's murder?"

"Of course not. I know you didn't, but technically we have to question anyone who has motive or might have information that can help with this case."

"Motive? Are you kidding me? Everyone who knew Jeremy had reason to want him dead. Does that mean you're bringing *everyone* in for questioning?"

"Come on, Amina. You know—"

"Did someone question you, Max? Because you had just as much motive as I did," she shot back. Her body was shaking with so much rage, Amina could barely contain herself. When he didn't say anything, only glared at her, she said, "I didn't think so. I can't believe you have him in here treating me like a two-bit criminal. I'm not answering any more questions."

"Answer me this," Zeke said. "Why did your phone number show up on Jeremy's personal cell phone call log five times in the last three weeks?"

The room went silent as Zeke and Maxwell stared at her and she stared right back at them.

"I have no idea what you're talking about. I haven't seen or talked to Jeremy in over six months."

"Do you have the phone records?" Maxwell asked the detective, and Zeke pulled papers from the folder that was on the table and handed them to him. "Why didn't you tell me sooner that Amina's phone number was on the list?"

"Would it have made a difference?" Zeke asked, attitude dripping from each word as his hard eyes bore into Maxwell. "Would you have done anything?"

Amina noticed that Maxwell didn't respond, only continued staring down at the papers in his hands. Clearly there was some tension between the men, and it was safe to say that they had discussed her...possibly being a suspect.

"These calls were only seconds long," Maxwell finally said.

"Seconds, minutes, I don't care. I'm telling you I didn't talk to him," Amina repeated.

Maxwell glanced up. "What about voice messages. Did Jeremy leave any?"

Amina sighed loudly. "No, I haven't..." Her voice trailed off as she recalled something. "Actually, that might've been around the time I was receiving calls, but no one said anything. I figured it was one of those computer-generated calls that take a while before a person starts speaking. I just hung up. After it kept happening, I blocked the caller."

"I wonder if he was calling to see if you were home. It could've been around one of those times that he snuck into your garage with the money."

She shrugged. "I don't know, maybe. All I do know is that I didn't talk to him. Now can I leave? I've had enough of this."

"Zeke, can you give us a minute?" Maxwell said. "Actually, never mind. Amina, let's head to my office." He opened the door for her, and she started to tell him to go to hell, but instead, followed him to his office.

The moment they were behind closed doors, she went off. "I can't be with someone who thinks I'm capable of murder."

"I never said that, and you know I don't believe that."

"Then what the heck was that all about in there, Max?"

"That was Zeke flexing. Don't take it personal. He was actually following departmental rules. We should've questioned you shortly after we realized that there'd been a hit out on Jay. Zeke wanted to, but I shot it down."

Maxwell gently cupped her face between his hands, and Amina couldn't pull away even if she wanted to. The love radiating in his eyes matched what she was feeling deep in her soul. She was in love with this man and knew he didn't actually think she had anything to do with Jeremy's case. After a stressful afternoon, he just happened to be the one she'd chosen to take her frustrations out on.

"I'm sorry if you doubted for one moment that I didn't trust or believe you because that wasn't the case. Whether a person is innocent or not, it's protocol for us to ask questions. That person might know something that'll get us that much closer to finding a killer.

"I know you've had a rough day," he said, "but you have to know that I will be by your side. And I will always come to your defense. I told you—I'm in this for the long haul. No matter what."

"I'm sorry. Zeke got me all riled up, which didn't take much considering what happened this afternoon. I'm so tired."

"I know, baby. Let me finish up here, and I'll take

you home…to my home, unless there's somewhere else you want to go."

"No. Wherever you are is where I want to be."

"Same here."

Maxwell covered her mouth with his, and Amina molded against him savoring his sweetness and the tender way he held her close. Her pulse sped up as shivers of delight pulsed through her body. With every lap of his tongue, he stirred something so sensual within her that went straight to her heart.

God, she loved this man. He had fallen back into her life when she needed him the most. He had offered her comfort after she'd been attacked the other day, and had offered a roof overhead after the break-in. He'd hugged away her tears and her fears.

"I love you so much," she said against his lips, and he froze.

Maxwell slowly lifted his head, and his eyes searched her as a smile kicked up the corners of his sexy lips. "I love you more, and going forward, I'm planning to show you just how much."

Someone knocked on the door, and a growl rumbled inside Maxwell. "I can't wait to get you out of here," he said, and placed a kiss on her forehead. Then he called out, "Come in."

"Sarge, we got something," Danny said from the doorway.

"Okay, give me a minute." Danny stepped out and Maxwell turned back to Amina. "I just need to see what's up, then I'll take you home."

Amina nodded and watched as he headed to the door. *Home.* She liked the sound of that.

* * *

"What do you have?" Maxwell asked the moment he walked out of his office and closed the door.

"We got a positive ID on the shooter. When Zeke noticed a telephone number kept popping up on Jeremy's cell phone records, he got our tech guys involved. I think he told you, but the number belonged to a burner phone. The tech guys were able to narrow down approximately when and where the phone was purchased based on when the calls started.

"Here's the owner of the phone," Danny said, and handed Maxwell a photo.

A hint of relief settled inside Maxwell as he studied the photo. They were getting closer to closing the case. The man in the picture was the same guy caught leaving the apartment building after Jeremy was shot. Except now they could see his face clearly.

"Who is he?"

"His name is David Murphy, and he's a former marine. He was enlisted for twelve years and has been out of the military for two. He was honorably discharged, but has been struggling to find full-time employment and has been picking up odd jobs here and there."

"Like hit jobs?" Maxwell asked. He was always impressed with Danny's and Zeke's thoroughness of solving a case even if he didn't always agree with their methods.

"No, like a day worker. He's been doing some construction work, demolition, painting and anything else he can get."

"Any arrests?"

"He's had a few minor infractions. Disorderly conduct for fighting in a homeless shelter, jaywalking and trespassing to name a few. We're having him brought in now, and he's already talking. He and Jeremy had a connection, but probably not in a way you would think. Guess who he's related to?"

Maxwell only hoped it wasn't Amina. She was more than ready to move on from anything involving Jeremy. "Who?"

"Rochelle Tillman. The fiancée."

# Chapter 25

"He gambled away my life's savings and made it seem as if it was no big deal," Rochelle was saying to Danny as Maxwell and Zeke listened from the other side of the one-way mirror.

Maxwell had to admit, she was a good actress. She came to the precinct the other day and put on a helluva show—the devastated fiancée. Based on what she was currently sharing, some parts of that visit hadn't been an act. According to her, she really hadn't known that Jeremy had a family or an ex-wife. What she had failed to tell them that day, though, was that she knew the killer—her cousin.

"I'm an executive assistant and before I started dating Jeremy, I was saving for a house. I worked my ass off to make something of myself and to accomplish my dream of buying a home. Then Jeremy came along saying all the right things and making me believe that we wanted the same things."

Maxwell gritted his teeth as he stood there listening to a familiar story. How many other women had Jeremy preyed on? Clearly Aaron had been right in worrying about his sister being with Jeremy.

*I'm glad Amina isn't here to hear any of this*, Maxwell thought.

Wanting to ride with Danny to pick up Rochelle, he had arranged for Trace to pick Amina up from the station. Not wanting her to be alone, Maxwell had suggested she hang out at Trinity and Gunner's place. Then he'd pick her up once he left work. Amina hadn't protested, which surprised him. According to her, she could use some family time, and hanging with his family was a close second to being with hers.

"For over a year, things were going good with me and Jeremy," Rochelle was saying. "We both were incredibly happy when Camille was born. That was when Jeremy and I started pooling our money. The plan was for us to save a little more money, then get married in a few months this fall. By that time, we would've been ready to buy some property."

"How is it that these beautiful, smart and successful women keep falling for guys like Jeremy?" Zeke asked, confusion in his tone. "I just don't get it."

"People see what they want to see and believe what they want to believe. Jeremy zeroed in on what the women wanted and were looking for in a mate, then became that man to them," Maxwell said. He knew Jeremy had always been good at getting female attention. He just hadn't known the lengths he'd go to screw with their worlds.

Maxwell zoned back in on the conversation on the other side of the mirror. Jeremy had stolen thirty thousand dollars of her money and gambled it away. That had been a few months ago. He promised he'd get it back, but she said he never did. Maxwell wondered if Jeremy had planned to reimburse her from the money he had stolen. Unfortunately, they would never know.

Rochelle went on to say how their relationship had started changing after that. She insisted that she didn't know the extent of his lies, and her only concern was taking care of her baby. Rochelle and David had come up with the plan for Jeremy to be shot while on duty, then she'd collect his benefits. She also had a three-hundred-thousand-dollar insurance policy on him. She'd said that had been Jeremy's idea when they learned that Rochelle was pregnant.

After Jeremy's death, Rochelle's plan was to move to Morocco, where she couldn't be extradited if it was found that she was connected to Jeremy's murder. She would live off the insurance money temporarily until she found a job.

Maxwell and Danny had found her at her apartment with bags packed and ready to leave town. According to her, she would've left the day after the funeral but didn't realize that it would take a couple of weeks to get the insurance money.

"Our whole relationship was a lie," Rochelle choked out as she broke down in tears. "I was such a fool. I fell for him and had a child with the man. If I could do everything over again, I'd do it differently. I never would've been with him."

"Why not just leave? Why have him killed?" Danny asked. They all wanted to know that.

"I was angry, but I didn't think my cousin would really kill Jeremy. One day, I was telling him what Jeremy had done. The conversation got way off track. I was letting off steam and talking silly when we came up with the plan. I didn't think David would actually go through with it. But when he really did it, I knew I had to get me and Camille out of the country."

"I've seen and heard some weird stuff being on the job, but this is just…sad," Zeke said, and left the room.

Maxwell stayed behind. He felt a little sorry for the woman. He didn't condone anything that Rochelle did for the sake of revenge or taking care of her daughter. But unfortunately, he could relate to how angry she was with Jeremy.

There had been a couple of times over the last few years that Maxwell had wanted to strangle the guy. The difference was, he hadn't acted on those strong emotions.

His mind went to Amina and all that she'd been through. She was lucky she had gotten out of her marriage when she had. And Maxwell was lucky that he was getting a second chance with her. Their connection was like nothing he had ever experienced with a woman, and he planned to spend the rest of his life building on that bond. Now that the case was closed, they could create the life that they both wanted…together.

*Three months later…*

"Amina, are you ready yet?" Maxwell called up the stairs.

"No, stay down there. I'll let you know when you can

come up here," she yelled back, and closed the bathroom door while she finished setting up.

Their bubble baths for two had become a weekly ritual since she'd moved in with him. Some days Amina still couldn't believe how her life had changed in such a short period of time. She never did live in her house again, opting to stay with Maxwell temporarily. But after her home sold within a week of being on the market, he had asked her to move in permanently and Amina agreed.

The man was like sunshine on the cloudiest day, bringing joy to every aspect of her life. Amina couldn't remember ever being as happy as she'd been over the last few months. She found herself wanting everyone to feel what she felt: an overabundance of joy and peace like nothing she had ever experienced before. She credited much of that to Maxwell's unconditional love.

She lit the last of the scented candles that were sitting on every available flat surface in the bathroom. To some, it would seem bizarre, all that she and Maxwell did to make their bubble baths special. They took the ritual seriously because it gave them a chance to relax together, regroup from a busy week, and the routine helped strengthen their bond. It was during these times that they talked about everything. No subject was off-limits, and tonight was extra special. They'd been officially dating for three months, and Amina wanted to celebrate the milestone.

The last few months had been wild and busy. David, Rochelle's cousin, was charged for a number of crimes, the main one being murder. Rochelle had been charged with conspiracy to commit murder and hiring someone to commit murder. She was still awaiting trial, but expected to do some years behind bars.

Financially, Amina was comfortable. So when she found out how much she was receiving from Jeremy's job, she put a plan in motion that centered around baby Camille.

The little girl was an innocent in all of this, but now she didn't have her mother or her father. She was currently with Rochelle's parents, who lived outside Los Angeles, and Amina didn't know what role Jeremy's family would play, especially since she wasn't in touch with them. Either way, she wanted to make sure Camille was taken care of financially. Amina sent the grandparents money for her now, and she also set up a trust fund for Camille to be made available to her on her twenty-first birthday.

"I hope you're ready in there because I'm tired of waiting downstairs." Maxwell's voice drifted through the bathroom door, and Amina laughed.

"Max, it hasn't been that long. I'm still setting up. You weren't supposed to come to the bedroom yet."

Amina tightened the belt around her short white satin robe and glanced around the large space. Freddie Jackson's "Have You Ever Loved Somebody" flowed through the Bluetooth speaker and the scent of lavender permeated the air. From the numerous candles to the dimmed lights, the space was romantic and as relaxing as a spa.

"Okay, I'm ready," she said, and swung open the door. "You need to start practicing patience because..." Amina's words died on her lips at the sight of Maxwell.

Dressed in a purple robe befitting a Nubian king, he looked like African royalty. But that wasn't what had her speechless. No, that had everything to do with seeing him on one knee holding open a small black velvet ring box.

Tears sprang to her eyes and her hands covered her mouth. Two months ago, the marriage topic came up and they discussed plans for their future. The number of kids they would have, where they'd live, where they wanted to be financially, and the list went on and on. Amina would've married him on the spot, but Maxwell hadn't asked.

"It's been three months, baby. For some people, that's not long enough to know if someone's right for you. But I've known from the first time we met that we were perfect for each other. So what if it took us years to get to this point. All that matters now is where we go from here. I love you. I want to spend the rest of my time on this earth…with you. Loving you, protecting you and defending you from jerks like Zeke who might try to throw you in jail."

Amina laughed through her tears and placed her hand over her heart that felt as if it was going to burst out of her chest.

"But seriously," Maxwell continued, "would you do me the honors of becoming my wife?"

"Yes," Amina said, and threw herself at him, practically knocking him over before he caught her around the waist. "Yes, I'll marry you. I love you so much."

"Not as much as I love you."

When Maxwell kissed her, it was different than all other kisses they'd shared. The passion and desire were there, but this one held something more. A promise of forever.

\* \* \* \* \*

*Don't miss Connie and Trace's story,*
*His to Protect,*
*Available now from Harlequin Romantic Suspense!*

## #2167 COLTON'S PURSUIT OF JUSTICE
*The Coltons of Colorado* • by Marie Ferrarella

Caleb Colton has dedicated his life to righting his father's wrongs, but when Nadine Sutherland needs his help proving an oil company took advantage of her father, he wonders if his priorities haven't skewed. Will he be willing to open his heart to Nadine? And will she live long enough to make it matter?

## #2168 CONARD COUNTY CONSPIRACY
*Conard County: The Next Generation*
by Rachel Lee

Widow Grace Hall experiences terrifying incidents at her isolated ranch: murdered sheep, arson, even attempted murder. Her late husband's best friend, Mitch Cantrell, is her greatest hope for protection. But the threat to Grace's life may be even closer than either of them believes...

## #2169 UNDERCOVER K-9 COWBOY
*Midnight Pass, Texas* • by Addison Fox

The instant a rogue FBI agent wants to use Reynolds Station for a stakeout, Arden Reynolds is skeptical of his motives—and his fine physique. She knows attraction is dangerous, but allowing Ryder Durant into her home and her life could prove deadly.

## #2170 PRISON BREAK HOSTAGE
*Honor Bound* • by Anna J. Stewart

When ER doctor Ashley McTavish stops to aid a bus crash, she finds herself taken hostage. Undercover federal agent Slade Palmer's investigation takes a dangerous turn when he vows to keep Ashley alive—even as he finds a new reason to survive himself.

---

*When ER doctor Ashley McTavish stops to aid a bus
crash, she finds herself taken hostage. Undercover
federal agent Slade Palmer's investigation takes a
dangerous turn when he vows to keep Ashley alive—
even as he finds a new reason to survive himself.*

*Read on for a sneak preview of*
*Prison Break Hostage,*
*the latest in Anna J. Stewart's Honor Bound series!*

"Sawyer?" Her voice sounded hoarse. She sat back on
her heels and looked behind her. He was a fair distance
away, moving more slowly than she'd have thought.
Ashley shoved to her feet, her knees wobbling as she
stepped back into the water and shouted for him. "You're
almost there! Come on!" But he was gasping for air, and
for a horrifying moment, he sank out of sight.

Panic seized her. It was pitch-black. Not even the moon
cast light on this side of the shore. No homes nearby, no
lights or guideposts. How would she ever find him?

But she would. He would not leave her like this. She
would not lose him. Not now. She waded into the water,
stumbled, nearly fell face-first, just as he surfaced. He
took a moment to wretch, his hand clutching his side as
he slowly moved toward her, water cascading from the
bag on his hip.

"What is it?" She'd seen enough injuries to know something was seriously wrong. She wedged herself under his arm and helped him walk the rest of the way to dry land. "Where are you hurt?"

"Doesn't matter," he wheezed as he dropped to the ground. He leaned back, still pressing a hand to his side. Blood soaked through his shirt and onto his fingers. "I'll be fine in a minute. We need to get moving."

She dragged his shirt up, tried to examine the wound. "I can't see anything other than blood."

"I know." He covered her hand with his, squeezed her fingers. "Ashley, listen to me. Valeri left with Mouse and Olena, but he ordered Taras and Javi to stay behind. They're coming after me, Ashley."

"Us. They're coming after us. Let me—"

"No. It's me they want. Which means you're in even more danger than you were before. You need to go on alone. Now. While it's still dark."

"I'm not leaving you." She slung his arm over her shoulders and, with enough effort that her feet sank into the dirt, helped him up. He let out a sound that told her he was trying not to show how hurt he really was.

"You have to."

"Hey." She gave him a hard squeeze. "You aren't in any condition to argue with me. I am not leaving you, Sawyer Paxton. So be quiet and let's move."

*Don't miss*
Prison Break Hostage *by Anna J. Stewart,*
*available February 2022 wherever*
*Harlequin Romantic Suspense*
*books and ebooks are sold.*

Harlequin.com

# Get 4 FREE REWARDS!

## We'll send you 2 FREE Books plus <u>2</u> FREE Mystery Gifts.

**Harlequin Romantic Suspense** books are heart-racing page-turners with unexpected plot twists and irresistible chemistry that will keep you guessing to the very end.

FREE Value Over $20

---